Leaving Paris

Copyright ©2022 A. Stanza. All rights reserved.

All rights reserved. No portion of this publication may be reproduced, distributed, stored in, or introduced into a retrieval system, or transmitted in any form or by any means (electronically, mechanical, photocopying, recording, or otherwise), except as permitted under Sections 107 or 108 of the 1976 United States Copyright Act, without the prior written permission of both the copyright owner and the publisher of this book.

This is a work of fiction. Names, characters, places and incidents are the product of the author's imagination, or, if an actual place, are used fictitiously and any resemblance to actual persons, living or dead, business establishments, events, or locales is entirely coincidental.

Beta Readers: Alicia Maggiore, Kelly Lord, Chloe Smith

Cover Illustration: Talita Asami

Editing: Kathy Bosman, Indie Editing Chick

Dedication

This book is dedicated to those who want to give love a chance because that shit is hard.

Chapter 1

ESTELLA

PAST

Something about the tune took me back. I couldn't place it—an original maybe—but it didn't matter. The mellow feel of the piano solo, note melting into note, moved me to simpler times. The warm lights of the jazz club made the place very welcoming. The waiters in black vests swept between the tables while jazz filled the air, inspiring friends or couples to enjoy each other's company.

I had expected this when Theo mentioned meeting at a jazz club, but better. It was called the Sunset Jazz Club. It was a cool hole-in-the-wall, with distressed wood, metal, and brick elements. The people were dressed smartly, but casually and overall, they looked friendly.

We wanted to see what Paris offered, and I didn't find myself disappointed. A waiter seated me at a table in the corner, handing me a small menu. I placed two fingers up and the waiter politely smiled as he placed another menu on the table.

Theo and I had bumped into each other during orientation. He came from Chicago and I came from Brooklyn. We debated on which pizza was better: deep dish or New-York-style. Enjoying our friendly debate, he suggested we go out to eat. We agreed on 9:00pm, and I had been waiting for thirty minutes—ten of those minutes were from my early arrival. I pulled my phone out, sending him a quick text.

After three unanswered calls and an hour later, I received a drunk picture of him at a club asking me to join him. I scoffed at the message and tossed my phone onto the table.

I hated nightclubs, and a date at one wasn't ideal. The loud, electronic dance music, the intoxicated, raving people, and all the pressing bodies sounded like torture. I loved being seated in a closed-off booth and listening to the piano solo. This was one of those places where the music

Leaving Paris

became more subdued over time and you left in the early morning.

The clarinet and mellow piano filled the room with breath-taking jazz. A pair of waiters were clearing out abandoned tables. At least I was able to appreciate the beauty of this hidden gem.

Based off of the sympathetic smile the waiter gave me, he figured I had been stood up. "Anything I can help you with? Another plate of calamari, a refill, an entrée?"

"Do you have cake?" I asked, defeated.

"We do, many kinds; anything specific?"

"Nope."

"I'll surprise you."

Little by little, the tables were cleared up, and I could see companions bidding farewell to each other and sauntering out to the waiting station to hail a cab or stumbling away into the dark, rainy night. I remained in the corner, alone, doodling on a scrunched-up napkin.

I tried not to look around, to become oblivious to the place was closing down for the night because I had been spellbound by the piano's lulling notes. The seduction of the beautiful instrument and my thoughts were all I needed that night.

Leaving Paris

As much as I wanted to stay, I couldn't keep the musicians and workers waiting. They clearly weren't going to dismiss me; I had to do it myself. They recognized that I was calling it a night, and slowly the song began to die down.

It was my time to go.

I reluctantly pushed away the drawing that I had made and turned to exit. At the same time, a dark figure emerged from the stage and he had caught my eye. It was the pianist. Our gaze lingered a second or two—not long, but unusually pleasant. Everything about him was beautiful: chocolate-brown curly hair, cognac-colored eyes behind tortoise-shell glasses, sun-kissed skin, and an inviting smirk. He made his way over to the corner, sliding his hands into his pockets.

"Did you enjoy the music?" he asked. His words had a slight accent—Italian maybe. He reached over and grabbed the singular peony from the vase, handing it to me.

Had he been watching me or was it a justified assumption considering that I was the only other person in the room?

"Of course, it was beautiful." I fiddled with the flower.

He sat across from me, not giving it another thought. I

smiled in approval, acknowledging his audacity with only a sideways glance.

"It's very nice," he said, looking at the sketch I had drawn on the napkin.

Insecurity crept in, and my fingers scurried over to the thin cloth, pulling it away from his sight. It was a silly drawing of a faceless woman with an array of instruments swirling around her.

"I was just doodling," I played off.

A waiter, with his vest half-buttoned, popped into the main area. "Sir, I'm the last one out. Would you like me to lock up?"

The man looked at me. "Do you have to go far?"

"I'll have to catch a cab," I said, noticing the time on my phone. "If there is one this late on a Monday at 1 a.m.," I whispered, doubtfully.

"Sir?" the waiter called.

"You can go home," the mysterious man responded. "I'll do it in a bit."

The waiter bowed his head and disappeared.

"I'd be glad to drive you. Walking in this rain wouldn't be too fun." He spoke sincerely and without hesitation. "I'll just need to get my keys from upstairs." He smiled kindly, and after a polite objection, and my polite insistence in return, we were walking together between the tables.

"Well, before I go with you…"

"Only for my keys," he assured.

"What is your name?" I asked.

"Ignacio," he said. "And yours?"

"Estella," I responded.

"What is an American doing in Paris?"

"I'm studying abroad for the semester."

"What are you studying?" he asked as he led me to the mahogany-lined elevator.

"I'm still figuring it out," I said honestly. "I came for an adventure, and I'm not sure what I'll end up with."

"Paris has a lot to offer," he said.

"You seem like you're speaking from experience."

"Not really." He chuckled.

"How can I trust you?" I asked playfully but concerned that I made the decision to retrieve keys with a complete stranger. He looked older than me by five years or so.

"I mean no harm," he said, seeming genuine.

Just then, the elevator opened, and he placed his hand over the frame of the elevator to allow me onto it. He pressed the only other number on the keypad, and the doors closed.

"You're lucky to live above the club, to hear beautiful music play every night."

"That is the exact reason I decided to become a co-owner and live here."

The elevator opened its doors in direct access to his studio. There wasn't much but a king-sized bed at the end of the room draped with a plush, blue comforter, half a kitchen, a gray couch, a wall lined with books, and a…

"Grand piano," I whispered in awe.

"Ah, yes, my prized possession. All of it really; it's my getaway," he said.

My gaze didn't part from the beautiful, glisten-black Fazioli piano. It was considered the best grand piano of all time. I'd always wanted to run my fingers across the inviting keys. I wasn't a professional by any means, but I taught myself how to play a couple of pieces with the help of online videos and a trusty old digital piano. I admired the art of piano playing and wished my parents had enrolled me in lessons when I was younger.

"You can try it out," Ignacio suggested, giving me a convincing smile.

"Are you sure?" I hesitated.

"Yes." He nodded.

Ignacio didn't have to tell me twice. I eagerly sat on the accompanied black bench and absorbed the view of the glorious keys. My heart swelled with elation by sitting in plain view of the piano. The music which would be created from the piano would be nothing short of magical.

My finger hovered over one of the keys, and I gasped when he opened his mouth. "I'm going to lock up until we are ready to go," he said. "Take your time."

Ignacio was willing to offer some privacy which I appreciated. From his earlier playing, I just knew he was a professional and I didn't want to make a fool out myself. With Ignacio's absence, I found it easier to gain the courage to play.

It was easy for me to lose all concept of time whenever I played the piano, but I was certain that Ignacio had been gone longer than needed. I lifted away from the piano bench and made my way to the elevator when it slowly came into sight.

"I'm sorry, I had to take a phone call. You play very well," he said.

All the blood rushed to my cheeks. Receiving compliments from Ignacio, a pianist, who also happened to be good-looking, made my stomach flutter.

"Do you mind if I show you some techniques?" Ignacio offered, rolling his sleeves up and unbuttoning the first two buttons of his white dress shirt. He had a rugged, academic look to him, and he pulled it off well. He looked like he waltzed out of a painting, or even a magazine.

Ignacio sat at the edge of the bench, his posture straight and upright, his arms relaxed and in front of him. His long fingers immediately lost themselves in the sea of ivory keys. They darted back and forth with so much poise. Ignacio was undoubtedly classically trained; even his style of music was a mixture of romantic and jazzy.

I couldn't recall the piece he was playing, but it would have been no surprise if it was an original. Ignacio had my undivided attention as he played the rest of the wistful piece. The music ended, and his hands landed on top of mine, guiding them over to the keys. His touch felt like fire, and it burned me so beautifully.

Ignacio spent the early morning hours teaching me the basics, refining my techniques, and a majority of the time being my personal pianist. I'd name a song or hum a tune and he'd add to it without hesitation. We even managed to create a little melody together. I admired his ability to play and stopped myself from fawning over him multiple times.

It wasn't easy for me to open up to people, especially men. I'd never had any luck with keeping a man's attention. I wasn't sure if it was me or them, but it always seemed like I was the problem. It was hard to believe that a talented—and super handsome—man was giving up his precious hours of sleep to entertain me. I gave him trusting looks, which I hoped he took as a personal compliment.

The muscles in his forearms and arms twitched as he extended them out to reach the high keys. His arm brushed against my breasts, and it created a whirlwind in my chest. Along with the scent of his cologne, it was difficult to pay attention.

I didn't want to physically show that I had been defeated by all our playing because I genuinely enjoyed spending time with him, but we all had our breaking points. I lifted my face upward, stretching my neck as I leaned back, feeling the strain on my shoulders that managed to support my frame for so long.

Ignacio noticed my exhaustion and flashed me a small smile. "We've been playing for five hours. Are you tired already?" he joked.

I removed myself from the bench and stretched my

limbs, losing myself in the wonderful sensation of a good stretch. "I don't know how you do it."

"When you've been professionally trained, you get used to it."

"You know," I said, taking small strides around the room to remind my body of its mobility, "I'd come every night. I really enjoy hearing you play."

"I appreciate it, but I don't play often."

"What? Why?"

"It's more of a hobby now."

I tried my best to hide the horror on my face, but Ignacio noticed it and smirked.

"I've changed my profession," he said, his long finger tracing the outline of the piano. There was a look on his face, a mixture of wistfulness, caution, and maybe pain. I wondered what urged him to change his profession, and I wanted to ask, but it wasn't my place. I was a stranger, who happened to be at his place in the wee hours of the morning, but still, nothing more. I couldn't overstep.

I wasn't sure if I was reading the room correctly, but the dynamic had changed. Ignacio wasn't playing on the piano; he was looking at it as if it was a regretful one-night stand, and I looked out the window, admiring the beautiful city view.

I pushed myself off the windowsill and walked back to Ignacio. "So, who do you think is the best composer of all time?" I asked, sitting beside him again but with my back towards the piano keys.

I had only known him for a couple of hours, but my gut told me he'd say…

"Beethoven," we both answered. I cocked my head to the side with an I-knew-it smile.

Ignacio looked taken aback. "How'd you know I'd say Beethoven?"

"The way you play; it's insistent, romantic, and dramatic like Beethoven. You almost surrender yourself to the piano. It's beautiful."

Ignacio looked at me with a quizzical expression. I couldn't tell if he wanted to say something to me. I bit down on my lip when Ignacio leaned over towards me, his eyes narrowed in on me. "Who do you think is the greatest composer of all time?"

"Debussy," I answered with certainty.

Ignacio tossed himself back and shook his head. "Right when I was starting to like you," he teased.

"Hey," I murmured, placing my hand on his bicep. It

was firm, pleasant under my fingertips, and inappropriate, considering we weren't friends. Blood rushed to my cheeks, and I immediately pulled my hand away to conceal my face, feigning a yawn, followed by a real one.

"Sleepy, huh? But the day has just begun," Ignacio stated as he played Moonlight Sonata.

"I'm sleepy, not dead. Can you not play a funeral march?"

"Oh, I'm sorry. Should I play something gentler and more poetic?" he asked, over-enthusiastically playing *Clair De Lune*. "Is this better? Do you feel like you're frolicking in the meadows?" His fingers played the beautiful composition as he looked at me with a smart-ass smile plastered on his face.

"Actually, I do. That is why Debussy is the greatest composer of all time. He makes life feel more than what it actually is."

The music came to a halt, and Ignacio drew closer to me, his gaze darting between my eyes and lips. The look he was giving me made my insides squirm, rendering me useless. "So," I whispered. "Are you firm on your decision with Beethoven, or have I managed to sway you?"

Ignacio eyes flickered away from my lips and back to

the piano. "To be honest, the best composer is my grandfather."

"Did he teach you?"

"He did." His beautiful smile faded away into a painful expression.

Once again, I found myself in the position where I had to be careful not to overstep because I didn't know Ignacio, and I didn't want to do more damage. I didn't want him to feel any worse, so I decided to share a little about myself to distract him.

"Can I tell you a secret?"

I piqued his interest, and he looked straight at me with a curiosity twinkling in his amber eyes. "Of course."

"I was supposed to be on a date tonight, but the guy stood me up." I played with the tips of my finger. "Before you pity me, I want to say I'm okay. I'm used to this type of behavior from guys."

Ignacio traced my hands with his long fingers. "Their loss," he responded. "Seriously, they don't know what they're missing out on."

I lowered my head, wanting to hide my blushing face. "You're just saying that to be nice." I chuckled nervously.

Ignacio's fingers cascaded up my arm and neck, and he

slid his hands through my hair, cradling my head on his palm.

"May I kiss you?" I heard him say, but I was sure I'd pulled those words from my imagination.

"What?" I whispered.

Ignacio withdrew an inch and had a contemplative look on his beautiful face. "May I take you home?" he asked, releasing his hold on me, pulling away completely. The distance between us wasn't pleasant. I wanted to be close to him again.

"Of course," I said, taking his hand.

I wasn't sure if it was the lack of sleep or if it was a universal sign, but there was a surge of electricity that passed between us.

As I stood up, his face grew closer to mine, and more of his shadow was cast upon me.

"Actually, that's not what I had asked," he said, shaking his head. "I'm sorry, I grow nervous whenever I look at you," he said, fiddling with the knuckles of my hand.

Oh... I made him nervous? I never made anyone nervous, if anything, most men made *me* nervous.

"What did you ask then?"

"If I could kiss you."

I nodded slowly but surely, because I wanted one kiss before I left.

Ignacio towered over my five-four frame perhaps by a good eight inches. He watched me as my eyes slowly closed, my lips parted, my chin raised slightly toward him, and my soft palm slid along his arm to his strong shoulder. His palms were now upon my cheek, and his lips traveled to mine, kissing them.

I had kissed only one boy in my life. Ignacio was not a boy. He was a man in all its essence. Tall, athletically lean, gorgeous thick curls, a chiseled chin, mesmerizing eyes that could break my heart in a second.

I hadn't imagined such soft, full lips, melding passionately with my own, his teeth gently nipping at mine and mine at his, and then his tongue colliding with mine in a passionate embrace. His kisses were surreal, like Heaven on Earth.

Ignacio released his gentle hold on me and my body ached for his closeness again. Seconds later, Ignacio reached for my fingers and I wondered if he also found discomfort in being apart. I laced his fingers with mine. Ignacio gave me a reassuring squeeze and led the way to the elevator.

"Thank you for making my night, Estella."

Leaving Paris

"No, I should be thanking you."

"Can I see you again?"

"I'd really like that," I said, tucking my hair behind my ear.

Ignacio led me to where he had parked, and opened the door for me.

The radio played in the background as I stared into space, watching the droplets race down the car window. I lightly played with my lower lip as I replayed the moment we kissed. Ignacio would be taking over all my thoughts and dreams because I'd never known a kiss could feel like that.

The car rolled towards the curb, and Ignacio turned off the vehicle. He jogged around the front of the car and finished opening the door for me. A friendly hand extended out, and I held onto it, being pulled into his chest.

The night was foggy, the rain pitter-pattered against the cobblestone sidewalks, and the yellow street lights flickered. Ignacio traced my jawline with his finger and tilted his head to the side as he examined every inch of my face. I'd never been looked at this way, and every passing second made my stomach jump.

"Tonight."

"What about tonight?" I asked.

"I want to see you tonight again."

"I'm sure I can find some time."

A beautiful smile appeared on his face. Droplets beaded his hair, and I ran my fingers through them, gripping his hair and leaning up to place a gentle kiss on his lips. I slowly pulled away, darting my eyes between his lips and eyes.

Ignacio held me tightly and pressed his lips against mine, placing a kiss so tender that time almost froze. There was a mutual need for each other, and for minutes, we kissed under the light rain.

Chapter 2

IGNACIO

PAST

My leg bounced up and down in anticipation, aching for the next five minutes to pass so I could rush out of the building and go meet Estella. That was how it had been for the last three weeks. I could entertain myself most of the day with work, but those last five minutes were painfully hard.

Bouncing my leg wasn't enough. I started tapping my pen against the table, drawing my father's attention. His fiery brown eyes narrowed at mine, and I lowered my pen, focusing my attention on Mattias, who was presenting a business model. Nothing was interesting about the real estate and construction world, but I was working side by side with my father because it was what we both thought it was best for me.

Mattias finished his presentation, and my father stood up, shaking his hand firmly and praising him for his work. My father never smiled at me with pride, even with all the piano competitions I had won. Nothing I did was ever good enough for him, and maybe that was one of the reasons I started working for him. I wanted to be close. No, I *needed* it after the last few months. After losing Nonna, who was more mother than my own, I needed that void to be filled.

Everyone gathered around the table, collecting their belongings and walking out of the office in unison. They were grouped together, all walking towards their elevator while they chit-chatted. I was usually the first to head out, but everyone eagerly made their way out quicker than I could.

"Will we be driving together or separately?" my father asked.

"Where?" I asked.

"Our corporate dinner—that's where everyone else is heading."

"I haven't heard about this dinner."

Leaving Paris

"You miss out on important information when you're racing out the door after every meeting. An email was also sent out a couple days ago."

Once the clock struck five, I wasn't going to waste another minute entertaining co-workers, projects, or anything else, but my father didn't see it that way. Alessio Amatore was a workaholic. Everything in his life revolved around work and he couldn't understand people who didn't have the same mentality.

"Well, I had other plans, so I'll miss this dinner."

"It doesn't look good for the CEO's son to not join the dinner, especially when he's working to take over his father's business someday."

"I'm sure people will understand or not care."

"I care, Ignacio. I care what they think about you because that reflects on me."

I stood in front of him and patted his shoulder. "Maybe you should care a little less about what other people think and a little more about what your son wants. *I* want to go, so goodbye."

Arguing with my father wasn't going to do anything. We were never going to be on the same page. I left him huffing and puffing, but I couldn't find the energy to care when Estella was on my agenda.

We always met at a quaint little café by a floral shop. We'd occasionally grab a little treat to eat before heading off to where her heart desired. Sometimes, she'd want to sit on the side and people-watch or go to an event that she'd read about online, but most of the time, she wanted to go to the jazz club and take her rightful spot in the booth where she sat the first time she visited. I'd sit next to her and we'd enjoy the musical entertainment for the night. She'd encourage me to join and when I declined, she'd tell me that I had to play for her when everyone left, which I obliged to because her beautiful, pure smile was worth it.

Tonight would be one of those nights. There was a singer tonight—Soprano, a talented new jazz singer and piano player, taking the stage for the first time. She was somewhere in her early twenties.

I wouldn't be surprised if Estella encouraged me to play alongside the singer. She enjoyed watching me on stage the night we met, and now, had these wild imaginations about me playing with the starring show.

I promised my father that I could give his business a fair chance without piano in the way. I loved playing for Estella and watching her admiration for the piano. That would never change. But that was all it had to be: piano playing for Estella.

I had my time and my supporters when I pursued a music path, but that was all over now. On the few occasions I'd spoken to my father while growing up, he'd always mention that he'd love for us to work together one day. I needed him more than ever since Nonna's passing a month ago. I had to escape from Italy, away from all the memories, and working at Amatore Inc sounded like a good enough escape.

I'd have to stand firm on my position with Estella. The confidence within me helped me stand straight up, but from a distance, I spotted Estella. The butterflies were blooming and my confidence dwindling. Then her whole body came into view.

Game over.

A green dress with floral detailing hugged her body, her long hair bouncing with every step, and her warm brown eyes filled with wonderment. There was no doubt that she had her earphones in. She had the same look every time she listened to music. It was one of my favorite looks on her, from head to toe.

Saying no would be harder than I thought. Estella could

convince me to do nearly anything with a bit of persistence. She had that type of effect on me. The way she spoke, carried herself and expressed herself, it weakened me. I was falling for her fast and hard.

Estella was definitely listening to music and so lost in it that she walked past me. In her defense, I wasn't in our usual spot. We usually met by the lamppost in front of the café, but today it was warmer than usual, and I stood under the roof canopy.

I lightly placed my hand on the small of her back as I stepped in front of her. Those brown eyes glazed over with excitement, and she cupped both of my cheeks as she gifted me a demanding kiss on my lips. I slowly gripped her waist, pulling her into my chest as our tongues worked with each other.

An old couple grunted as they walked past us, and Estella immediately withdrew. She placed her fingertips on her lips and looked down, trying to conceal her blushed cheeks. Estella wasn't one for public displays of affections, but when she kissed me, I couldn't help but reciprocate a little more.

"They're gone," I assured her.

"That was embarrassing."

Leaving Paris

"Not for me."

Estella playfully rolled her eyes and tucked a strand of hair behind her ear.

"What are you listening to?" I asked, pulling out one of the buds and placing it into my ear.

Estella watched me with curious eyes as a reminiscent song filled my ears. *Bésame mucho* by Andrea Bocelli. A classic, and one of Nonna's favorite songs. I used to play a Latin jazz rendition of the song for Nonna, and it always got her up and moving. Listening to the song made me want to play for her again.

But I'd never be given a chance again.

Estella plucked the earbud out of my ear and wound it around her phone. "Not a fan of Andrea Bocelli—noted."

"I am, it's just, he was my nonna's favorite singer. She passed recently, and the wound is still fresh."

Estella pouted her lower lip and cupped my face with her soft hands. "God, I'm so sorry."

I closed my eyes and found solace in her touch. I'd never been touched this way by another woman and wouldn't want it any other way. Estella was the one for me, and it didn't take three weeks to realize it. I knew it the moment our eyes met for the first time.

Leaving Paris

My hands covered hers, and I kissed them. "We have thirty minutes until I need to open up. Soprano needs an hour to set up before the show begins. What would you like to do until then?"

"Soprano!" Estella squealed. She squeezed my hands tightly and led the way towards the jazz club. Estella was unstoppable when she put her mind to it. She zig-zagged through the pedestrians, dodged cars as she raced through streets, and still managed to keep me at arm's length.

I handed Estella the keys to the club and she gleamed like a schoolgirl; opening the club was her favorite. It was the simple things that created the biggest smile for her. Estella took a couple steps into the dark space, and I gradually turned on the lights, finding her already seated on the bench of the piano on stage.

"You know, I really miss home, but the piano, this club, you, it all kind of feels like another version of home."

"Then," I said, taking long strides towards her, "let this be your home for as long as you need."

"Really?"

"But only on one condition."

"Hm?"

"You need to *bésame mucho*." I leaned over and stole a

kiss. Kissing her was my favorite pastime.

Estella smiled from ear to ear and shook her head. "You're so cheesy."

"You must accept my cheesiness and my kisses."

"Deal."

The music swelled, and the tone of it hit me with great force. The melody produced by the singer and the musicians spoke to me, and my heart thumped with every beat. Soprano's delivery and my newfound feelings of love arising, it was impossible to not admire it. Her voice rose and lowered as she hit the outro of the song, amplifying the feelings that I had.

It turned out so right for strangers in the night.

Estella had her chin resting on her hand as she mouthed along with Soprano.

The musicians faded out the music and the audience erupted into claps and whistles, Estella being the loudest. The bashful singer bowed and broke into a grand smile. Soprano loved making people feel what she wanted us to feel. Musicians were magicians. They decided which instruments would be used, what notes would be played, and composed riffs on the spot. It was what I loved about playing the piano and writing songs.

Leaving Paris

Estella cocked her head to the side, reading my face. "Do you get it now? This is what I want for you." She focused her attention on Soprano and gave another loud round of applause.

Soprano brought the mic back to her lips. "And a big thank you to Ignacio, who decided to take a chance on me and allowed me to use his stage to perform."

Everyone's eyes were on me, and I gave them and Soprano a firm nod. There was no longer a place for me in the music industry, but I wanted to support whoever dreamed of being a part of it. Nothing brought me more joy (other than Estella) than to kick start a dream.

My gaze finally landed on Estella, and she gave me an appreciative smile, but there was a little bit of sadness in her eyes. It wasn't the right time to ask her what was wrong, but I planned on asking after the adrenaline died down.

The piano notes slowed down, the crew started to clear out the empty tables, and the busy clatter in the kitchen let me know that everyone was rushing to go home. I understood, considering we closed at 2 a.m. and had to commute. My living quarters were above me (which homed my precious Fazioli), and the lady I was falling in love with had her head on my shoulder, and she sleepily twirled a peony flower. The two most important things in my life were all in this building.

The last two guests were out the door, arm in arm. Louis rushed to the entrance door and locked it a second after they stepped out.

"What are you thinking about, *stella mia*?" I pressed my lips against her hair, inhaling the scent of strawberries and cream.

"A little worried about you."

"About what?"

"I think you belong in the music world, not the corporate world."

"I understand."

I really did. For a while, there was a possibility of becoming big in the music world, but I let it all go. With Nonna dying, leaving Italy, and an opportunity to work at a place that guaranteed success, it made sense to stop pursuing a musical career.

Estella sighed. "What about your dream to be a film composer?"

"It's on pause. I will see how far I can go in the corporate world." I could succeed and become an asset to my father's company.

Estella closed her eyes in defeat.

"No matter what path I take, I'll always be your personal piano player. I will play just for you—no one else, ever. Can that be enough for you right now?" My finger slid down the edge of her jaw, and I pulled her chin towards me, so I could read her face.

"I just want you to be happy, Ignacio."

"I am happy. You make me happy, and all I want to do is make music for you." My eyes flickered to her pink lips and I placed a tender kiss onto them.

"Just for me, Ignacio?" she breathed against my lips.

"*Per sempre.*" Forever.

Estella sat upright and slinked an arm around my neck as I delivered hot kisses into her neck. This was right. Us, hands on each other, in our little booth in the corner of the jazz club. Estella straddled me, rolling her hips on my lap as her hands traveled through my hair. I kissed her neck, up to her jaw, and slammed my lips against her. Every kiss was followed by another kiss.

"Ignacio, I want you," she whispered. "Please."

Estella's scent, her voice, and her body were driving me insane. All I wanted was her.

I exited the booth and carried her towards the elevator,

unable to keep my lips away from her. She tried to pull away when Louis saw us, but I shooed him, telling him that I would lock up if he left. He didn't think twice.

Our lips stumbled over each other as we hastily undressed ourselves in the elevator and made our way to my bed. Cradling her head in my hands as I kissed her, I pushed her head against the pillow beneath her. I drew away for a moment to confirm with another glance that this was really happening, to take note that her legs had parted to allow my knee between her thighs and that my hips were pressed achingly against her pelvis.

My hands slid from her face to her shoulders, then along the lengths of her arms until I gripped her wrists above her head and buried my mouth in the curve of her neck, kissing, gently biting and leaving moist rings to glisten in the dim light.

I suddenly felt her hands on my head, fingernails gently latching onto my hair. As she involuntarily pushed my face downward, I complied, delivering kisses along the way to her lower rib cage, her stomach, her navel, the soft parts of her thighs, and at last, the narrow silky patch of cloth.

I paused to look into Estella's eyes for a moment, and my finger glided down her cheek. "Are you sure?"

Estella nodded.

I pulled my eyebrows, and I focused on making this a memorable evening for both of us. My fingers gripped the sides of her panties and I pulled them down, taking a deep breath in through my nose. Estella's hands glided over my chest, then wrapped around my neck, pulling me to her lips. We kept kissing, allowing any free hands to roam unfamiliar territory. We were nearly breathless from all the exploring, but we continued.

We were rolling over each other, kissing different patches of skin, occasionally bumping into each other and fumbling, but it was everything I imagined it to be. My insides blazed with unadulterated bliss. My senses were overwhelmed to the point that I couldn't think straight, but I continued to plunge my mind, body, and soul into Estella.

***

I awoke with a jolt, tangled in the sheets with Estella nuzzled next to me. I peeked over, brushing her hair off her face and taking in her sweet, innocent expression. My hand reached over to pull the comforter over us but froze midway at the sound of a loud clang coming from the kitchen.

I slipped away from the bed, trying my best not to disturb Estella. I didn't want her peace to be disrupted while I checked the noise downstairs. I figured that maybe a pan or a cup had been stacked awkwardly and fell.

The kitchen lights were still on, and I walked in, reaching for a cup on the rack. My lips eagerly met the rim of the glass, and I sighed deeply with relief after satisfying my thirst. I walked over to the backdoor and locked it three hours late, but nothing happened around our part of town.

I placed the cup in the sink and turned around, only to find a man with a bat swinging directly into my gut. My body fell to the ground, and I started gasping for air, grasping at whatever I could because my only concern was Estella. The man hovered over me again, and he gave me one last final blow before I collapsed onto the ground, unconscious.

Chapter 3

IGNACIO

PRESENT

Marcelo knew that I was lying. He knew that I wasn't ready to be back so close to home. I had been raised across the lake in a village called Castellara. It was a cliffside village known for its beautiful harbor, wines, hikes, and vineyards. Grandmothers were selling delicious sweets, artists showcasing their finished products, restaurants with homemade Italian food, and genuine people.

It was where I was born and raised and also where I had been broken. The last time I had stepped foot there was five years ago, after Nonna's passing. It still seemed too soon to be back.

Leaving Paris

I had been succeeding in my father's company for the past five years, owned a villa and a car, and had been making a name for myself before the age of thirty. It was a dream many wanted to live. All I needed was a woman, my father would tell me.

Marcelo placed a perfect grilled Tuscan steak onto my plate and topped it with grilled onions and grilled potatoes. That was the one best perk of having a best friend who was a Michelin-star chef: perfectly cooked food. Marcelo had never disappointed, which was why he succeeded in all his restaurants. Two, to be exact, but they were growing. His goal was to have three restaurants opened by thirty. He was three months shy of hitting his deadline.

"This villa is phenomenal," he praised. "I can't believe you waited months to move in."

"There were a lot of electrical issues, plumbing too." I shoved a tender piece of steak into my mouth to prevent myself from discussing this topic any further.

Marcelo eyed me, a smirk appearing. "Okay."

For the past five and a half months, I lived with Marcelo in his villa. I could've lived in my own villa in Lilla, but instead, I lied about the state of the house. When my father first gifted it to me, it still needed some minor renovations, but once those were fixed, I lied that there were more ongoing issues.

"Do you know any good honeymoon spots? Camilla and I have been arguing about the location. I prefer keeping it close, but she wants something distinctive and classically romantic."

Marcelo had only dated Camilla for a couple of months until he decided to propose to her. I thought he would regret it in the long run, but that was another goal of his: to be married by the age of thirty.

"Paris. She wants Paris," he scoffed.

Paris.

I hadn't been there in five years. I refused to go back to the city of reckless mistakes. If Marcelo and Camilla were to go there, then I'd be fully convinced that it would be an evil omen for divorce.

There was so much chaos during my stay in Paris, but there was one shining evening that would never escape my mind—when I first met Estella. She left an indelible mark on me.

She was extraordinarily beautiful with her dark eyes and hair, her slender body. She had been alone at a table, hidden in the back, her chin in her hands, sketching something on her napkin.

I had approached her with the intention of watching her enjoy the music and offering her a safe means of transportation. All my senses jumped out the window when I saw her eyes glisten in adoration at the sight of my beloved Fazioli. Other than my grandfather and instructors, I hadn't met anyone else with an immense fascination with piano or classical music in general.

I had taught a handful of rich kids who only studied piano for their parents' approval, and none of them appreciated the lessons. Estella absorbed every word, every move, every ounce of life that the piano created. I had connected with her in a way that I never thought possible.

With her posture upright and her thick, brown hair spilling over her left shoulder, it was hard to resist her, especially with her strawberry-and-cream scent intoxicating my senses. There was no way I could teach her just once and let her go. I kept seeing her, spending most evenings at the jazz club and losing myself in her presence. She had been one of the best things that had happened in my life, and it all had vanished in a blink of an eye.

"Are you sure you'll be okay here?" Marcelo asked, noticing that I had wandered off into my own thoughts.

"It'll be fine. I'm fine," I assured him.

"Well, if there happen to be any other issues with the villa, you're more than welcome to come back to my place." He winked and stuffed a roasted potato into his mouth.

I gave him a nod of appreciation. Marcelo picked the conversation back up and started to discuss his plan to open a third restaurant soon. I tried to concentrate on the topic because I believed in him and his strategy, but it was difficult. All I could think about was Estella and our nights in Paris.

I looked out across the vast, blue lake. Estella had set my standards too high for other women. They had to look like her, be fascinated by and passionate about music like her, and have the quiet confidence that she had.

I will always want her—forever.

Chapter 4

ESTELLA

PRESENT

I smiled as I watched Salem hang the last wall art, the final touch needed in her new café. There was something about her spirit that made me feel at home. At the age of twenty-five, Salem Russo and I decided to move to Italy for a year just for the experience. There wasn't much for us back home other than family.

And a toxic ex-boyfriend that I needed to be oceans apart from.

I was pretty hesitant about moving to another country because the last time I went to a foreign country, I had fallen in love with a man who ended up ghosting me after we slept together. My first sexual experience ended up being a tragedy. So, this time around, I vowed to myself that I wouldn't delve into the world of romance. Italy was my fresh start—to create a new me. Estella 2.0 who didn't fall for men like Mr. Pianist or ex-boyfriends named Cesar.

To my surprise, my parents urged me to move to Italy. They were tired of seeing me work in their tiny Latin market during the day and as a waitress at Mr. Russo's restaurant at night, cooped up in my bedroom, and most importantly, they wanted me away from Cesar. They knew that he wasn't a good boyfriend, but they never knew the true extent of it.

"Norah's Panetteria is going down!" Salem grunted.

"Salem, shame on you. That's your nonna!"

"Nonna or not, I will ensure my bakery is the talk of the town."

"Everyone already knows about it because Nonna Norah passed it down to you."

Salem batted her eyelashes, and her lips formed a tight line. "What do you gain from saying all of this?"

I shrugged. "Riling you up is a pleasure."

"So disrespectful," she said, shaking her head.

"*Ciao, mie belle nipotine!*" Nonna Norah greeted,

entering the café. *Hello, my beautiful granddaughters!*

Nonna Norah was a small, round woman with gray hair twirled up into a bun. I wasn't her granddaughter, but she insisted on calling me one since I befriended Salem in sixth grade. Salem wasn't biologically related to her either; she was adopted into the Russo family at the age of four. The only traces of her old life were her name and that she was also born in Salem, Massachusetts.

"Nonna!" Salem smiled, running over to her grandmother to embrace her. "I was telling Estella here that we could never really compete with you. You've been here for twenty years, creating a name for yourself. We are frauds, really." Salem placed a dramatic hand over her chest.

Nonna wasn't buying it. "I'm sure that is exactly what you said." Nonna handed Salem a thick, brown book.

"Yes, thank you!" Salem cheered, running over to the counter to look through all of Nonna's most beloved desserts. She intended on baking the same sweets to keep the old customers around.

Nonna walked over to the end of the café and gazed at our shelves of ceramic art pieces. "Estella, did you make all of these?" she said in awe.

"Yes."

"So beautiful," she said, reaching over to a piece that I had made of a young woman playing the piano alongside a fox wearing a top hat.

Story of my life. Literally.

I specialized in making customized knickknacks, plates, mugs and anything ceramic. New York was too large of a state to make a name for myself, so I decided to bring my talent to the small city of Castellara, Italy. I had seen many painters and needleworkers, but no sculptors. There wouldn't be any competition for me here. Then again, I wasn't planning on launching a massive business. I aimed to create art in the backroom of Salem's restaurant and renovate it into my own little studio.

"I love this one," she said, picking up a cherub figurine. "Consider it your first sale," she declared, handing me twenty euros.

"Thank you." I beamed.

"Well, I'm off to my book club. I will let the ladies know that you're opening tomorrow; it might be our new spot." Nonna wiggled her eyebrows in delight. She had been working nonstop until a month ago. She ached for a slower pace of life, and honestly, she deserved it. She was a busy woman, so she still wanted to work and be involved but not take the reins. I respected that.

"I can't wait to see you around," I said, wrapping an arm around her shoulder.

She was four inches shorter than me and went on the tips of her toes to place a rough kiss on my temple. "My sweet Estella."

Salem had been too enthralled by the cookbook to say her goodbyes. "I'm going to have to stay here until midnight in order to perfect all of Nonna's treats," she huffed.

"This is *your* bakery, Salem. Make it you. Make all the treats that you're great at creating. Cupcakes, donuts, macarons, cookies, and maybe add three of Nonna's special items for a touch of Italy."

"Maybe." She hesitated. "Will you help me figure out what three special menu items we should add?"

"Of course, I can even help you make them, but after my Italian class."

Salem collapsed onto the counter and groaned. "I need help now."

"It'll only be an hour or two," I reminded her. "I need to be there in thirty minutes."

"I told you that I could help you with your Italian."

"I need to know more than curse words if I'm living here for a year."

"Curse words are the foundation of a language."

"Bye, Salem," I said, waving my fingers.

"Ugh, fine, leave me," she whined.

I slipped on my brown, leather backpack and headed out through the back of the café. My sky-blue Vespa scooter waited for me, and I eagerly plopped my helmet onto my head. Salem and I had both received gently used scooters for our travels around the city. It was a gift from Nonna Norah, but Salem said that an admirer of Nonna's had bought it for us. Nonna was a secretive lady so I believed it. Either way, I was grateful for whoever bought it.

Castellara was picture-perfect. The population was about three thousand, and everyone knew everyone eventually. The lake was vast and bluer than the sky. The sun was out with great fortitude, and the water glistened as I rode down the path to the small community college.

I wasn't used to being in the countryside, but the breath of fresh air was delightful. It was nice to escape the city smog, the blaring car horns, the phone-obsessed pedestrians, and the fast-paced life. New York City always seemed too rushed for me. In this little, old city, the kids were outdoors playing with grand smiles plastered on their faces, people bicycling with each other, birds fluttering above and singing beautiful songs. You'd be lucky to hear a bird sing this well in Brooklyn. The poor birds had their lungs infected from all the air pollution.

The community college was a small-sized building made out of red bricks with two archways that led to the only level of the building. It was the tallest building I had seen in the city but definitely paled in comparison to the properties that were across the lake.

I parked my scooter by the edge of one of the building's walls where everyone else had theirs lined up. There was a young man playing the guitar by the entrance of the college, and he flashed charming smiles to all the girls that walked past him. His light brown eyes met my gaze, and he winked. I gave him a polite smile and walked away.

No love, no romance.

The building had an old-town feel to it, but it was refreshing for me. I had grown tired of seeing industrial buildings taking over the city, so seeing a city with its original architecture had me appreciate the culture a lot more. I easily found the library in it, as well.

Leaving Paris

Leonardo, my Italian tutor, had informed me that he was sitting in the back corner of the library, so I walked around until I found someone that looked around my age. Nonna Norah had referred him to me for a tutor but never gave me a physical description. I tilted my head quizzically at the man I suspected to be my tutor. He glanced up, smiling widely. It had to be him.

"Estella?" he asked.

"*Si*! Leonardo?"

"*Si*," he said, appreciative of my Italian response. "Should we start?"

"*Si*."

"*Bene!*" he said, clapping his hands together and signaling to the table.

Leonardo deserved more than what I was paying him, and I insisted on paying more, but he happily objected. I stumbled over words, had him repeat himself over twenty times, and probably made an already painful experience even more aggravating. I thought only learning to converse instead of learning all the grammatical technicities would have been easier, but I proved myself wrong.

We went over the basics: *hi, how are you; what's your name; what would you like to order?* All the basic phrases that

Leaving Paris

I would need to say at Salem's café. I understood that Salem was the baker and had to stay in the back most of the time, but it didn't make sense to have someone who didn't know Italian work at the front.

"I've heard a couple students talk about the café," Leonardo said. "They are excited for the opening especially since it'll be the most updated place around here."

"Oh no," I whispered.

He looked at me in bewilderment.

"I mean, I'm happy but I'm nervous. I'll be doing most of the talking."

"It'll be okay," he assured. "I'll make sure you're prepared. On the bright side, most people here speak English and will find any opportunity to speak it."

"How about you come in tomorrow, and I will give you a treat on the house? It's the least I can do for all of this."

"On the house?" he asked, tilting his head and his light gray eyes searching mine for an answer. I took a minute to appreciate his looks. For the past hour that we had been studying, I had been too stiff to absorb his facial features. Looking at him with a newfound peace of mind, he was actually quite handsome.

"*Gratis*," I said.

"Ah, okay," he said, nodding in approval.

"See you on Wednesday?" I asked.

He confirmed with a solid nod.

"*Ciao!*" I hollered, slinging my backpack over my shoulder.

The singer was no longer outside when I left the small college; it would've been nice to hear him play the guitar again. I always appreciated a musician, just not too much or too personally.

I hopped onto my scooter and had my helmet hovering over my head when my ears were hit with a beautiful melody. I lowered my helmet and searched the open area for the direction in which the music came from but couldn't determine it.

I entered the building again, the music sounding stronger but still untraceable. The music created a beautifully haunting tone as I walked down the vacant hallways. It definitely wasn't an original; I'd heard the song before. I couldn't pinpoint it, and it was virtually impossible to know the name when I'd listened to thousands of classic songs.

After walking farther into the building, I heard the music fill the hallways with vibrations, and that's when I knew I was close to the source. I hadn't been this captivated by piano playing in the last five years, since Paris. Every ounce of logic told me to back away, to not even tempt myself with the sight of who was playing. It could be *him*.

No, impossible. In a world of 7.6 billion, what are the odds we'd meet again?

I peeked into a room, and to my surprise, found an older gentleman playing on the piano. His body swayed from left to right as his fingers danced along the keys, his back somewhat hunched over. I pressed half of my body against the door frame and admired the talent that the man exuded. It was clear that this wasn't just his career; it was his life.

The song ended as quickly as it began, and I waited for him to play another song, but instead, he closed the piano and sat in silence.

The man sighed deeply and swirled around only to find me staring at him. His amber eyes widened in shock. He clearly wasn't expecting an audience.

"*Mi dispiace,*" I apologized. "I didn't mean to startle you…" I continued to fumble over my words as the man stared at me. "*Non parlo Italiano.*"

"I speak English," he said, placing his hand on his lap.

He had an accent but not as thick as everyone else in the town.

I placed my hand over my chest in relief. "I'm sorry, I didn't mean to eavesdrop. I heard you playing from outside and had to follow the music."

"Do you play?" he asked.

"Oh, no. I haven't touched a piano in years."

"Why?"

How do I explain to a stranger that I associated the piano with an absolute jerk who stole my heart? So much pleasure, so much pain. This wasn't information you shared with anyone but a best friend because it was ludicrous and downright embarrassing.

"Work," I answered simply.

"Too much talent has been lost because of business," he said as if he spoke from experience.

"Probably." I sighed. "You're amazing though."

"I'm not too bad," he said, humbling himself. "I've only composed for a number of films and shows." A simple brag. I appreciated it.

My mouth dropped open and I started to grow nervous. "Oh, my God," I whispered.

"Would you like to hear more?" he asked, his smile

widely enthusiastic. It seemed like he needed this more than I did.

"It'd be a pleasure," I said, entering the room and walking toward a nearby chair. "What's your name?"

"Emile," he responded as his fingers moved swiftly into a more playful tone. "And yours?"

"Estella."

"Star," he smiled. "Lovely name."

"*Grazie*," I said.

"What brings you to an old city in Italy?"

"A journey of self-discovery."

"It is the perfect place for that."

"How about you? A man of your talent should be in New York performing concerts."

"I'm too old for all the traveling and back-to-back performances." He stopped playing and began to rub his hands and wrists. "My body is beginning to fail me."

I looked down at my hands and couldn't imagine what Emile was going through. I wasn't a pianist, but I was a sculptor and needed my hands in order to create visual art as he needed his to create auditory art. To be betrayed by your own body was heart-wrenching.

"Now, I'm left to offer piano classes because I have the

need to teach, yet no one in this town is interested. I've only taught one person who loved it with true passion, but they got swept away into business many years ago."

We remained silent, and I noticed that he was truly grieving the loss of that student.

"Teach me," I said without thinking; the words just slipped out of my mouth. "I may not turn out to be a famous composer, but the art would be appreciated." A part of me doubted myself because I wouldn't be able to pick up scales easily as someone younger or well-practiced. I had to mentally convince myself that this was a part of self-discovery. To try, to learn, to fail, to get back up again.

"I believe you," he said. "We start tomorrow."

Chapter 5

IGNACIO

"I believe this is it," Marcelo announced, stepping out of the car and putting his sunglasses on. "Salem's Café," he said, simply.

I eyed the exterior and stared at Marcelo. "You could hire any bakery in the world to make your wedding cake—you do know, that right?" It wasn't even a bakery; it was a café.

"It's a cake," he said, bored. "Also, I'm doing my due diligence by hiring local businesses. I heard this place has the right people for the job."

"By whom?"

Marcelo raised an eyebrow and shrugged. "People."

"Right," I said, giving the bakery one more stare.

"Let's just get this over with."

Camilla was nothing like Marcelo, and had it not been for their ulterior motives, then they wouldn't have entertained each other. Camilla was the daughter of Marcelo's culinary role model, Massimo Russo. I didn't exactly know what Camilla's motives were, but it was clear that when she looked at Marcelo, she certainly had one.

We entered the small botanical café. The nutty aroma of the fresh coffee immediately hit us. I wasn't a fan of coffee, but I enjoyed the scent and the nostalgia that came along with it.

The restaurant was different from the other shops around the area. The walls were painted with a rough coat of white over the brick walls which gave more texture to the color. Wooden shelves held plants, printed-out poems, paintings, and knickknacks.

"Alright, be safe," someone hollered into the backroom.

A girl with raven hair, that slightly grazed her shoulders, appeared from the curtains and flashed a welcoming smile. It was clear that she was American from the way she spoke and the way she dressed. She had a plain black T-shirt paired with light blue shorts and other black accessories. It had the minimal look that I would see when

Leaving Paris

I traveled back to the States to visit my mom in New York.

"Benvenuto al caffè di Salem!"

"Are you Salem?" Marcelo asked in English. If he had the opportunity to speak in English, he took it. He wanted to make sure his English was flawless. Unlike me, I had an American mother and Italian father, and I bounced from using both English and Italian. I didn't have too much of an accent when speaking English. I only used to exaggerate it when I wanted to feel like somebody else.

"Yes, sir," she replied, happily.

"I'm having a wedding, and I'm looking for a local café…bakery to make it for me. Would this be possible?"

"I'd be happy to do that for you! When is the wedding?"

"In a month and a half."

"For how many people?"

"About two hundred," he said. "We don't have the location set so don't worry about transportation—just the cake."

Salem's face dropped in surprise. "Ookaay," she whispered. It was her grand opening day, and Marcelo had slapped a hefty job on her plate.

"And I'd like a small cake for the rehearsal dinner party. That'll be in a month and for about seventy people."

Salem frantically started to jot down the information on a small notepad. She huffed in confusion and scratched the top of her head with the back of the pen. "That's definitely doable, but a large order on such short notice will be a pretty penny." She was casual and direct; Marcelo probably appreciated her forwardness.

Marcelo reached in for his wallet from his blazer and pulled out his credit card. "I'm ready when you are," he said.

I rolled my eyes and turned on my heels to look at the figurines on the shelves by the large window. There were cherubs, angelic women, wedding toppers, plates, cups, and an odd one of a fox with a top hat playing the piano with a young woman sitting on the shared bench. I picked it up to take a closer look at it. Whoever made it took their time to make the piece; the piano seemed to have all its details.

There was a name handwritten on the back which read **E. SALVADOR**. So, Salem didn't make them.

"Everyone loves that one," Salem said from the counter.

"That's pretty funny." Marcelo chuckled.

Was it funny? At first glance, it seemed lighthearted, but I wondered if there was a specific story behind it. It was too out of place with the other figurines to just have a comical purpose.

"Yeah," I said, placing it back.

"Are we all done here?" Marcelo asked.

"Yes, sir," she answered.

"Sounds good," he said and allowed his signature smirk to make an appearance. Marcelo was trying to hit on her, and she wasn't necessarily buying it.

"She was hot," Marcelo commented the second we stepped outside. "Makes me wish I wasn't getting married."

"Really?" I sighed as I traced the long scratch on the side of my Mercedes Benz. I never cared about labels or fancy cars, but my father did and if he saw me driving it around with a scratch, he'd throw a fit.

"No one drives a car to Castellara," Marcelo said. "Let alone a luxury car—maybe a fiat but not a Mercedes."

"You weren't saying anything when I drove you here for your cake."

Marcelo shrugged and slipped into the passenger seat.

I didn't open my door. I simply turned on my heels without warning and headed back to the café.

"Welcome back!" Salem greeted. "Everything alright?"

I made a beeline straight to the piano/fox figurine and

took it to the counter. "I'd like to buy this," I said, pulling out a one hundred euro note.

"That'll be seventy-five euros," she said, grabbing it.

I nodded, and she wrapped the figurine in tissue paper and placed it in a small gift bag. "The change can be a tip to the artist."

"She will appreciate it. Enjoy," Salem said, handing me the bag.

I headed back to my car and sat in the driver's seat, placing the bag in the backseat. I expected Marcelo to ask about my purchase and throw judgment, but he had eyes fixated on the screen of his phone as his fingers typed rapidly.

"Fuck, she's coming two days early," Marcelo groaned. "She'll be here at 8 p.m. today."

"Camilla?" I asked, starting up the car.

"She doesn't trust me with handling my wedding to-do list," he grumbled, stuffing his phone back into his pockets.

There wasn't much advice I could give him considering that most of my encounters with women had failed miserably. Marriage wasn't likely for me, and Marcelo was doing an outstanding job at solidifying it.

"Let's go to the bar," Marcelo suggested. "I'd rather be

hammered when she comes, so I couldn't care less about her rants." He had about five hours to drink his sorrows; it was doable.

"Very well," I said, taking us back to Lilla.

Chapter 6

ESTELLA

My lesson with Emile was a splendid experience, and the high that came from learning from a master didn't wear off until I was a minute away from Salem's café. When I had left my work shift, I accidentally scratched a Mercedes Benz when I turned the corner. I was too excited about the lesson and wasn't paying attention when I made a sharp turn. Granted, the luxury car shouldn't have parked on the side of the building, but what did rich people care?

To my luck, the car was no longer there. I parked my scooter by the back door and opened the door to enter. Salem stood by the front counter, flicking through photos on her phone. Through our large window, I could see her hunched over. Anybody could look into the kitchen if they wanted to do so.

I popped out from the black curtain and stood next to her. "Busy day?"

Salem jumped up and clapped. "We had a lot of business today."

"Like what?" I asked, putting my apron back on.

"Three thousand worth of business."

"What?" I squealed.

"These two hot guys came in, and one of them is getting married. He wants two cakes, one for the wedding consisting of two hundred people and another smaller cake. We hit the jackpot!"

For a small business that was an astronomical amount of money especially with it being the first official day.

"That's going to be a lot of work, Salem. You've made cakes for fifty people, but two-hundred?"

She shrugged, not too worried. "It's doable, and he wants it relatively simple. Nonna and Maria will be on it, too; they won't disappoint."

"Good, we'll need all the help we can get."

Salem walked out from the counter area and to the shelves that displayed my work. She pointed to an empty space on the shelf. "The other hot guy bought your piano-playing fox."

"Really?" I whispered, scanning all the shelves to confirm the purchase.

"Yeah! Keep them coming!" she said, pulling out change from her pocket and handing it to me. "A tip from the buyer."

I stood there in utter disbelief that one of my most significant figurines had been purchased by a complete stranger. It was a figurine I made to cope with the heartbreaking relationship that I had in Paris when I was twenty. The piano player was such a gentleman on the keys and in bed, which is why the fox wore a top hat, but he was nothing more than a fox. Mischievous, untrusting, cunning, and transformative. He made me believe that we had a genuine connection, but that was proven wrong when he left before I woke up.

I want this forever.

The words replayed in my head like a haunting lullaby, making the little hairs on my arms rise. Those were the words he'd said to me after we finished making love and he kissed me tenderly. I believed him, but I blamed that on naivety. Men will say what you want to hear in order to get in between your legs. My foolish heart fell for it.

"You okay there, bud?" Salem asked, noticing that I hadn't moved.

"Yeah," I said, snapping myself out of my thoughts and tying my hair back.

Salem knew about that night, but we never talked about it after it happened. It was such an embarrassing and low point in my life that I didn't want to discuss it again. We promised to bury it and never let it out again or let it happen again.

"I'll be in my studio," I said, heading through the white drapes that led to my sanctuary.

It was a medium-sized storage room transformed into a ceramic art studio. It had a wooden table in the corner, where I would sit to work out details on a piece, wooden shelves on the walls to hold all my materials, a drying rack, a potter's wheel, and a small kiln. It was the right amount of perfect to satisfy me.

Time seemed irrelevant at the moment; all I could do was sit on my barstool and look at the clay in front of me. Ignacio was on my mind, and I desperately wanted him out of it. He had preoccupied too much of my life, emotions, and time already.

There was only one way that I could deal with all of it.

All of him. I placed my earbuds in and pressed play on *Fool That I Am* by Etta James. Her rich, raspy voice blasted on repeat as I worked on the potter's wheel.

Two hours went by, and I had accomplished absolutely nothing. My hands would move up and down the wet clay, only to smash it back down. If I did create something remotely decent, I'd stare at it until I convinced myself otherwise and destroy it.

"Why can't I get you out of my mind?" I said, staring at the mess before me. Thinking about Ignacio had hindered my ability to accomplish anything.

Salem peeked her head into my studio. "Ready to go?" she asked. "Nonna said to head to her place; she's making pizza."

"Give me five minutes," I said, taking my apron off and looking at the mess I had to clean up.

At least there wasn't anything food couldn't fix.

***

People like to believe that the older you get, the uglier you will be, but the ladies in front of me showed that all it was fake talk. Nonna Norah and her friends radiated beauty at their age, probably at their peak, in my opinion. Their gray hairs glistened under the light, their faces tan and blushed, their laughter causing a beautiful storm, their grins as wide Lake Castellara. I envied their happy and carefree attitude. Obviously, they had all gone through the tumultuous journey of life and deserved the calm.

"Estella, I heard that you're taking classes with Signore Emile," Antonella said, eyeing Nonna Norah with a flirtatious look.

"Oh stop," Nonna Norah said, swatting her look away.

"Ah, is that Nonna's admirer?" Salem cooed.

Antonella didn't say anything, but her child-like eyes made it clear that something was going on between Nonna Norah and Emile.

"Ignore these two," Nonna said and looked at me. "How are the lessons going?"

"They're great," I chimed. "He's an amazing teacher. I'm learning how to read sheets."

"Outstanding. I hope I can hear you play one day," Nonna said.

"When I'm good," I assured her.

"I wonder if she's learning the song that he wrote for you on your birthday," Stefania chimed in, snickering with

Antonella.

"Oh, hush, you two," Nonna Norah said, trying to diffuse all the rumors.

All four of the women at the table bickered back and forth, making assumptions about their relationship, recalling memories and other tidbits that put a smile on my face. Nonna Norah seemed annoyed, but it was all harmless. I think she even enjoyed all the attention despite her shushing.

He played a love song once, and I wondered if it was the same song he played for Nonna Norah. Emile never mentioned her even when I told him that I worked at Salem's café, and everyone knew she was Nonna Norah's granddaughter.

He never told me how long ago he composed the song, just that it was about a man who desperately wanted to be in love but was afraid of the heartbreak. At the end of the song, he finally conceded to love and realized that he had nothing to fear. They were both widowers, so they had all the reasons to want to avoid love again.

The song was called *Fammi Innamorare*, translated in English as *Let Me Fall in Love*.

Everyone could relate to the song at some point in their

lives, and I was in that current situation. Ever since Paris, it had been difficult for me to emotionally give myself away to a man, only because I was afraid that they were the next fox wanting to steal all the joy from me. My ex-boyfriend didn't help with my existing issue; he actually magnified them.

Two weeks before coming to Italy, I had broken up with a boy named Cesar. We dated for about six months, then I quickly realized that he was a mistake. While he was pursuing me, he was the definition of a perfect boyfriend; even Salem liked him. Once we made it official, he started to demand sex, got drunk often and spat nasty names, and constantly humiliated me. I never told anyone the extent of his abuse, but Salem and my family started picking up on my hesitation to be around him. Cesar was rude, narcissistic, unapologetic and I hated being around him, but I didn't know how to leave him.

There were many sleepless nights consisting of curling up in a ball and asking the universe to change him because I didn't feel strong enough to leave.

Then the day came.

Cesar wanted to celebrate since we had been dating for half a year and I had been excited but nervous about meeting him. We'd had a fight a couple days before, and he had been giving me the silent treatment. He didn't like that I went to a bar with Salem for her birthday. He expected every weekend to be about him, but I drew the line for Salem. I had to make time for my best friend. He had blocked my number and all my social media accounts so I could have a taste of what my life would be like without him.

It wasn't relieving. If anything, it was more anxiety-inducing because I was made out to be a villain just for trying to celebrate with my best friend. Salem told me to never contact him again and when I was with her, I dared to look forward, but whenever she left my side, I became weak again. She had left early one day to go to work, and I stayed home, which was when Cesar came by with a bouquet of flowers. He asked me to join him that night for dinner and left.

I met him for dinner at a fancy restaurant, and he immediately made a scene about my scandalous outfit.

"I didn't expect you to dress like that," he said, eyeing me from head to toe.

"Like what?"

"A whore," he mumbled and walked ahead as the hostess

motioned us to the dining area. "Is that how you dressed when you went to the bar?"

I looked down at my blue dress and shook my head no. "Of course not."

"Good girl."

I hated those words; I felt beneath him every time he uttered them. Sometimes, he'd pat me whenever he said them, and I could feel my skin burn, but not in a good way.

"So, how have you—"

"I'm getting impatient with you, Twinkle," Cesar interrupted.

"What did I do?" My voice was barely a whisper.

"It's what you're not doing. I'm not waiting much longer for you."

I wanted to play dumb, but I knew what he was talking about. We'd been together for six months and I still hadn't slept with him. Cesar always got what he wanted, and every time I tell him I can't take the next step, all Hell breaks loose.

"Do you hear me?" he growled. "If you loved me, you wouldn't make me wait anymore."

"I'm sorry." After that night in Paris, I never gained the courage to sleep with another man. It was terrifying to become intimate with another man after the first one fell off the face of the Earth.

"You better be." Cesar scanned the menu. "Keep it light. You look like you've put on some weight the past few days."

I shifted uncomfortably in my seat and tried to adjust my dress so it didn't cling too much onto my body. If anything, I had lost weight from all the stress and anxiety that he had caused when he kept ignoring me. Cesar was good at making me feel like the bad guy, even when I logically knew that I wasn't, but he always won.

"You're still pretty—you have a nice face and all that—just need to work on your body a little more."

"And you need to work on your manners," I responded, the words slipping out of my mouth. I rarely snapped back at Cesar, but I had grown exhausted of all his pressures and inconsiderateness.

Cesar lowered his menu and looked straight at me, his black eyes penetrating me. "What?"

"Nothing."

"Didn't sound like nothing," he spat.

"It was nothing." My voice was trembling, my hands were sweating, and I could feel the bile rising up my throat.

Cesar lurched out of his seat, grabbed my wrist, and pulled me down a block before pinning me against a wall in a hidden alley. He grabbed my jaw and clenched it tightly as he brought my face forward. "Who do you think you're talking to?"

Silence. I couldn't say another word, not only because he was crushing my jaw but because all that courage I had a minute ago had disappeared. It was just me, him, and a dark alley. People were walking by, but they were too lost in their own world to see that mine was crashing.

"I'm sorry, I'm sorry," I mumbled incoherently.

Cesar crooked his head to the side and admired the fear that had been radiating out of me. He got off on my pain. There was no love in him. He wasn't capable of loving anyone but himself.

"Good girl," he said, releasing me.

I gingerly held onto my jaw as I kept the tears at bay. This was the first time Cesar had put his hands on me, and I knew that it wouldn't be the last. Whenever he crossed a line, he would always find the next one to cross.

"I'm hungry; I'm going to buy a sub." He wrapped his arm around my waist and kept me pressed against his hip as we walked a couple of blocks to his favorite sub shop.

"Hey Stanley, one Philly steak to go," he shouted as he entered the deli.

"You got it," Stanley responded. "Anything for you, Estellita?"

"She's not too hungry," Cesar responded. *"Why don't you go to the bathroom and clean-up your face? It's a mess,"* Cesar ordered, whispering into my ear.

I walked towards the back of the deli and into the run-down bathroom. The floor was covered in dirt, toilet paper, and wrappers. The bathroom was absolutely disgusting, but it was a saving grace. Between the toilet and sink there was a window.

It was a small window and on a normal day, I probably wouldn't have fit, but with my lack of food intake and drive to survive, I forced myself in. I squirmed and wiggled until I plopped five feet onto the dirty, alley floor. It wasn't pleasant, but it was freedom and I wasn't going to undermine that.

The police station should've been my first destination, but instead, I ran to the Russo's restaurant. Salem was working double that night, but I flung my arms around her the second I saw her. She took me to the back of the kitchen and ordered one of the line cooks to make me a meal and watch over me until she finished work.

I stayed with her for a couple days, and that is when she devised a plan to run away to Italy "for the hell of it", but I knew she just wanted us out of Brooklyn. We went to my parents and we didn't even have to sell the plan to them; they were completely on board. Two weeks later, we were on a plane to

Italy, and I hadn't seen Cesar since that night.

"What's on your mind?" Nonna Norah asked, placing her soft hand over mine.

"Oh." I sighed, trying to come up with a lie. "I'm wondering what cheese you used on these delicious pizzas."

"Mozzarella!" all the girls hollered in unison and erupted in laughter.

"Of course." I nervously chuckled. Not only did I make it clear that I was lying, but that I was an idiot as well.

"Are you feeling okay?" Nonna Norah asked.

"I'm actually exhausted," I said. "I think I'm going to head back to the cottage."

"Okay, it's not a problem," she said.

"I should be there in an hour or so," Salem said. "After we get some answers from Nonna here." She gave Nonna a mischievous look, and Nonna ignored her by looking in the opposite direction.

"*Buonanotte*," I said, excusing myself.

There were three cottages near the lake shore, hidden amongst tall, luscious trees. One of the cottages belonged to Nonna, the other one was abandoned but still had good bones, and the other one belonged to me and Salem. It was a small, cute house that had enough integrity to support two girls in their twenties.

I dragged my feet across the grass and towards the cobblestoned ledge to look out into the lake. During the day, the blistering-hot sun would project down into the turquoise-blue water and welcome its visitors, but at night, it looked ominous, especially with the emptiness of the space around it. The moonlight shone down on the face of the lake, and the water in the spotlight twinkled with clarity. The nearing autumn wind tousled my hair, and I closed my eyes, inhaling deeply through my nose and exhaling through my mouth.

There was no point in tormenting myself about the past. I came to the small, quiet town of Castellara to move forward. I couldn't let myself fall into the habit of overthinking about unchangeable.

This trip was for me. I wasn't going to let anyone get in the way of it—especially not the ghosts of my past. Nobody was looking for me or at me; it was just me against myself.

Chapter 7

IGNACIO

One would expect the piano room to be my most beloved spot, but that was far from the truth. It had been designed perfectly to compliment the famous Fazioli, and yet, it looked almost abandoned because the piano had been draped by a large, white cloth. I hadn't played it ever since Paris, or any piano for that matter.

There was no way I could get rid of it even if it tormented me day and night. It carried too much value; it was everything that reminded me of Estella. All the laughter, stories told near it, and the kisses shared on it. I didn't want it to lose its musical beauty, so the only time it was played was when I hired someone to tune it once a year. The Fazioli had an upcoming appointment, and I wondered if it was time to do the job myself.

My hand hovered over the ghostly drape, and before I could pick it up to reveal the object of all my wistful memories, my phone rang loudly.

"Nonno," I answered. "How are you doing?"

My nonno, Emile Amatore, was a world-renowned pianist and the man who taught me everything I knew about piano. He was more of a father to me than my own father, and I appreciated everything that he had done for me. Nonno and I were pretty much inseparable until I decided to work at my father's business about five years ago and deserted the world of music. Nonno claimed that I broke his heart, and although I believed he was exaggerating, things had never been the same for us even after I moved to the neighboring city.

"My hands are failing me a little more every day; what is new?" he said with a light chuckle.

Nonno was diagnosed with carpal tunnel syndrome about five years ago—around the same time I decided to end my musical career—and it made his life a little more difficult every day. Most of the time, doing simple day-to-day tasks wouldn't cause any harm, but if he played the piano for too long, then it would flare up.

"Is there anything you need help with?" I asked. "I don't mind going into Castellara to check on you."

"I'm not that old of a man," he scolded. "But I do need your help."

"Sure."

"I'm teaching a young lady to play the piano, and I've enjoyed my sessions with her—"

"You shouldn't be playing," I said, clearly upset.

"Don't interrupt me," he warned and continued to scold me in Italian. *I'm your grandfather and I demand enough respect to not be interrupted.*

He wasn't upset that I interrupted him; he was upset that I was holding him accountable for disobeying doctor's orders. Nonno was a stubborn man and unwilling to let go of his passion for piano even if it meant putting his health at risk. As much as I didn't want him in pain, I also knew that not playing caused more harm than good.

"I'm sorry."

"My wrist isn't doing well, and I can't teach her today. This is the last session for the week, and I'll let my wrist heal until the next session. I don't want to cancel on her; she is very passionate and a quick learner. I don't think she'd give you any issues. You need to be in the music room in an hour."

I rubbed my forehead with my free hand. "Nonno, I haven't played in five years."

"Talent like yours never disappears," he said.

"It's not that I'm not capable," I said.

"What is it? Speak then."

I can't bear playing the piano anymore, especially with another woman.

"It's complicated."

"I won't tell your father," he said. "Is that it? Fear that he will reprimand you as a grown adult?"

I scowled at him. Nonno barely spoke to my father after I stopped playing because he believed my father influenced my decision. He wasn't completely wrong—my father was offering a large fortune if I joined him in his business, but it was so much more complicated. I had been suffocated with the need to succeed.

"He wouldn't care because I'm still working for him."

"Shame," he whispered.

"I won't be able to do it," I answered. "I'm sorry, Nonno, please do not be upset with me."

He muttered under his breath before hanging up: *I'm not upset; I'm disappointed.*

Leaving Paris

Everyone knew that being disappointed in someone was far worse than being upset or angry. Worst of all, he had every right to be disappointed. He constantly gave, and all he wanted was a fraction of his deserved returns.

I gripped my phone and stared at the covered piano. How did I let myself part ways with something that I loved so much? The money wasn't worth it, and it wasn't like money was ever a concern for me. The Amatore family were millionaires, and by default, I was one, as well. It was my need for validation from my father, to prove myself invaluable that dug me into the miserable position that I was currently in.

The world convinces you that if you have money, a home, a business, and a legacy, the world can be yours, but nothing has been easy or joyous. None of it mattered if you didn't have anyone to share it with. The only real family I had was Nonno, and even then, we still weren't as close as we were before. I hadn't seen him in months, and I hadn't been at his cottage for years.

My fingers hovered over the keyboard on my phone, and it was a mental battle between wanting to let go of my past with the piano and also not wanting to disappoint the only man that I respected.

Me: I'll be there.

There was an immediate response.

Nonno: I knew you'd make the right choice.

I'd also be lying if I said I wasn't curious about this mystery lady that had impressed my grandfather. He was a judgmental man, and most of the time, he believed that the majority of people weren't made for the piano. The only time I heard him praise someone was when he spoke about me to a close friend of his who played the violin. They were discussing their best students, and I was the first and only one he mentioned.

I arrived five minutes late to the session which wasn't too bad, but if Nonno found out, he would lecture me for hours. He instilled punctuality in all his students because time was critical in the world of music.

The first thing I expected to see from the student was a scowl on her face to show her disapproval of my tardiness. Instead, I stood by the door frame and noticed her playing a song that made my heart beat hard against my chest. A rush of memories surfaced with the help of the composition. I'd only heard it once before, five years ago in Paris.

Every timid step I took toward the piano caused my

heart to pound even more intensely. The pressure of it urged me to leave the room, to convince Nonno and myself that I never arrived at the small college. The music and the heartbeats were so deafening, I almost lost my balance, but I remained unknown to the girl playing the piano. She was too immersed in the piano to recognize that I was behind her.

I wanted to see her face. I wanted to confirm it was Estella. I also wanted to run out of the room and toward the hill. How, after five years, did our worlds collide in an old part of Italy that people couldn't even point to on a map? Was it fate, destiny, an alignment of the universe, a curse, a second chance?

My eyes scanned her straight posture that accentuated the soft curves of her body, the length of her chocolate-brown hair cascading down her back, and her delicacy. All I needed was to see her beautiful face, and that would confirm that the woman who'd haunted all my dreams was in Italy, in the same classroom, now a foot away from me.

The song ended, and her gentle arms fell to her side, her body slouching slightly. She didn't move and neither did I. I couldn't have been breathing. If it was Estella, what would she say? What would she do? What would I say or do?

Apologize profusely, I reminded myself.

Her body slowly moved, and I knew that the time had come when we would meet face to face. I composed myself despite my mind being in a complete frenzy, and I waited for the moment our eyes met. There was no chance of hiding, and I had to accept the consequences of my past actions, or lack of actions, to be more accurate.

Her innocent face couldn't have hidden her emotions: shock, anger, shock, uncertainty, and then anger again. The pain was evident from the way her brow creased and the downward curve of her full lips. Betrayal swirled around in the mix of her brown eyes. As I looked into them, I just knew that she hated me.

Estella's eyes turned glossy, and her lip quivered.

"Estella," I whispered with ten layers of guilt in my voice.

Estella sat in place, rubbed her arm, and then pinched herself. No, this wasn't a dream; it was a nightmare.

When the realization hit her, she shuffled off of the piano and hastily grabbed her bag that had been on the ground. She tried to rush past me, but my hand shot up and wrapped around her wrist just enough to not let her escape me so easily.

Leaving Paris

Her gaze traveled all over my face, and mine all over hers.

"I'm sorry," was all I could muster.

"Just don't," she seethed, trying to pull away.

"Let me explain, Estella," I begged.

Half of her body was touching mine, our faces inches away from each other, our scents intermingling. She no longer smelled like strawberries and cream; it was something more alluring, more sensual, more mature. I was no longer dealing with the young girl I met in Paris; I was dealing with a girl who had been hurt, broken, scarred, and unwilling to let that happen again.

"I don't want to hear it," she spat.

"That's not true."

"Let go, now."

"Not again," I responded.

That made her react a little differently, but she grounded herself again.

"Leave me alone."

And before I could release her, there was a loud knock on the door that took me off guard, and she managed to slip away. I turned around to find a blond-haired boy around her age who held a phone in his hand.

"Estella, you left your phone at the library," he said, his gaze bouncing between the two of us. The whole situation didn't look good—because it wasn't—and I slid my hands into my pockets. I shouldn't have touched her.

Estella tucked a loose strand of hair behind her ear and walked toward him. "Thank you," she said, grabbing it and slipping past him.

A part of me wanted to run down the hallway and catch up with Estella, but I knew that she needed that time to process the situation and perhaps, grieve.

The thought of having to tell Nonno that the lesson didn't go well would disappoint him, and that was the last thing I wanted to do, especially after all these years.

Most importantly, the thought of Estella living across from me was going to haunt me.

Chapter 8

ESTELLA

What were the odds of bumping into the man you dated for three weeks and slept with half a decade ago?

Almost zero.

My body moved through the motions of flight, but my mind was frozen. I returned to the cottage with every intention of chucking all of my belongings into my suitcase and heading straight to the airport. I couldn't be in Castellara anymore knowing that *he* was here.

"Damn it!" I cried, throwing myself onto the bed.

All I wanted from this year-long trip was to find myself, fall in love with my passions, and discover another town other than Brooklyn. Four weeks into the trip, of course, I had to collide with the man who had obliterated my foolish, naïve heart. I fell in love with, made love with him, all for it to be thrown away without a trace.

My mistake for ever believing him.

Many questions raced through my mind: Did he live here? Was he on vacation? Did he follow me? The last one gave me the creeps.

I still hadn't forgotten a single etching carved in his deviously handsome face. The man had hardly aged in the past five years. His hair was shorter, and he'd upgraded his glasses to silver, retro frames that gave him a hot-professor look which, unfortunately, turned me on.

Every part of me felt on fire, and I couldn't tell if it was due to hate or lust. They were nearly the same emotion—consumable and full of passion.

It had nearly been over an hour after my encounter, and I still lay in bed contemplating my next move. I desperately wanted to leave, to ensure that I wouldn't see him again, but there was a lot going for me already in Castellara. Salem's café was booming, people loved my work, I adored being taught by a famous pianist, and being out of a busy, loud city allowed me to live in peace for once.

My phone lit up, and I noticed that Emile's name appeared on the screen. I held my phone tightly in my hand

and pressed it against my lip. What did Ignacio say to him, if anything? Do I tell Emile the truth, but that would involve so much history that it almost seemed unnecessary? The phone stopped ringing and went to voicemail. I expected him to call again, but he didn't.

More time passed, and I realized that this wasn't a subject I could address in one night. I had to take care of my responsibilities at the café first before deciding on what to do, and I had to discuss it with Salem. I had to relive it all over again.

From the outside of the café, I noticed that it was busier than usual. I swerved around the corner, noticing a red convertible sports car, and parked the scooter in my usual spot. Even from the outside, I could hear the hustle and bustle of the café. I entered, throwing my baking apron on, as I took my place behind the cash register.

"Took you long enough," Salem whispered. "We have a surprise visitor," she grunted.

"Who?" I asked, my heart thumping against my chest at an abnormal rate.

It couldn't be him again? I really hated my odds today.

"Camilla." She gagged.

Before I could respond, a tall, model-like woman

appeared from the restrooms and sashayed toward the cash register. Camilla Russo was the type of girl that everyone envied in high school—in fact, I was one of those girls who did the envying—with sun-kissed skin, silky, light brown hair, flawless bone structure, an hourglass figure. She wore an all-black lady's suit and accessorized with gold earrings and necklaces for a luxurious touch.

"Oh my, Estella, you've had better days," she said, giving my chin a little shake. "I missed you, darling."

With her condescending words, I was reminded of why Salem hated her cousin. The rivalry between them ran so deep. It had started with their fathers—two brothers who wanted to excel in the culinary world, but only one of them made it to the top. Massimo Russo, Camilla's father, ended up being a three-star Michelin chef with numerous restaurants all over the world, TV shows, and an undefeatable culinary empire.

The real rivalry between Salem and Camilla began when they were thirteen, and Camilla had stated that Salem wouldn't ever succeed in the culinary world, like her father, and shouldn't try. Those hurtful words never left Salem's mind.

"Your little café is so…cute," Camilla said, hesitantly.

"I'm surprised you decided to come to Castellara."

"Oh no, I'm surprised *you* came to this part of town. Lilla seems more your speed," Salem said. "Considering you like everything fake," she mumbled low enough only for me to hear.

"Well, my fiancé is on the other side of town for now. Marcelo Moretti—I'm sure you've heard of him. He's going to be Daddy's next prodigy," she prided, flipping her salon-styled hair over her shoulder.

Salem started to frantically hit my hand under the counter. It was clear she was sending me a signal, but I couldn't decipher it, so I slapped her hand away.

"Anyway, I'm getting married next month, and Nonna will only come if you go," she informed, retrieving an invitation from her Hermes bag and tossing it onto the counter. "You know, she's afraid of planes and all. She needs a companion, and I'll be too busy. Estella, you're more than welcome to join, as well."

"Thank you for your kind invitation," I said, trying my best to sound grateful. The longer she stayed, the more irritating she became, and as much as we wanted to push her out the door, we couldn't. Camilla had the power to shut down the café and any of Salem's future franchises if we so dared to look at her the wrong way.

"Alright, dolls, I must go plan a wedding." She laughed as she promenaded out of the café.

"Have I ever told you I loathe her?" Salem grunted.

"Many times." I sighed.

"Oh, and I was slapping your hand because that high-dollar cake we are making was requested by Marcelo Moretti, her fiancé. And Michelin-star chef, if I may add!"

"What? That's incredible, but do you think she knows?"

"Oh, no way. If she did, we would be out the door. We can't let her find out for another month." Salem placed her head on my shoulder. "She literally raised my blood pressure. Thank God you're here."

It wasn't the best time for me to run for the hills, but I had to inform Salem about my conundrum.

We worked until closing time—7 p.m.—the time most cafés closed in Castellara—and made our way back to our little home. As soon as we jumped off our scooters, right then and there, I stood in front of her with a defeated look on my face. Salem cupped my shoulders as she looked into my conflicted eyes. I told Salem everything—everything that had happened in Paris and everything that happened today.

Leaving Paris

We eventually sat at the edge of the lake, skipping rocks to ease the situation. Every fear, concern, and embarrassing memory cascaded out of my mouth.

Thinking about it all, having to actually vocalize all the emotions I felt five years ago, had me on the verge of tears. I locked all the good, bad, and ugly memories from Paris into a little box and shoved it in the back of my mind. It was devastating and traumatic, to say the least. I did everything I could to make sure none of it resurfaced.

"Estella." Salem sighed, placing her hand over mine. "What do you want to do?"

"All I know is that I don't want to see him again."

"Well, I'd love to see him because I would flick him off."

I choked on the bubble of laughter, and it caused all the accumulated mucus to unleash. "Sorry," I said, laughing and crying at the same time as I reached for a tissue that I had in my bag.

"Don't apologize," Salem said. "Just let it out. You're constantly bottling everything you feel, especially the bad. You'll distract yourself by working, studying, or hiding in the shadows when in reality, you're struggling. Look at everything that happened with Cesar. Stop drowning yourself in tasks to prevent yourself from feeling. Keep crying," she said, patting my back.

"What am I really supposed to do?" I asked, cleaning my nose.

I knew nothing about Ignacio and his intentions with me now that we had collided. It seemed like he had a lot more to say to me, and I wasn't going to allow him to deceive me again. How would I be able to decipher a truth from a lie?

"I'd say, continue to live your life, and if you ever meet again, tell him you have no intentions of interacting with him. If he's at the café, I'll do my best to ignore him. I will help you through this, but Estella, you can't run away from this—your problems."

"I know." I sighed.

"Do you want me to make some sweets and watch a Disney movie? Your favorite, *The Princess and the Frog*?" Salem bumped her arm into mine, trying to cheer me up.

"Sure, but can we just sit here for a while more?"

We continued to sit out on the edge of the water until we could only see the whites of our eyes. The night consisted of a bright, full moon, large boats sailing across the water, and two friends who had each other's back. It

Leaving Paris

might've been a crap beginning of the day, but it ended on a better note.

And for once, I wasn't suffering in silence.

Chapter 9

IGNACIO

ONE WEEK

It had been one long week since my last encounter with Estella. Castellara wasn't that populated, but it was an earthy slab of land. There were parts of the city that had the majority of the residents, and the others lived in the mountains with their acres of land surrounding their homes. There was no sure way to find her except by visiting the small college during the times she was expected to take her piano lessons.

Even then, I couldn't do that to her. I wasn't going to ambush her, not when she did me the favor of lying to Nonno about the lesson and saving me from a lecture. She had told him that the session went decently but she preferred his teaching style. If I visited them after their lesson, Nonno would be able to sense the tension, and then we would be questioned. She lied for a reason, and I wanted to respect that despite my need to just come clean to Nonno.

I had called out of work every day this week and told them a lie about having a horrible stomach bug. Seeing Estella after all these years—after convincing myself that I'd never see her again—had rendered me useless. Mentally, I had zeroed out. There hadn't been a day this week when my father hadn't called to request my return. He didn't ask if I was okay or if I needed anything. He just declared that he needed me at the company.

Thinking about my father's company and not being able to talk to Estella had drained me. I found myself hopping around different shops in Castellara to ease my mind. I came across Salem's café once again and wanted to see what ceramics pieces were on display. The fox-and-piano figurine that I had previously purchased rested on top of my Fazioli.

There was a new line of work displayed on the shelf. It was a beautiful pink-peony-patterned ceramic tableware set with a gold rim. It was truly a work of art; every detail had been thought through. The petals of the peony edged out just slightly to give it texture. It was remarkable, and of course, it reminded me of Estella. I had given her a peony that night in Paris, five years ago.

"Will you be buying this, as well?" Salem, the owner, appeared beside me, snapping me out of my memory.

"No," I answered honestly. As stunning as it was, I had no use for it. "But, I would like to tip them."

Salem smiled widely. "Wow, I'm sure she'd appreciate that."

I handed her the bills that were in my wallet. "One hundred."

"May I ask what moved you to be so generous?"

I looked back at the set, and a faint flicker of a smile crossed my face. "It reminded me of a girl I liked a couple years ago."

"You know what, I'll be back," she said before disappearing.

She returned shortly with a takeout bag with cannoli inside. "A thank you for supporting the café and my friend's art. She really needs the support right now."

"Well, we artists have to support each other."

Leaving Paris

Salem nodded and then tilted her head to the side, looking at me with some sort of motive. "You know, my friend will be back soon. You should give her the tip yourself."

I nervously scratched the back of my head. Was she really trying to set me up with the artist? I appreciated her efforts, but I couldn't entertain another woman romantically, not when Estella was in town.

"Maybe some other time. I have somewhere to be," I said, looking at my watch. "Thank you again."

I exited the café and was greeted by sprinkles of droplets. Every fiber of my body wanted to continue aimlessly walking around hoping to stumble into Estella, but the rain started to fall harder. I ran back to my car, and sat in place, thinking about where she could be right now.

Seconds before driving off, a light blue Vespa whipped around the corner and barely brushed past my car. I couldn't see the driver's face, but I noticed how her brown hair whipped around in the air as she drove, albeit a little recklessly. I wondered if she was were the one who'd scratched my car, but I didn't intend to approach her.

Today had been long enough, and I decided I would let it all go and hope for the best in tomorrow's search.

Chapter 10

ESTELLA

On Sundays, most businesses in Castellara either opened late or didn't open at all. Salem and I would spend the day resting in the cottage, catching up on shows, talking to our parents from back home, or hanging out with Nonna Norah.

On this specific Sunday, we were getting ready for church. Growing up, our parents considered themselves Catholic but never attended church, not even for the holidays. Nonna Norah wanted us to attend the service on this specific day because she was going to sing. Emile was going to accompany her, as well, and everyone believed that this was their way of making their relationship public.

We decided to sit in the middle of the church; it was the

perfect way to say that 'we are here' but 'don't want to be in sight of the preacher.' Nonna Norah was on stage, wearing a light blue, suit dress, and mid-heel, black pumps, speaking to Emile who had been seated on the piano looking pretty dashing himself. They gave each other reassuring smiles as everyone began to settle down in their seats.

I had been skimming through the Bible when I heard Salem hum in appreciation. I peered up to find a tall, lean male figure walking down the aisle to the second row. All I could see was his back, but even that was enough to know that he was attractive. He wore navy blue suit pants, which perfectly emphasized his behind, and a lighter-shade-of-blue blazer.

I wasn't sure what was appropriate behavior at church, but visually undressing a man in church had to be a sin. I diverted my attention away from the fine specimen and looked around, taking in the beauty of the stained-glass windows that displayed Mary and Jesus. My gaze wavered around to find Leonardo, my Italian tutor, looking in my direction. He lifted his hand, giving me a simple wave, and I returned the greeting by smiling at him.

"Oh, who's that?"

"Leonardo."

"Damn, that's Leonardo?" Salem whispered. "Is he single?"

"I don't know." I chuckled.

"You should try to find out."

Leonardo definitely caught the eyes of other young ladies at the church. He wore a white, polo shirt that put his biceps on display, and his boyish smile had the ability to make you feel something. He was a good friend of mine, and I'd be lying if I said that I wasn't attracted to him. Though, I realized that in this year-long journey of self-discovery, it would be best to learn about myself without being in a relationship. I didn't need to complicate my life even more than it was.

The preacher took his place on the podium and watched his audience. The second he spoke, I realized that I would be confused for the duration of the service. My lessons with Leonardo were going well, but surely, I wouldn't be able to translate a sermon.

"Nonna is going to sing now," Salem informed.

Emile played the first few notes, and I instantly knew that Nonna Norah was going to sing Ave Maria. A string of emotions escaped her as she started to sing to the church.

Leaving Paris

I've heard Nonna Norah quietly sing while cooking or humming as she did chores, but I never knew that she had the voice of an angel. She was keeping her special talent secret, and honestly, it was the best way to reveal her relationship with Emile.

I had been completely captivated by Nonna's singing that the sudden crash of piano keys snapped me out of the heaven that I was experiencing. There were whispers in the church, everyone unsure of what was happening. Nonna Norah and Emile exchanged worried glances as Emile started to rub his right wrist.

"Oh no, it's his carpal tunnel," I whispered to Salem.

Even the preacher didn't know how to react; he kept hovering over the chair as if Emile would bounce back, but he didn't. A male figure emerged from the crowd and walked up onto the stage to briefly speak to Emile and Nonna. They both looked relieved; and with one pat on the back, Emile left the bench and the male with the impeccable outfit had taken his place.

The man shimmied off his blazer and handed it to Emile, allowing the crowd to get a glimpse of his profile. The whispers behind us grew louder and had giggles added to the mix. The side of the face was all I needed to know that the one who replaced Emile was Ignacio.

What was going on?

Ignacio picked up a little before where Emile had stopped, and Nonna knew exactly where to continue her singing. My chest felt tight with anger and sadness, but I knew he was doing nothing harmful at that moment. If anything, he saved Emile and Norah's performance—the event that made their relationship public—which made him look somewhat decent.

Nonna Norah finished the song, and then everyone erupted in adulation. Ignacio took advantage of the distraction to jog down the stairs nearing the walls of the church to leave. I turned back to continue watching him leave, along with a couple of curious churchgoers, such as Salem, and he gave the church one last glance before exiting.

"Oh my God, he's the guy that bought your fox-and-piano figurine and tipped you the hundred dollars."

I nearly choked on that revelation.

It was the perfect opportunity to tell Salem that he was the man who'd shattered my heart, but instead, I remained utterly silent. I couldn't tell Salem the truth now; it'd have to wait till after church. Now all I could think about was

Leaving Paris

Ignacio's relationship with Emile, and what did that mean for me?

Chapter 11

IGNACIO

All I wanted to do was return to my villa after that church performance, but I promised Nonno that I would attend the intimate lunch gathering after church. He wanted to formally introduce me to the new woman in his life. I was happy for him—proud even—because he'd decided to give love another chance regardless of the results of his last relationship.

I stood in front of the cottage and envisioned myself playing soccer with a then-black-haired Nonno and a very lively Nonna. It was where I would live for most of my summer breaks when my father decided to take his heaviest load of work. He wouldn't even step foot out of the car to help with my luggage or to hug me goodbye. He was excitedly waiting for me to not be his responsibility and focus on what he actually loved most: work.

Leaving Paris

And the worst part? I was happy when he left. What kind of child feels relief from seeing their parent leave? A child that never felt loved in the first place. Mom was constantly traveling to play her parts as an actress, Dad breathed work, and I just wanted someone to look at me. I wanted to matter, and I always mattered to Nonno.

The cottage didn't seem that bent out of shape, better than I had expected. After Nonna died, it was just four slabs of discolored brick walls. All the vines in front of the house had died, the plants in the front were wilted, and those who lived inside it didn't have much will to live.

A single tear escaped my eye, and I wasn't quick to wipe it away. I didn't let anyone see me cry, but I knew that I was alone. I had never let myself fully grieve Nonna's death. Nonno wanted nothing more than to join her, but I had to remain strong for him. I had to give him some reason to keep living, and after I did, I left.

Nonna would have slapped me across the head for abandoning him. She had no problem putting me in my place considering she constantly had to do it; she was more of a real mother than my own. Norah had the same fiery energy as Nonna; I could see her trying to set me straight.

Spotting Nonno's olive-green Fiat had snapped me out of all the reminiscing and internal ranting. I noticed one red and one light-blue-colored Vespa trailing behind his car. I couldn't identify their faces from where I was standing.

Nonno stepped out of the car and happily waved at me, a goofy smile plastered on his face as he headed toward the entrance of his cottage. I was still too far from his guests, standing under one of the great trees that my nonna used to host picnics under. As I strode toward them, one of them huddled in front of Emile and entered the house.

I reached the cottage and Emile and Norah were lingering by the front door.

Emile shot me a nervous smile. "Ignacio, I didn't expect you to meet Norah the way you did, but here's to a second chance."

I extended my hand out to shake Norah's hand, and she grabbed it, only to pull me into a tight hug. Emile couldn't contain his laugh; I could only imagine the awkward face I made that caused him to bellow out like a child. I missed hearing him laugh.

"It's so nice to meet you, Ignacio. Your nonno told me so much about you." She had her hand on my shoulder.

"I'm not sure if that's a good or bad thing," I joked.

Norah laughed and patted my arm. "All good things, mostly."

Emile smiled and clasped his hands together. "Well, should we put the lasagna in the oven?"

"Yes, of course. I told Estella and Salem to preheat the oven," she said and walked through the doorway.

Leaving Paris

Estella's name caught me off guard, causing my whole body to stiffen. A million questions raced through my head and down to my mouth. I wanted to ask Nonno but didn't know where to begin.

"Are you okay there, boy?" Nonno asked, slapping my arm, jolting me back to reality.

"Yes," I lied. There was a whirlwind in my head. I wasn't okay knowing that Estella and I would be under the same roof. She hated me and appeared to be Norah's granddaughter. I didn't expect family drama so soon.

"Let's go introduce you to the girls," Nonno said, guiding me into the cottage.

I hadn't stepped foot in the cottage for almost five years. After I had left nonno, I had stopped attempting to make music my career and dealt in the world of business with my father. Life had been more than complicated since then.

Everything remained the same: the gaudy furniture that Nonna adored; the countryside paintings hung unevenly on the walls; the bouquet of smells—old wood, Italian food, powder, and wildflowers, and dust. It was unpleasant, to say the least, but the memories were so far from that.

There was chitchat coming from the kitchen, and I wondered if Estella was warning them about me. I peeked into the kitchen, watching Estella combine ingredients into a salad bowl.

I may have been smiling at her, but she looked over her shoulder and shot me a nasty scowl that made every positive feeling in me instantly die. Her brown eyes turned cold, wicked even; they looked like they were prepared for murder and I was her victim. She snapped her head away and continued to prepare the salad.

There was still so much unresolved pain behind those eyes. If I gave her my truth, then maybe it would help her, but she didn't want to talk to me. She'd made it clear as day.

How could we have known that we would be in this situation? It seemed that the universe was persistent in having us meet again. I expected Estella to have been out the door by now, but she was staying for the same reason I was: respect for our elders and family.

Substituting for Nonno at the church had filled me with an uncomfortable feeling. I hadn't played the piano ever since my last night with Estella, and I didn't intend on having my first time in years to be in front of a crowd.

The whispers of the churchgoers echoed in my mind.
He left the man who raised him for his despicable father. What a foolish boy. What does he think he's doing now?

Nothing in this town was kept secret. Everyone knew what my father had done and had reservations about me leaving Emile. The town may have thought they knew my story, but they didn't. I was a man who just wanted a relationship with his estranged workaholic father, yet I was seen as the bad guy. I didn't want to be the bad guy anymore.

Norah noticed that I stood by the kitchen archway. "Don't be shy," she said, smiling. "Come in here and meet my girls."

Why did they have to be related?

I was raised in this cottage, yet Norah seemed far more comfortable than me. She reached over for my arm and fluttered her eyelashes. "Girls, I would love you to meet my hero and Emile's grandson, Ignacio."

From the corner of my eye, I saw Estella roll her eyes.

"We've met before, actually," Salem said, squeezing my hand a little too tight. I watched her gray eyes turn into steel.

She knows about me and hates me for hurting her best friend. Great start, Ignacio.

"Oh, how?" Norah asked with a big smile.

"The café," she said simply, but her eyes were telling another story.

"Oh, how nice! And that's Estella."

I know.

Estella stood at the end of the kitchen and flashed a pirated smile that disappeared as soon as it appeared, then lowered her head back down to the salad bowl.

"Pleasure to meet you two," I said.

"Well, we have forty minutes until the lasagna is ready. Let's sit down and get to know each other," Norah chimed, walking out of the kitchen.

Salem sent me a death glare and then faced Estella, extending her hand out. Estella held it tightly, and Salem brushed past me without another thought.

***

Nonno walked us out to the garden terrace and asked everyone to take a seat. We bounced in and out of conversation but nothing substantial. Estella and Salem excused themselves out of the conversation to walk around the spacious backyard. I took the opportunity to escape the heavy tension and went to the piano room.

It was one of my favorite rooms growing up. The honey-colored walls complemented the dark-stoned chimney, his chestnut grand piano, a brown two-seater where Nonna and Nonno would sit once I felt practiced enough with a composition, and rows of books about the great pianists in history and stacks of Nonno's own masterpieces.

There was still a lingering aroma of the cigars that he used to smoke. He stopped smoking the day Nonna passed away. Nonno told us he went to smoke in the backyard because Nonna never liked to see him smoke, and she decided to water the plants in the front. When he was done with his cigar, he went to see her in the front, but she had collapsed on the floor.

Leaving Paris

She had a heart attack while she watered the plants. It took Nonno weeks to pick up the watering can that had fallen from Nonna's hand. He blamed himself for her death or at least, not being there with her while she suffered. He threw away all the cigars that he had on hand and never looked back. I believed it was Nonna's way of keeping Nonno on Earth for a bit longer. He would've been on the brink of lung cancer had he not stopped.

A timer went off in the kitchen, and I closed one of Nonno's leather composition journals to tend to the lasagna. I reached the kitchen but stopped dead in my tracks when Estella stood before me. She placed the lasagna on the counter and slid off the old, green oven mitts.

Estella's gaze darted over my shoulder and to the archway that led back into the hallway.

"I'm sorry," I said, stepping aside to let her out. I wasn't only apologizing for being in her way, but was sorry for everything that had happened between us.

She stepped back, crossing her arms around her chest, only to trudge forward. Her arm brushed against mine, and I spoke to her again. "I can go, if it makes it easier," I offered, softly.

"It's okay," she whispered. "I'm not actually related to Norah; I mean, neither is Salem, but that's not the point." She paused for a moment and huffed. She became noticeably flustered and placed her hands over her blushed cheeks. "I'm not a Russo or an Amatore. I'm a Salvador. I should be offering to leave."

Thank God she wasn't related to Norah. Fewer complications.

"Salvador?" I whispered, the surname sounding familiar. "Are you E. Salvador?"

"Yes," she exhaled, deeply. "You bought my figurine and tipped me."

"The fox on the piano, is that me?" It all started to make sense now. The fox on the piano with a beautiful young woman that looked like her, and then the peony ceramic set, the same kind of flower that I had given to her that night in Paris.

"You tell me."

Her body was positioned to face mine, and I breathed her presence. She was so close, yet so far from me. I had craved this moment for the last five years.

"Don't go," I responded, sensing her need to get away from me.

Please, stay here. I need you near.

"I'm staying, only because I know how important this is for Nonna Norah and Emile."

I nodded in agreement.

I expected her to dart out of the door, but she didn't move and neither did I. This closeness felt *so* good. I only wished that I could give her the same feeling. If only I could've explained myself to her.

"I *need* to explain my side of that night, Estella." I sighed.

Leaving Paris

Her breath hitched, and she pulled away. "No, I don't want to hear it."

"Please," I begged.

"Ignacio," she sighed, exhausted. "No."

"Estella, I haven't been able to get you out of my mind," I expelled. She had to know that I never forgot about her. Those nights in Paris were the best nights of my life. The connection we had was otherworldly.

She placed her hand up, firmly shielding us. "I don't want to hear it. Not today."

Not today. There was still hope.

"Would you like me to return the figurine?" I asked, just wanting to hear a little more from her.

Estella tore her chocolate-brown eyes away from me and headed into the hallway. I heard the back door open, and the door proceeded to close. I looked out the window, and Estella pointed to the cottage and everyone cheered.

I was sure that Estella wasn't going to speak to me for the rest of the night but knowing she would be in the same room was enough for now.

Chapter 12

ESTELLA

The lasagna came out phenomenal, and dinner went smoothly. Ignacio didn't overstep; if anything, he remained quiet most of the time. He would answer Nonna's questions but kept talking to a minimum. He didn't like talking about himself.

I tried not to make eye contact with Ignacio, but at times, I caught myself stealing glances. We made eye contact one time throughout the dinner, and it startled me. I could harbor all the hate in the world for him and still find him undeniably handsome. He lowered his gaze, and the corner of his lips turned upward.

Crap, he caught me.

"Should we do dessert now?" Norah asked us. "It's

tiramisu."

Everyone agreed with mumbled yeses and head nods.

Emile went into the fridge to retrieve the dessert and placed a perfectly cut piece onto each plate. Nonna Norah handed us each a plate and sat down, glancing at Emile with a serious expression.

"So," Emile started. "The incident at the church."

With that line, Emile had all of Ignacio's undivided attention.

"I wanted to thank you, Ignacio, for rising to the occasion. It's not a mystery that my hands are starting to fail me." He sighed. "I was speaking to Norah while you all were roaming around, and I've decided to take a break from playing the piano." It was clear that his words pained him. Asking a pianist to live without the piano was similar to asking a human to live without their heart. It wasn't possible.

But this also meant that my lessons were ending. Emile watched me process his words and form all the connections.

"I'm sorry, Estella," Emile huffed. "There is a lot of potential, but I can't do it," he said, lifting his hands in disappointment.

"It's okay, I understand," I responded, softly.

"But that only means the end of us, but when one door closes, another one opens," he said and turned to Ignacio who sat up straight. "I know you two had a lesson together. You both agreed that it went decently, correct?" His gaze moved between the two of us.

Ignacio and I nodded our heads, unsure.

"Well, I believe that with more practice, you two will make a terrific duo. Ignacio learned from me, and Estella, he can teach you what I know and more."

Oh no.

"Nonno," Ignacio mumbled and craned his neck to the side.

Emile glared at him. "Yes?"

"I go back to work tomorrow," he said.

He was trying to say no. Good.

Emile didn't conceal his annoyance at Ignacio's response. "You do not work; you are kissing your father's ass. Big difference."

Ignacio opened his mouth and inhaled, but he bit his tongue and shook his head as his neck began to turn red.

"Is it money? Is it fear? Why is it that you insist on working for him? Ignacio, you are not him. You are a man of music, not business."

Both men looked annoyed with each other. It seemed that Ignacio working for his father was a sensitive topic. By the looks on their faces, there were some unresolved issues. I remembered the conversation I had with Emile when we first met and how he lost one of his best pianists to business. It all made sense. He was talking about Ignacio.

Ignacio kept his eyes locked on his plate of untouched cake. "This is the route I'm taking now. I'm sorry for disappointing you, Nonno."

I winced at his words, sensing the guilt in them. He apologized to me earlier, and I wasn't sure if it was for anything in specific, or sorry for everything. Hearing the same painful apology again, I could vouch for the fact that he was apologizing for everything.

Emile ignored his apology, just like I did. But, I didn't feel good about it.

"It's okay, Emile. I'm going to be busy with orders and helping Salem. Maybe it's for the best." I had to say something to steer the conversation away from Ignacio. No one deserved to be jabbed at in front of other people.

"Non-sense," Emile protested. "Are you passionate about learning?"

I nodded.

"Then we will figure it out, okay?

"Okay."

I wanted to learn how to play the piano, but I only wanted to learn from Emile. I couldn't be in the same setting as Ignacio; it would be too much for me to handle. It would remind me of *that* night, and I didn't want to do that to myself. Everything that I adored about Ignacio five years ago was still present. His looks. His talent. His presence. It *all* made me weak. I wouldn't stand a chance if we were in close proximity.

This was supposed to be the time to free myself. To roam like a butterfly, learning about myself and the world, but it didn't feel possible anymore. I wanted to continue playing the piano; every time I played, I felt in control of my life again. It was the one thing I didn't want to be taken away from me right now, and now it was gone.

"Well, that was all delicious," Salem interjected.

"It was," Nonna Norah said, collecting everyone's plates.

Somehow, I felt responsible for the tension in the room. It was all because of my piano lessons. I had to move on and find another interest. Maybe it was for the best to leave the piano behind, along with all its associations.

"I will clean up," I offered.

"No, it's fine. Ignacio can do that," Emile said.

"It's okay," I insisted.

"Help the girl," Emile ordered Ignacio and headed out of the kitchen.

"Ignacio, he's upset about his hand. Please, don't take his words to heart," Nonna Norah said, noticing that Ignacio had been affected by everything Emile had spewed. "Salem, come with me and tell him that joke about the hunters. Maybe it will lighten his mood."

Salem looked at me with a conflicted expression. If Nonna Norah needed her, she had to go with him. I gave Salem a little nod to confirm that I would be okay with Ignacio. She turned to Ignacio and flashed him a warning with her sharp eyes.

I collected the remainder of the plates and placed them in the sink. "I'll wash, and you can dry them."

Ignacio didn't respond, and I didn't turn my attention toward him to see if he nodded. I had just finished cleaning the first plate when Ignacio appeared next to me with a towel in hand. I handed him the plate, and he took it, dried it, and placed it in the cabinet.

Leaving Paris

The water ran, the dishes clattered, the cabinets opened and closed, but the silence between us was deafening. We worked through the chore without exchanging any words. We barely acknowledged each other. He kept his distance, standing a foot away from me, and kept his eyes on the dish on hand. The only part of him that came in contact with me was his warm and woody cologne that invaded my personal space.

God.

He smelled absolutely devouring. His cologne brimmed with the sweet notes of all things feminine and masculine. Leather, rum, cigar wrappers, spice, vanilla. It wasn't the same cologne from years ago, but it reminded me of Sunset Jazz Club.

Ignacio set the towel to the side and slid his hands into his pocket as he leaned against the counter, unsure of what to do next.

I was also unsure of what to do and decided that maybe asking him a question about his childhood would alleviate the tension.

"Your nonno's cottage is very nice," I said, my voice sounding small. "Did you come here often as a child?"

"I did. I would visit in the summer as a child, but once

Leaving Paris

I turned ten, I had to move in permanently when my mother's career and father's business were thriving. It was best if I was out of their way." He kept his eyes on the floor and his voice low. "I'm sorry. I don't know why I shared all that."

The whole sentence itself was heartbreaking. My heart started to feel heavy, and I wanted to scold myself for making matters worse again. I didn't want to feel sorry for the man who had hurt me, but I also didn't want to hurt him. His issues ran deeper and much longer than mine, and right now, I didn't want to hold onto the grudge that I was holding against him.

"I'm sorry," I murmured.

"For what?"

"Asking that question. I didn't mean for it to lead to a sensitive topic."

"It's okay, you wouldn't have known."

"Right," I whispered. "I know it doesn't feel good."

Ignacio raised his head, and his amber eyes flickered in my direction. "Could you tell Emile that I left?"

I nodded and watched him leave the kitchen, then heard the front door close behind me.

My heart hammered against my chest, and even without

Ignacio in the same room as me, I found it difficult to breathe. This was his childhood home; his scent still lingered in the air; his words echoed in my head.

I inhaled deeply and walked to the garden terrace to inform Emile about Ignacio's departure. Nonna Norah and Salem were taking pictures of a bird on a tree while Emile sat on a wicker loveseat, facing them but mentally somewhere else.

"He left, didn't he?" Emile asked, his eyes still locked ahead.

"Yes."

"My boy," he whispered and looked down at his hands. "I hate being upset with him, especially when it comes to his father."

"Is his father your son?" I asked.

"Yes."

"What happened, if I may ask?"

Emile snorted, but none of it was humorous. "I wouldn't know where to begin, Estella."

I wasn't sure if that was his way of shutting down the conversation, or if he was waiting for me to ask for specifics. I shouldn't pry, but a part of me wanted to know about all the hurt that Ignacio had gone through.

Leaving Paris

"He said he was raised here," I said, giving us a place to start.

"That's correct. He moved in with us the day he turned ten. Alessio, my son, and his father always saw Ignacio as an inconvenience. Alessio is a businessman and Florence, Ignacio's mother, is an actress. I worked with her decades ago, and I introduced her to Alessio because they had the same passion and drive. Work, money, status were their top priorities. I thought it would have been the perfect match, and it was until Ignacio was born."

"They didn't plan on being parents," I figured.

"Exactly. They didn't want children, and I thought it was some ridiculous claim they made, but they were right. They were incapable of thinking about anyone else other than themselves and money. They made a mutual decision to have him live with us until he was eighteen. His mother would take him for some time in the summer, but other than that, they rarely made contact."

I had no words. I couldn't imagine not having my parents around. Even though we were four thousand miles away, I spoke to my parents more now than I had when I lived with them.

"That's pretty devastating for a child to experience."

"It is, and yet he ran back to him as if the man didn't abandon him. I know Alessio is my son, but he is one of the smartest and most manipulative men I know. He knows exactly how to play with Ignacio's emotions."

He shook his head in disgust. Emile didn't share anymore, but his pensive expression solidified that he had only told me a fraction of their issues.

And for some reason, I wanted to know more.

Chapter 13

IGNACIO

The next morning, I began my commute to Amatore Industries much earlier than usual. I wasn't a morning person. Add in having to attend an early meeting at my father's company after having a fight with my grandfather, while the most amazing woman was present, it was hellish and embarrassing. It left a bitter taste in my mouth. My father sent me an email with a debrief about the meeting. We were going to speak with potential investors for our upcoming project.

I was his right-hand man, the COO of Amatore Industries, and had to attend the meeting since he couldn't. When he called me five and a half years ago asking me to join his company, I did everything I could to prove that he'd made the right decision by involving me. I showed my father that I was an asset to the company by acquiring any degrees or certification.

But, years later, I hated it. I hated the work, the people, the goals, every single bit. I tried to convince myself that this career path could be for me, but I was miserable.

I loathed sitting at one end of the long, wooden desks, leaning back on a chair worth way too much, and watching two employees trying to persuade investors to do what they do best. This was hell. There was nothing captivating about international real estate and construction, yet here I was, my first day back in the office after my month-long break.

Rambling, rambling, and more rambling. The investors lost interest, and so did I, but the rambling continued.

"These two might look similar, but the key difference between Model A and Model B is—"

"Who fucking cares?" I murmured, leaning forward.

All eyes were on me, and I leaned forward, inhaling deeply. They all heard me. There was no point in backing out now. "They're clearly not interested, and none of this matters anymore."

I pushed myself away from the desk, and was confident in my firm decision to end the meeting, but it wasn't until

Leaving Paris

I stepped foot out of the office that I hesitated, realizing my father was going to hear about this shortly. I could feel the disapproval already.

There were three consecutive knocks on the door, followed by the door opening. My father and his assistant Serena entered the premises. Serena led the way, wearing a tight, black dress, that accentuated her sashaying hips, and she held an iPad that covered her chest. My father followed closely behind with no expression what so ever, which was never good.

Father wore his favorite crisp, gray business suit, and it was laced with power. He had told me that it was his suit of fortune and had never lost a deal when wearing it.

Until today, because of me.

"Ignacio, it's wonderful to see you," he greeted, flashing an artificial smile. "How's Emile and everyone in town?"

"Your *father* is doing fantastic," I said, emphasizing the term that probably meant nothing to him. "And the town...well, they still don't like you."

He corrected his tie and stared blankly at me. "Ah, little town people love the drama."

Father strode around my desk and picked up one silver ball from the cradle balance pendulum, then released it. "I heard what happened," he said, sitting on the edge of the desk and folding his arms across his chest.

There it was.

"We were wasting time."

"Did you visit your nonno yesterday?" he asked, completely ignoring my explanation.

"Yes?"

"Ah, I understand now." He bobbed his head. "The old man got to you, didn't he?"

"No, not necessarily."

Father scoffed. "Let me ask you, do you desire to be a COO?"

I didn't immediately respond, but that was enough of an answer for him.

"When you wake up in the morning, do you crave money, power, and label?"

"No, not everyone has the desire to chase money or status," I informed.

"Ah, yes, the commoners. They're complacent with having no real talent or drive. Is that what you are? Less of a man? What are you doing here if you can't handle the position?"

Father had the ability to pick at his opponent's flaws

and question them in a manner that didn't seem like a direct attack but still punctured the ego. The man should've been a lawyer instead of the CEO of a real-estate-and-construction firm. Though, I'd learned to have a thick skin around him, so his strikes didn't do much harm. They were nothing compared to the betrayal he committed when I was ten. He left me for the empire that he created for himself.

"Should I demote you to a more manageable position, such as a real estate agent?" he asked without letting me answer his previous question. "That will prove to me what a failure you already are, and I won't have to worry about being further disappointed."

I clenched my jaw tightly, attempting to swallow down his hateful words.

Father shrugged. "I don't think you are meant to be a COO."

"I have *one* slip-up, and you sound like you want to dispose of me."

"Because you are disposable. If you can't show me that you are reliable and dedicated to the company, then you have no place here. This isn't a place for your hissy fits."

His cold words were a slap to the face, and all I wanted

was to display the hurt I suffered from that blow, but I remained still. When I was a child, he never showed me that he was reliable or dedicated to his role as a father. Why would I give him the same when I never received it? And without it, why did I torment myself to keep him in my life? He never deserved being in it.

Father noticed that I had processed his words into another meaning despite my stoic demeanor.

"It's business, Ignacio. If those beneath us are useless to the superiors, then we terminate them."

Father delivered his words in a more sensible voice, but no tone could ever hide the atrocity of his words. In his eyes, everyone was beneath him.

It was a harsh realization, and I wanted to retaliate by cursing him and insulting him, cutting him with my words laced with pain. But he wouldn't understand; he would never admit that he was a neglectful father. He wasn't someone to argue with. It wouldn't be worth it.

I inhaled deeply and stared into his fiery, copper eyes. "I'm leaving the company."

Father furrowed his eyebrows and leaned back, analyzing me. He was going to fire me, I just knew. What he didn't expect was that *I* released myself from the job. He didn't get the satisfaction of seeing me beg or defend myself.

"I expected that from you," he retorted. "Sign your discharge forms with Serena and go on your way," he said, lifting himself away from the desk and walking towards the door. He stopped for a moment—there was a sliver of hope that he'd take it all back, that our relationship trumped business. He stood in place with his fists clenched tightly, then proceeded to exit.

Father lost in this game that he created, but I know that I lost a lot more. I wanted to hate my father for never being there for me, but I couldn't. Despite it all, I couldn't hate him.

"You've upset your father," Serena said, lowering her iPad and pulling up the necessary forms.

"I won't be a problem for him anymore," I said.

"I hope you find what you're looking for," she responded, handing the iPad in my direction.

"Thank you," I said, signing my name with a pen. "And, Serena, if you are with my father, I'm telling you to run far away. He will break you."

There were rumors about them developing a relationship. There was no way someone would want to engage in a romantic relationship with my father. I never believed in the rumors until I saw Serena's face fall.

Serena walked away with her head hung low in guilt and embarrassment.

I gave the lifeless office one more scan before leaving for good. I didn't care for any of my belongings and left them for others to claim. Unlike my father, I didn't care about the superficial things. Money was nice to have, but it wasn't meant to be loved.

***

"*Benvenuto,*" greeted one of the hostesses from Marcelo's restaurant, Villa Mia. "I can seat you at the bar, and I'll inform Marcelo of your arrival," she said in Italian.

It was his home, his child, his heart. It was a modern rustic-themed restaurant with glossed-wood panels as walls, industrial-like tables and chairs, bright lights that lined the restaurant, and a spacious feel even though it met max capacity most of the time.

The hostess guided me to my usual spot at the bar and handed me a drink menu, but she and everyone else knew that all I ever ordered was a glass of whiskey.

Leaving Paris

The bartender greeted me and made my original order without asking me, which was fine by me because I appreciated those who read my mind. A large gulp later, I received another refill, and Marcelo managed to escape the kitchen.

"So, you finally left?" he asked, flinging a towel over his shoulder.

"Gone for good." I cheered.

"I'm relieved to hear that." Marcelo smiled. "I need to go back in there, but celebrate throughout the week for me, though. You're finally ridding yourself of your old man. If only I could get rid of my own baggage."

"You don't have to marry Camilla," I responded. "You could call off the wedding."

"Wedding or not, I'm bound to her now."

I suspiciously narrowed my eyes at him. "How so?" He never spoke about her in that way.

"She's six weeks pregnant," he said, no excitement in his voice.

"Are you sure?" I asked.

"Yes, she received a positive yesterday, and we went to the doctors today to confirm."

"I meant, are you sure it's yours?" I asked, flatly.

"She's a pain in the ass, but I wouldn't peg her for a cheater."

I placed the rim of the glass along my lips and mumbled, "Don't be too sure."

"Keep your life simple, man, while you can. Stay far away from relationships," Marcelo said, glancing back into the kitchen. "I need to go. I'll see you later."

My second drink had been obliterated within seconds.

"Another?" the bartender asked.

I shook my head and placed a fifty euro note on the bar before heading out. Another drink would've been pleasant, but I had to head back to Castellara and have a much-needed conversation with my nonno.

***

"Have you heard from Estella?" Nonno asked, leading the way to the piano room.

"No."

I knew she wouldn't reach out to me, but Nonno didn't know that. He didn't know our history, and every part of me wanted to tell him the truth. I didn't like deceiving my nonno and giving him the false hope of working with

Estella. I bit my tongue despite the guilt.

"I will call her and let her know that you're no longer working; maybe she can find some free time and work with you," he suggested.

I didn't respond.

Nonno sat on the bench and his hands hovered over all the keys. "Did you know that I was Angelica's piano teacher? Ah, she was so young, beautiful, and vibrant, and aching to learn more about the art. It was practically a match made in Heaven."

A wistful smile crossed his old face. He wanted to talk about her. He wanted to talk about Nonna.

"How old was she when you two met?"

"She was twenty," he responded. "Had no musical abilities, but she really wanted to learn. Estella reminds me of her."

I closed my eyes and thought about the melody that Estella had composed that night. It wasn't long, but it took us hours to compose. Those were hours well-spent and still treasured to this day.

I opened my eyes, and Nonno fixed his eyes on me, a smile spreading across his face. "What's her name?"

"What are you talking about?"

Leaving Paris

He rolled his eyes and chuckled. "You're not a teenager anymore, Ignacio Lorenzo. You don't have to feel ashamed for sharing about your love life."

"I don't have one."

"Maybe not now, but it seems like you *had* one."

"It was five years ago, in Paris," I shared. "She came into a club I co-owned at the time, stayed there until closing, and we played on the piano until sunrise. I had to keep seeing her, and I did every night for three weeks. I fell in love with her, hard and fast."

"Sounds like she left a mark on you."

"She did."

God, she really fucking did. Her passion for music was one of her sexiest qualities, her ability to absorb information and handle critiques was admirable, her giggles were gold, her voice was angelic, and her concern for my future was touching.

"What happened?"

"I was jumped in the kitchen of the club, and Dad's security found me and took me to the hospital. Dad had also been admitted—someone broke into his home. We were targeted by one of Dad's many rivals. We had to stay low-profile for a month. When I returned, she was gone. I didn't know her last name, where she was staying, or anything. I never saw her again, and it's my fault."

"It is not, Ignacio. That was not something you could've predicted."

"Had I locked the door right after closing, it wouldn't have happened."

"Ignacio, if they were truly after you, they would've found a way in, regardless. I'm sorry that you went through all that. I never knew you were in the hospital."

"Dad didn't want the word to get out, not even with you. I tried not to think much about it since we weren't talking back then."

Nonno's eyes misted over. "I'm sorry we stopped talking. I was mad after you left, to your father's nonetheless, but I wished you told me. You're practically my son."

After five years, it was my turn to give Nonno a much-deserved apology. "Nonno, I'm sorry for leaving you after Nonna died."

Nonno inhaled deeply. "I know, my boy. You did what you had to do."

I brushed my face and passed my hands through my hair. "After she died, I couldn't be here anymore. I just couldn't. I was desperate for an escape, but I didn't take you with me. I'm sorry for abandoning you."

Nonno nodded, accepting my apology. "I forgive you. You're here now, and that's all that matters." I didn't deserve Nonno either, but here he was, accepting me and my faults.

We exchanged a few more words before I left.

I drove down the dirt-path road along the edge of the town and headed toward the bridge that would take me back to Lilla. I looked around the darkened evening and noticed a light-blue-colored Vespa parked by a mini-market. The only person I'd seen on a Vespa similar to that one was Estella.

My car made a sharp turn into the mini-market, and I stepped out of the car without another thought. Deep down inside, I knew that I shouldn't have stopped to check Estella if was the owner of the Vespa, but I needed to see her again.

An old Italian man with a bored expression on his face gave me the side-eye before redirecting his attention to the TV screen hanging on the adjacent wall. Below the TV, I saw a figure of a woman looking at the showcase of frozen seafood.

Leaving Paris

I walked down the small aisle dedicated to treats and headed to the back of the minimart. She had a green basket looped around her arm as she spoke to the man behind the seafood. He handed her a bag of shrimps, and she offered him a soft smile before placing it in her basket.

She turned around and was taken aback at the sight of me.

"Hi," I breathed.

Seeing her again, wearing a delicate, light blue dress that gave her an angelic look, it nearly took my breath away. I had yearned for this moment—the longing and contemplative stare that was exchanged between the two of us. She felt that connection. I knew she did.

"What are you doing here?" she asked, doing her best to not offend me.

I wanted to see you.

"I stopped for a drink before heading onto the bridge."

Estella's eyes narrowed in as I reached over for a drink.

"Do you not have water at home?" she questioned.

I looked at the bottle and placed it back on the shelf. One look at her and my mind was in shambles. I selected another drink, something I'd never heard of.

Estella made her way down the aisle and placed her bag

of shrimp, a small wheel of cheese, and two Balconi cake snacks onto the checkout counter.

"*Venti*," the clerk responded.

I stepped in and placed my drink on the counter, along with the cash needed to pay for everything.

"No, no," Estella said, handing the man her cash.

The clerk looked at me with confusion but continued to process my payment.

Estella bit down on her lip and placed the cash back into her wallet. "You didn't have to do that," she mumbled.

"Yes, I did."

I opened the door, allowing her to go ahead, and I walked behind her as she made her way to the Vespa.

"I no longer have a job, and Emile might call you to inform you of that. He wants us to work together, but I figured I'd warn you."

"Thank you." She snapped her helmet on.

"I'm sorry."

"For what, exactly?"

"Everything, really."

She shook her head and turned on the Vespa.

"Have a safe ride home, Estella."

Estella stalled for a moment, her gaze bouncing

Leaving Paris

between me and the ground.

"Can I ask you something?" she asked softly.

"Anything," I said, trying not to sound too eager. I didn't want to scare her.

Estella looked at me and then tightened up. She gripped the handles of the Vespa and bit down on her lip. Whatever she wanted to ask, she was unsure of how to, or maybe she was mulling it over. Either way, with every passing second, I became more unsettled. I would sit and answer all her questions if she asked.

"Never mind, Ignacio. Have a goodnight."

Without saying another word, Estella jetted away, leaving me to ache for her even more.

Chapter 14

ESTELLA

Emile called me twice that week. He asked about my days, my business, and if I had any free time to meet with Ignacio to continue my piano lessons. I appreciated his persistence. He knew that learning how to play the piano was important to me, but I only wished I could tell him the truth instead of lying to him about my availability.

The thought of sitting next to Ignacio on a piano bench and watching him play made me weak. Every part of my body reacted a different way. My brain told me to stay clear of him, my heart told me to try being his friend, and my body craved him. Worst of all, when I was near him, my heart, my brain, and my body turned into butter.

I closed my eyes and took a long, deep breath. I allowed

the wind to clear my mind from everything Ignacio. I opened my eyes again and concentrated on my surroundings. People walked around the market, fishermen parked their small boats on the side of the harbor, and children splashed in the nearby ocean.

The harbor was filled with booths and tents of delicious foods, beautiful arts and crafts, hand-made clothes, and antiques. I scanned through the colorful array of fruits and vegetables, and my hand reached for three, bright yellow lemons.

I pulled out my wallet for the third time within ten minutes and handed the vendor the cash I had on hand. He handed me the change, and I turned to place my wallet back into my purse, noticing a two-year-old boy staring up at me.

"*Ciao!*" I greeted, kneeling down and flashing a smile.

He was small and tan with honey-colored eyes and hair. The boy reached for my hair and smiled, revealing a little dimple on his cheek. I cupped his little hand and looked around to see if his parents were anywhere near, but no one had their eyes on the kid.

"*Dovo sono mamma è papà?*" I asked.

The little boy looked over his shoulders and then

shrugged.

"*Ti sei perso?*" *Are you lost?*

The little boy shrugged.

"Oh God," I muttered.

The little boy reached over to grab a red apple from the cart.

"*Affamato*," he responded, frowning.

He was hungry.

"*Mangia*," I said, motioning him to eat it.

The vendor looked down at us and cleared his throat. I riffled through my purse and handed the vendor his payment.

I watched the little boy chomp through the apple. He wore an outfit with a matching shirt and shorts, white tennis shoes, and his hair combed to the side. Someone clearly took the time to get him ready.

I wanted to ask him where his parents were or who he came with, but I didn't know enough Italian to communicate with him on that level. Leonardo never prepared lesson plans on what to say or do if I found a lost child near the harbor.

"*Camminiamo un po'?*" I asked the boy. *Let's walk a little.*

He happily grabbed my hand and continued to carry

the apple with his other free hand, occasionally taking messy bites. As we walked, I would point to someone and ask if he knew them, but he shook his head no. I circled the whole harbor, and he rejected every person.

All the faces started to blur together, and I couldn't even remember who I had or hadn't asked. There were no police officers, no distraught parents running around, nothing. I walked us to an empty bench by the waterside and pulled out my phone. I needed help; I had to figure out what to do with the boy.

I called Salem but no answer.

I called Norah but received her voicemail.

I called Emile, and his phone didn't ring.

My finger hovered over Leonardo's name, but I debated on whether or not to call him. He was a friend but nothing more. If it didn't revolve around tutoring, then we wouldn't see each other. I turned my head and watched the little boy staring off as he swung his legs. He didn't seem the least bit worried. I was worried, though, and I needed help.

I looked up at the clear, blue sky. "Send help, please. Anybody."

From the corner of my eye, I noticed the little boy look

up at the sky. "Anybody," he yelped.

A faint smile crept on my face and I watched more people walking by without a care in the world.

"Estella?" I heard someone call from behind.

I turned my head back, and my heart stopped beating for a second. It took me a second to recognize the man, but with a closer inspection, I knew him.

"Are you okay?" Ignacio asked, pulling out an earbud from his ear and cocking his head to the side.

Ignacio wore a tight, gray shirt that showcased his toned body, gym shorts, running shoes, and I guessed he had contacts on. He almost looked like a completely different person without his silver-rimmed glasses. It was more intimidating to look at him; there was no barrier between our gazes. His light eyes emanated fire. Ignacio was fire. Hot, strong, intense.

Gah, stop ogling; you're in a crisis.

"No," I said, shaking my head. "This little boy is lost. He found me, and I've been walking around the whole harbor in search of his parents, or somebody. I've been looking for almost an hour. Can you help me?" I never expected to ask Ignacio for help, but once I did, a subtle amount of relief washed over me.

"Of course," he said. "What's his name?"

I waved his question away. "I don't even know," I mouthed. I had been so anxious that it hadn't occurred to me to ask the boy for his name.

Ignacio knelt in front of him and started to communicate with him in Italian. All the words flowed out, and he was able to extract more information from the boy in one minute than I did in an hour. I couldn't understand everything they were saying, but I could tell the little boy liked him. Ignacio even made the boy laugh.

"His name is Luca; he said he came here with his father and aunt. He was at the beach but walked away because he was hungry. You gave him an apple, he liked walking around with you, and now he is thirsty," Ignacio said with a small smile.

I exhaled in relief that we had some information, so relieved that I almost wanted to hug Ignacio for helping me, but I stopped myself.

"*Ho sete*," Luca whined.

"Let's get him some water and head to the beach," I said.

Ignacio stopped to get himself and Luca a water bottle from a vendor. He asked me if I wanted anything, but I politely declined.

Leaving Paris

We walked away from the harbor and down the waterside to the beach. It was nearing October, but there were plenty of people occupying the small beach. I didn't blame them; it was seventy degrees outside, but the bright, sunny day and the luring blue color of the water would make anyone want to go swimming.

Luca stopped in front of us and knelt down to grab sand, then handed it to Ignacio. "*Mangia!*"

Ignacio pretended to take a bite. "*Delizioso, grazie,*" he said, smiling with his eyes and mouth.

Whenever we were together, the air was thick and intense, but it was different today. There shouldn't have been this type of peace while looking for the parents of a two-year-old, but there I was witnessing the gentleness in Ignacio.

A woman laughed in the distance, and it captured Luca's attention. "Zia," he shrieked. *Aunt.*

Luca's aunt danced along the shore, blowing kisses to the man taking a picture of her. The man encouraged her to do more poses as he gave her compliments.

"*E papà!*" Luca clapped.

Ignacio and I glanced at each other with the same puzzled expression. We didn't know anything about Luca other than what we'd been told and witnessed, but it was difficult to not jump to conclusions. Luca's father was being flirtatious with Luca's aunt and they had been so lost in their own world that they hadn't realized that Luca wandered off.

Luca waddled away with a beaming smile and ran into his father's leg. The father glanced down for a second to pat Luca's head and walked away from him to kiss the woman. They pulled away only to look through the pictures in the camera, and Luca stood on the shore, neglected. My heart ached for the little boy.

"Ignacio!" I called, watching him storm toward the couple.

Ignacio yanked the camera out of the man's hand and catapulted it far into the ocean. Luca's father balled his hand into a fist and directed it to Ignacio's face, but Ignacio caught it and pushed the man away. Ignacio's face was as hard as steel as he lectured the man. I couldn't understand everything he said, but it was full of detestation.

Ignacio's fingers briefly brushed Luca's hair as he walked away from the beach. I slowly waved goodbye to Luca and ran behind Ignacio. He had stormed off, several feet ahead of me. I thought that I'd lost him, but he stopped in his tracks, and I wrapped my hand around his arm.

Ignacio turned to me, gazing down at me with tender eyes. "I'm sorry you had to see that, but men like him disgust me—fathers who neglect their children only to chase after their own wishes. The selfishness of it is unbelievable. They'll never understand what that does to a child."

"It seems like you're speaking from experience," I shared in a soft voice, recalling the conversation I'd had with Emile.

Ignacio leaned against a bricked wall and looked down to the ground.

"I'm sorry, I shouldn't have said anything," I murmured, realizing that I shouldn't have exposed him.

"It's fine," he responded.

"Thank you for helping me with Luca," I said. "I'm not sure what I wouldn't have done without you." I did ask the universe to send me *anybody*, but why Ignacio? I didn't question it much longer and decided to let it be and move forward.

I walked away from Ignacio but slowly turned to face him when he called after me.

"Estella, when can we speak?" His voice was low and

genuine. "You don't know the guilt I'm plagued with for leaving you that night in Paris."

My heart felt like it had been turned slowly, a rattling doorknob for a door that had to stay closed. I never properly moved on from that incident in Paris, and as much as I wanted to gain closure for that night, it was terrifying. I didn't know if I wanted to feel all those ugly emotions again. All I had for the men I had been romantically involved in were ugly feelings.

"Ignacio." I sighed.

"Fine." He nodded. "When you're ready."

I nodded slowly and walked away. I'd always thought about the possibility of receiving an apology from Mr. Pianist, but I never thought about how much it would impact me. It was an apology—just words that placed a bandage over a gaping wound, but they were *his* words. His words did something to me that I wish they didn't. They made me stop in my tracks and think about the possibilities.

"The universe had us cross paths again, Estella. We should do something with that," he shared.

I wasn't sure what the universe wanted from us, let alone what it wanted from me, but it was giving me a massive headache. I continued walking back to my cottage with Ignacio's words on repeat.

Chapter 15

ESTELLA

My room was in shambles, and it was due to my indecisiveness about what to wear. I reminded myself that I put myself in this situation.

Ignacio's words echoed in my mind throughout the night and the following morning. I rehearsed what I would say to Emile and Ignacio, and I called them as a brief wave of confidence surged through my body.

I instantly regretted it.

I told them that I wanted to meet for a piano lesson, and Emile praised me for continuing my journey in learning music. Ignacio didn't say much; he was probably as stunned as me.

"Screw it," I said, zipping off the dress and tossing it

onto a large pile that rested on an armchair in the corner of my room.

I decided on wearing a white midi dress that had a small slit on the side. It was a casual dress, but it had a little bit of personality to it. I analyzed myself in the mirror, and before I could change my mind again for the seventh time, I headed out the front door. After all, this wasn't a date.

The drive to Emile's cottage was more than dreamy, and the jazz music that blasted in my ear emphasized the wondrous feeling. I should've been more nervous of the upcoming interaction, but with Emile being there, I wasn't as worried. Nothing could happen if we were being supervised, and even then, I wouldn't let anything happen. I couldn't let myself be that vulnerable again.

Ignacio had beat me to the cottage despite being ten minutes early. I knocked on the door three times, and Emile answered with a cheery smile. Seeing him smile made me smile. Emile reminded me of my grandpa who passed away three years ago, so interacting with him was easy.

"Just in time for the challenge," he said, a wicked smile creeping up.

"What?" I chuckled.

Leaving Paris

He closed the door and walked two steps ahead of me. "The blindfold challenge. As a child, I would blindfold Ignacio and have him perform a piece he was comfortable with, and if he won, I gifted him with whatever he pleased. He hated it, still does, but it's entertaining and beneficial to his motor skills."

"Oh interesting," I said. "What piece will he play now?"

"He isn't too sure; he keeps saying he is rusty, but I know that's a lie," Emile said, walking into the study. "We have an audience today." Emile beamed, clapping his hand.

Ignacio was seated on the bench, his body straight and broad. The sun shone through the windows and onto him and the piano, showing off the beauty of the remarkable duo. The brown hue of the piano glistened yet accentuated its structure and form. Ignacio looked amazing, as usual, with his sleeves rolled up, his white dress-shirt loose, and careless waves barely grazing his face.

"Estella." He sighed, causing the butterflies in my stomach to be resurrected. The way he said my name made me flustered and frenzied. "It's nice seeing you again."

"It's nice seeing you again too," I responded, softly.

"Have you picked a song yet, boy?" Emile said.

"Yes," he declared. "'Moonlight Sonata, third

movement. Let's keep it simple."

Of course, he'd choose Beethoven.

"Outstanding choice, but are you sure? For someone who is unpracticed, it may be difficult." Emile enjoyed taunting him, and I enjoyed seeing Ignacio's reaction.

"I'm positive."

"Estella, do you mind placing the blindfold on him."

"I could do it, Nonno," Ignacio said.

"No, the blindfold must always be placed on you to ensure that it's secure, and I've already made myself comfortable," he said, grabbing his mug and placing it in his hands as he comfortably sat in his armchair.

"Where is it?" I asked.

"In the drawer under that bookshelf," he said, pointing.

I retrieved it and walked behind Ignacio. Ignacio removed his silver frames and placed them on top of the piano. I covered his eyes with the black, thick blindfold. I secured it tightly around his head and waved my hand in front of his eyes and got no reaction.

"I think he's good to go," I said.

"We're ready when you are," Emile hollered.

"I'm blindfolded, not deaf, Nonno," Ignacio responded.

Emile clapped his hand and expelled a loud laugh. "I'm

sorry."

I decided to stand behind him to get a good shot of all the action. His back was tense, and his fingers hovered the keys, determining where to start. I could never imagine myself playing a song blindfolded, let alone the third movement of "Moonlight Sonata." My hands could never work at that speed even with years of practice.

Ignacio's fingers bounced around the keys momentarily; he was getting himself accustomed to the keys again. The initial start of the song startled me, causing me to step back. Ignacio's fingers jumped from key to key; it almost looked like he wasn't touching the keys. The chord progression of the piece was deemed incredible by me, a beginner. Ignacio had no problem projecting force, and I could feel the intense energy radiating off of the piano. He hadn't missed a beat, a tone, or his composure.

Emile laid back on his armchair and twirled his finger up in the air as he was regaled by watching his protégé play a spectacular piece with ease. Ignacio was on his final minute and showed no signs of failure, and it gave me hope that I could learn from him despite our past. After all, that was how he captivated me in the first place.

Ignacio ended the piece with forceful grace and

whipped off the blindfold. "Jesus." He sighed. "I honestly didn't think I would make it."

"That was incredible," I said in awe, placing my hand on his arm and scooting him toward one end of the bench.

"You'll learn to get there in time," Emile said, smiling.

"How long?"

"Eight years or so."

My eyes widened in disbelief. "Oh, okay," I said, somewhat deflated.

"You're receptive, so I think it won't take that long." Ignacio leaned over, making it sound more like a statement to me and more of a whisper to Emile.

His wondrous scent made me lose my breath for a second. How could I simultaneously harbor negative feelings for someone yet feel so attracted to them?

"Where should we begin? I didn't know where to begin. I haven't played in five years."

"Five years?" I muttered. "Why?

His eyes watched me wistfully, making my cheeks heat up. *You know why.*

"It was his father," Emile chimed in.

"What have you taught her?" Ignacio asked, ignoring Emile's comment and staying on topic.

"She knows the key names, whole steps, half steps, chords, scales, et cetera," Emile said. "We're learning to read basic songs and will work upward."

"Okay, great. I remembered that you knew how to play a few advanced songs by ear, but I guess we want to create a foundation," Ignacio said.

"You remembered?" I asked, puzzled that he would retain random information about me.

"Of course, *Canon in D* and forty seconds of *Clair du Lune*." He chuckled. "Along with the melody that you created some time ago," he said, his voice low. I had a couple of chords down, but ultimately, *we* were the ones who created the melody.

My cheeks were on fire. These were all facts that he remembered, and it caught me completely off guard. I didn't actually expect him to remember anything about me or those nights. When he was able to walk away from it all without a single trance, it was hard to believe any of it mattered.

Honestly, it would've been easier to move on had he just forgotten about me. It was clear that I wasn't going to be able to move on without closure, and that's not something I wanted to address right now. This was all too much for me.

"You look a little pale. Do you need some water?" Ignacio asked.

"I will get some," Emile said, quick to get on his toes and out the door.

"I don't think I can do this," I whispered. "It's feeling all a little too much." I placed my hand on my head and tried to take a deep breath, but the air felt thick.

"Estella," he breathed and tried to reach out.

"I'm sorry, but I think I need to go," I said, sliding out of the bench and rushing out of the cottage.

I was overwhelmed and had to distance myself. I wanted to try and give Ignacio a second chance, but it almost seemed impossible to do so. The way he looked, the way he smelled, the way he carried himself, every fiber of his being repulsed and attracted me. I could feel my heart tugging in opposite directions.

It was idiotic of me to even believe that this situation would work. It didn't matter if Emile was a couple feet away from us, it was Ignacio being barely inches away from me that made the biggest impact. He surely didn't forget about our nights in Paris, but that didn't help his case. Did he expect me to swoon over him for remembering me? No, if anything, it infuriated me that he remembered those nights as clearly as I did but wasn't left with the aftermath of broken feelings.

Why did I let him affect me like this?

I fell hard for him in Paris. I admired, adored, and loved him. I slept with him. I lost my innocence to him.

I felt stupid that following morning and felt even stupider now for giving him a second chance and even worse that, despite it all, I didn't hate him. If anything, my body craved him. It craved comfort from the first man who had broken my trust and heart.

Stupid, stupid heart.

Chapter 16

IGNACIO

Days passed, and neither Emile nor I had heard from Estella. Emile was beyond confused, wondering what would have caused her to run out of the cottage the way she did. I was the cause, and the guilt continued to spiral inwardly. Maybe recalling those small details about her wasn't the best choice, but I just wanted to show her that she hadn't left my mind.

Nonno wanted answers, but he wasn't a confrontational person and left her a voicemail stating that he was willing to talk to her whenever she was ready. I, however, decided to take matters into my own hands and visit the café. She had every right to hate me, to not want to talk to me, or wish me dead, but it was time to set the record straight.

I entered the café and placed my wet umbrella in the designated spot.

Salem's smile had been wiped clean as I walked into the café. She was Estella's best friend, and I appreciated how much she cared for Estella. I fully accepted the withering stare that she was giving me.

"I'd like one cappuccino, please," I said, looking behind her and into the window that gave everyone a view of the kitchen. I couldn't see Estella in the back.

"You can't be here."

"I understand your dislike for me, but I need to talk to Estella."

"Estella needs space."

"Estella needs the truth." I leaned against the counter.

Salem closed her eyes and exhaled deeply. She knew that Estella needed the truth; she couldn't keep running from her problems forever.

I pressed my hands hard against the counter. "Salem, please," I pleaded. "She deserves the truth. I'll tell her everything and if she still wants to see me as the bad guy, then so be it."

Salem glanced at me and looked toward the black

curtains near the shelves that displayed all of Estella's work. She seemed uncomfortable with the whole situation but understanding. I assumed Salem, out of everyone, knew exactly how much damage had been done.

"She's terrified...of the truth, her feelings, men in general."

"She doesn't have to be afraid of me. All I want to do is apologize, and then I'll leave her alone."

Salem swallowed hard and watched me with contemplative eyes. "Fine, ten minutes, and then I'm going in."

"Thank you," I whispered and walked toward the black curtains.

I pulled the curtain to the side and watched Estella on the potter's wheel. Her beautiful brown hair had been pulled into a loose bun with a couple of stray hairs framing her oval face. She was a classical beauty and knew how to make a man stop in his tracks. She looked at peace, and all I wanted to do was watch her lose herself in her art.

Estella raised her head, pushed the strands of hair away from her face with her wrists, and noticed me watching her.

"What are you doing here?" Estella asked.

"I came to talk to you."

She shook her head and reached over for the towel that was on the floor. She wiped her hands and removed the earbuds from her ear. "What?" she asked, annoyed.

"We need to talk," I repeated.

"I'm working, Ignacio."

Even when she was upset with me, my name coming out of her lips sounded like a song.

"Estella, you know that it's time for us to talk. We can't keep pushing this conversation away."

Estella stood up, her body displaying a strong, confident, and grounded woman. "Excuse me? You came into *my* studio, during *my* work hours, and *you're* telling me to stop pushing you away?" She now had her finger pressed against my chest and her face inches away from me.

"Don't push me away," I whispered.

Estella's jaw tightened, and she glanced up at me with hurt in her eyes. "Stop talking," she whispered, walking over to the sink and running the water. She placed her hands under the stream, gazing ahead.

"Estella, I don't want to continue living this way, and neither do you. I need to tell you everything that happened that night."

"Stop talking."

"You need to know what happened."

"You left me," she whispered angrily, turning her body towards me. "You used me and left me alone in the studio," she muttered, her eyes no longer on me. "We spent twenty-one days together—playing music, eating sweets, sharing our dreams, you whispered all these sweet nothings in my ear, we slept together, and then you were gone. As if it meant nothing."

"Estella, those nights meant everything to me. I came back for you," I whispered, my hand slowly moving upward to wipe away the tear that ran down her cheek.

"I don't believe you."

"I did."

Our voices were in whispers, but our hearts thundered against our chests, begging for release. A bolt of lightning ripped through the sky, but it didn't faze us because we were in our own storm of emotions.

"I don't want to hurt you anymore," I murmured softly into her ear. I wanted to lift her head and kiss her sincerely, to let her know that I wanted her five years ago and even more now, but I restrained myself. The truth had to come first.

Estella motioned me to the large, wooden table in the

corner of the room and pulled out the wooden bar stools.

I sat down and faced her. "I don't know where to begin." I spent five years thinking about this moment and how I'd tell Estella the truth should I ever crossed paths with her again. Everything I ever wanted to say was gone.

"What happened *that* night?" Our last night together.

"I woke up after our night together and heard a loud crash downstairs. I figured one of the busboys placed a cup awkwardly and it had fallen. I went downstairs to check out the noise and also lock the doors because I hadn't done so that night." I ran my fingers through my hair and shook my head. "I still don't know how it happened, but someone broke in and attacked me."

Estella was shocked; maybe there was disbelief in the mix. I wouldn't blame her for not believing me. She had probably spent years coming up with scenarios as to why I left, portraying me as the bad guy.

"Both my dad and I were admitted to the hospital, and after that, we went incognito for a month because my dad wasn't sure who had orchestrated it. We were in a little cottage in the middle of nowhere with no technology, no communication with the outside world for four weeks. God, Estella, all I could do was stare out the window or sit outside and think about you. Those were the longest days of my life. When we were given the green light to return to Paris, I immediately went to our spot in the café. I waited there and when you didn't show up, I ran to the jazz club. You didn't come around to our spots. I went looking everywhere else for you around Paris for weeks, and I never saw you again."

"Ignacio," she breathed.

Estella's remorseful eyes couldn't meet mine as I searched her face. It was easy to be filled with anger and resentment when all you had was your side of the story, when you believed what you wanted to believe, but she must have realized that she'd been wrong about me. I didn't run away from her; I was taken away from her.

"Estella, you had owned my heart from the start, I would've never left you behind. Where were you, *stella mia*? I searched everywhere."

"After that night, I was devastated, but it didn't stop me from going to our spots. With every step I took to each location, all I could think about was seeing you again. I did it for three weeks and hated that I hadn't seen you or heard from you." Estella took a deep breath and continued. "I really did think you were done with me, and music all together because the workers from café hadn't heard from you either. And then, one day, I had been called into the financial aid office and was told I could no longer be at the university due to tuition issues. My study-abroad scholarship was no longer accepted. I didn't have the money to continue my stay, and honestly, I didn't fight to stay. I figured you were gone, I was ashamed, and I left."

We were staring at each other, dumbfounded by the whole situation. We parted our lips, in hopes that we could exchange something, but we were both short of words. Five years gone because of circumstances that were out of our control.

She pressed her hands against her face. "This is unbelievable." I thought giving her the truth would liberate her, but it conflicted her.

"I'm sorry that you're feeling conflicted. That wasn't my intention."

"I know, I know." She sighed, still hiding her face. "It's just, I've convinced myself the last five years that you were the bad guy and now...you're not."

I nodded, understanding her.

"Are you okay?" she asked, softly. "After being attacked?"

The corner of my lip turned up. "I'm okay. I was bruised and had minor headaches the first couple of weeks, but nothing major. Losing you was harder."

Estella sighed and leaned against the wooden table. "Unbelievable," she whispered.

"You should look into what the university did to you. It was unfair of them to decline your scholarships weeks in."

"That was five years ago. It doesn't matter anymore."

"Had I been there, I hope you know I would've paid for you to stay."

"That never crossed my mind, but thank you."

I nodded.

The tension in the room was thick but not suffocating. We were just lost in the truth and unsure where to go from here. It would have added a lot of pressure to both verbally acknowledge it, so we sat with it.

The black curtains moved to the side, and Salem stood by the doorway with a cautious expression on her face. "Everything alright?"

Estella softly smiled. "Yeah."

"Do you think you can lend a hand? Maria had to go home early."

"Sure."

Leaving Paris

Salem left us alone again, and Estella stood up to remove her apron. Her movements were slow, maybe even cautious. She hung her apron and gently turned on her heels to meet my gaze.

"I suppose I'll see you around?"

I wanted to do more than just see her around, but all this information was new. Five years could change a person, and maybe she still felt the connection we once had or maybe it was gone.

"Of course."

I held onto every bit of hope that she wanted this second chance. In a world of seven billion people, we'd ended up in the same old town in the middle of nowhere. That had to mean something.

Chapter 17

ESTELLA

I believed in second chances, but the repercussions of love had exhausted and terrified me. I moved to Italy to put the past behind me, except now, an important man from my past was taking over my present. Ignacio meant the world to me years ago, and I'd be lying to myself if I said that he still didn't mean something to me.

I had to take it slow with him, whatever I decided to do, but being friends was a start.

I knocked on the cottage door, waiting for someone to answer the door. I wanted to apologize to Emile for ignoring him the past few weeks. Ignacio's car was also in the driveway and I debated on whether to go back home. I pushed past that need to run away. We weren't on bad terms anymore, and he didn't deserve the cold shoulder.

The sun was shining, the flowers were still in bloom, the wind made its gentle entrance, and the birds sang at a distance.

Everything is okay.

Emile opened the door and smiled from ear to ear. I adored his child-like grin. "Estella, I didn't expect you on this nice Sunday."

"Hello! I know, and I'm sorry for intruding," I said, holding a delicately wrapped present tightly in my hand.

"No intrusion at all."

I handed him the present as I gave a sheepish smile. "Also, apologies for running out of the cottage and ignoring you. It's just been a tough few weeks, emotionally and mentally." I started to rabble on until Emile gave my arm a gentle pat.

"Say no more. I'm glad you're doing better."

I pulled my cardigan tightly against myself. "You can open your gift now, if you'd like."

Emile didn't spare a second more and tore the brown packaging away to expose four, black-to-white-gradient, night-sky expresso mugs that I made for him. It was a part of my new night-sky-themed collection. Emile wrapped an arm around my shoulder and thanked me with sincere gratitude.

"You are very talented," he said. "I'm going to put it to good use and make some decaffeinated *caffè espresso*. Come in and share a cup with me."

"Of course," I said. I didn't mind having a cup of coffee with Emile; he reminded me of my late grandfather. We didn't see each other often, but when we did, we would talk and drink coffee with a side of *pan dulce*. Delicious, sweet bread.

"Handwash only, by the way."

"I don't have a dishwasher, so that won't be a problem." He smiled widely, chuckling.

"Oh, right." I had washed dishes with Ignacio once. It seemed that my interaction with Ignacio last night had a bigger effect on me than I realized. It was hard to focus on anything; I'd been going through my day in a daze.

Emile scooped coffee grounds into the Moka pot and placed it on the stovetop. He pulled a wooden tray from under the sink and delicately placed three of the mugs on top. The sound of paper rustling at a distance captured my attention. Seconds later, piano music started.

"Ignacio is here. He's helping me organize all my pieces.

That room is a mess."

"I saw his car here. I can go, if you'd like? I don't want to intrude into your family time."

"No, no. Actually, I think it'd be fun to listen to my old compositions together."

The thought of being with Ignacio made me nervous, but I couldn't pass the opportunity up. I enjoyed Emile's playing style and pieces; they captured a lot of emotion. Emile had an impressionist approach to his playing whereas Ignacio was more romantic.

"Go ahead, I'll be there with our drinks," Emile said.

I walked into the piano room and absorbed the sight of Ignacio reading music sheets. He looked at peace. His face was studious, but his energy was lighter. Music was his passion—there was no doubt about that.

Ignacio was startled for a moment. He looked me straight in the eye with caution before composing himself again.

"I didn't mean to spook you."

"It's not a problem. What brings you here?"

"I stopped by to deliver cups that I had made for Emile."

"Very nice," he said, the corner of his lips turning upward.

"What are you reading?" I asked, walking slowly toward the piano.

"Some of Emile's older compositions," he said with a light smile. "I believe it's the song he wrote for my nonna."

"Do you mind if I see it?" I asked. It was still a bit difficult to read music, but the feeling of the final composition in my hands was another experience. It felt more real, rawer. That was the exact reason I also loved pottery so much.

"Here," he said, handing it to me and making room for me on the bench.

It was titled *Per Sempre* which translated to *Forever*.

I placed the sheets on the music rack and studied them. My right hand hovered above the piano keys, trying to determine where to start. It was beyond my learning skills, but I was a beginner and didn't expect to succeed. I just wanted to try, even if it meant making a fool of myself.

Ignacio moved my hand over the desired area and slowly pulled his hand away. We stared at each other, and I liked how he didn't look away until I did.

I started to read and play the music, out of sync, and read a couple of notes wrong. After a couple of failed attempts, I exhaled in frustration.

Leaving Paris

"Let me help you," Ignacio said and shared a few tips.

I analyzed the composition and slowly pieced the notes together, playing the first line successfully after listening to him closely.

"Very good," Ignacio said. "Left hand?"

"Sure."

"It's ready," Emile said, entering the room with a tray of expresso and chocolate sweets. He walked over to me, handing me a cup, and I turned to pass it to Ignacio. His fingers brushed against mine as we both held onto the cup.

"Thank you, Estella."

My eyes couldn't resist looking at his lips after saying my name. My stomach somersaulted at the brief flashback from years ago, when we used to kiss in front of the café. That was our spot.

Ignacio revealed one of his first secrets to me there: he hated coffee. Never told a soul because he didn't want to be that Italian that didn't like coffee. I enjoyed a cup of coffee here and there, and although he hated it, he would always buy one for himself. He wanted to be a part of something that I enjoyed.

"Carry on. I need to do one more thing before I settle down," Emile said.

"Let's continue?"

"Sure." I smiled.

For a while, Ignacio played the low end as I played the melody of the song while I grew comfortable with the melody. Once I became comfortable, I added in the base notes and played a couple of notes without error. I clapped with joy, genuinely feeling accomplished.

"Great teamwork," Emile said, already seated and holding his cup of expresso. I had been so lost in the lesson that I didn't notice Emile had joined us. "I knew you two would make a great match." He lowered his lips to the rim of the cup and took a tiny sip while Ignacio and I glanced at each other. Emile wasn't wrong, but if only he knew our history.

"Well, what do you two say?" Emile said. "A clean slate?"

Ignacio gazed at me with his warm eyes.

If only Emile knew.

"We can keep going today and play it by ear," I said.

Emile clapped his hands together. "*Perfetto!*"

We sat together, reading over the notes and working on the song by sections. There was no doubt that Ignacio could perform it on his own within minutes, but he worked with me at my own pace. He even laughed at his own errors which made my stomach twist in delight. I wanted him to keep laughing because it made everything between us feel almost normal. Like we were just two strangers.

There was no such thing as time when we were both playing together. Our dynamic—my eagerness to learn and his willingness to teach—worked well. I flourished under his guidance, absorbing more material than I ever had before.

Ignacio glimpsed at his watch. "It's five o'clock," he said, noticing that Emile had fallen asleep. "We should wake him or else he won't sleep at night."

I laughed and appreciated his joke—like a friend would do.

"He's like a toddler," he said. "I'm sure he'll also be hungry."

"Ah yes, close to dinnertime."

"I'm sorry, that went on longer than expected. I enjoy playing with you, and it doesn't feel like teaching."

"Thank you." I blushed and changed the topic to stop the butterflies from fluttering every time he complimented me. "I'm sorry for taking up your time. I know you were supposed to help him with organizing, not teaching."

"I don't mind."

"I'm sure he will."

Ignacio shook his head. "No, he won't, and neither do I."

My mind lingered on his words, repeating them and activating the butterflies in my stomach again. Ignacio leaned forward, inches away from my face. My eyes narrowed onto his plush lips, and I could feel the heat rise up my neck and onto my cheeks.

"I think we should play one more song before waking him up. What do you suggest?" His voice was almost a whisper.

"*Clair de Lune*."

"Still think Debussy is the best composer?" he asked.

"Of course."

A warm smile spread across Ignacio's face. His hands graced the keys with a combination of delicacy and firmness. The duality of it all took my breath away. The evening sunrays projected down onto his hands. Those same hands once traveled up and down my body.

My mind wandered to that night in Paris when I rode him, his strong hands grasping my breasts, covering them with ease. I remembered the way his hands slid up my chest and around my neck, his fingers spreading around the nape of my neck.

Those damn hands were talented in many ways.

And before I knew it, the piece had ended. I sat in place, feeling a sensation cascade between my thighs and my nipples harden. A soft sigh escaped my lips.

"I hope you enjoyed."

"I thoroughly did," I said, composing myself.

"We plan on making dinner; would you like to join?" he asked casually as he stood up. "Unless you have other plans. I don't want to pry."

"No plans tonight—just another Sunday evening."

"Great," he said, followed by a gentle smile.

***

Emile appeared behind me, placing a gentle hand on my shoulder. "You cooked; I will clean," he said, releasing me of my duties.

"If you say so," I said, wiping my hands dry on a hand towel.

"Who taught you how to cook, Estella?" Emile asked. "That was very delicious."

"My mom."

"I'd love for her to teach me one day."

"He needs all the help he can get," Ignacio chimed in.

The two men chuckled. They had near-identical smiles, and even their tones matched perfectly. They had light golden-brown eyes, oval-shaped heads, and similar facial features. I'd heard of grandchildren resembling their grandparents, but these two were peas from the same pod.

"Well, it's almost seven and dark out. Ignacio, do you mind dropping Estella off at home?" Emile asked, looking over his shoulder at us as he wiped down the counters.

Ignacio's eyes widened for a second, either amused or anxious about the situation. Maybe both. "I don't mind, but it's Estella's choice."

"It's not a problem, really. I have the Vespa." We'd had a great night, and for the first time, I could see us maybe being friends, but I didn't trust being in the car with him. Too many dirty thoughts have resurfaced and being alone with him would be risky. If he touched me when I was at my weakest, I'd unfold right then and there.

"Nonsense. It's too long of a ride at this time, especially since we are more in the countryside." Emile's tone sounded fatherly, and I appreciated his concern for me.

I exhaled and rubbed my arm. "Alright," I complied. I

wasn't sure how I would survive a car ride with Ignacio.

"Leave your key on the table. I will have someone drop it off by 8 a.m."

I twisted off the Vespa key and reluctantly placed it on the table.

"Are you ready to head out?" Ignacio asked.

"If you are."

Ignacio lifted himself off of the chair, and I moved to follow him out. I walked over to Emile to give him a pat on the back as a farewell.

"I will see you two on Tuesday," he said, smiling at both of us.

"But I—"

"Goodnight, Nonno," Ignacio said, opening the front door for me and not allowing me to finish my sentence.

The autumn wind danced around the bare skin on my arms, making me shiver. We were one day away from October, and it already felt like we were hitting the low 50s. I wouldn't have been able to bear the chills of the night had I ridden my Vespa. Emile's suggestion was a blessing in disguise, but I worried about being in close proximity to Ignacio.

Ignacio opened the passenger door for me and waited

for me to slip in to close the door. He appeared in the driver's seat and started the car, immediately turning on the heat.

We began cruising down the road, and Ignacio fiddled around with his radio, searching for a specific station. He sighed in relief at the sound of a piano and violins playing. The instrumental piece had a wistfully romantic harmony to it.

We didn't speak, and I did my best to keep my eyes averted from him. I couldn't look at him, especially in this state of mind. I had to focus to push the images of me straddling him, his hard chest, and his smoldering expression, out of my head every time I caught a whiff of his tantalizing scent.

God, I needed a distraction.

The car jolted downward, and Ignacio made a sudden jerk to the side, parking on the grassy terrain. I placed my hand over my chest and looked out all the windows to see what caused him to make an unexpected stop. There was nothing. The country roads were bare; there were no people or animals nearby.

"Shit, shit," Ignacio mumbled as he unbuckled his seatbelt, exited the car, and stood on the front corner of the driver's side.

I scrabbled out of the car to see what had concerned Ignacio. His arms were crossed over his chest, looking as deflated as the tire.

"Oh, yikes," I mumbled.

It wasn't the type of distraction that I wanted, considering it prolonged my time with Ignacio, but I got what I asked for. It was just my luck.

"That damn pothole," Ignacio muttered under his breath as rolled up the sleeves of his button-down shirt and motioned me to the back of the trunk.

He popped it open and my eyes flickered to a scratch on the side of his car. That was my doing, from when I was running late for my Italian lesson. In my defense, he shouldn't have parked where he had.

"I did that," I blurted out, pointing to the scratch. "I'm sorry."

Ignacio paused for a moment. "Oh, that. Don't worry about it."

I stared at the organized compartment, unsure of what I was looking at. I had never changed a tire before; I never had a car of my own in Brooklyn. There was no need for it, and now, I wished I'd had that experience, so I could feel somewhat confident about this new situation.

Ignacio walked in front of me and grabbed a bulky, black tool—a jack, I supposed. He went back to his workstation and took a brief glance over his shoulder, then groaned deeply.

"It's going to get dark soon," he mumbled.

"Let me help," I said, lowering myself down next to Ignacio. "I've never done this before, but I'm a quick learner."

The corner of Ignacio's lip turned up slightly. "I know."

Ignacio instructed me on how to help him, explaining every single step. We assembled the jack, raised the car, unscrewed the lug nuts, and we scrambled to not lose them. It had become too dark to see and I used my phone as a flashlight when Ignacio had to pull off the flattened tire.

"Careful, careful," I whispered, watching Ignacio lift the spare tire and place it in its rightful spot.

Ignacio exhaled deeply; it sounded as if he had been holding his breath during the entire process. He worked feverishly and was brief with his instruction on how to install the tire. I probably appeared deeply focused on the tire, but all my attention was on Ignacio, not the installation process. There was something very appealing about Ignacio using his hands to do something more rugged.

He walked back, stood next to me, and checked the tire out.

"Not bad," I said, admiring our work.

"Thank you for your help." He was being kind because I didn't help at all; I just watched him do all the work as I hummed, somewhat taking mental notes.

"Thank you for teaching me."

"I don't mind," he said, reaching for a rag and wiping his hands.

Ignacio tossed the rag into the trunk and walked around the car to open the passenger door for me. "Alright, let's get you home."

We settled into our seats, back to our usual deafening silence for the remainder of the car ride. I fiddled with my fingers, unsure of what to do with myself. Ignacio eyed my unsettled hands and extended his fingers out, maybe with the desire to actually reach out to me, but then retracted them, wrapping them around the gear stick.

Just pretend that didn't happen, Estella.

"That's me," I said, pointing to the cottage.

"I'll walk you to the door," he said, parking the car and

unbuckling his seatbelt.

"Oh, you don't..." He opened his door and closed it again. "...Have to," I finished with a sigh.

Ignacio placed his hands into his pockets as he walked towards the edge of the water. "Wow," he said, looking across the body of water and to the brightly lit city of Lilla. "We live across from each other."

"What?" I asked, surprised. "That yellow villa is yours?"

"Mhm."

I inched closer to him. "It's a gorgeous house, grand and lit up. It must be nice."

Ignacio's shoulder twitched. "It's okay."

Ignacio started walking away from the water and toward the cottage. We stood near the lit lantern by the door. It didn't provide a whole lot of light, but it was enough to see that Ignacio had his eyes on every inch of me.

"Do you remember asking if I was okay after being attacked?"

"Yes, and you said you were okay for the most part."

"Can I admit something to you?" His voice was low, ready to whisper his secret.

I nodded.

"I'm a bit afraid of the dark after being attacked."

"I'm sorry you had to go through that."

"I'm just glad they didn't hurt you."

I peered at him slowly, and I nearly forgot how to breathe when I gazed into his fiery eyes.

Ignacio's finger traced the outline of my face, and his eyes studied me, and I studied him back. I wasn't sure what he was reading because my mind was in a frenzy, but his face said everything he wanted. He wanted to know if I'd let him kiss me.

Ignacio set my insides ablaze, and as much as I feared the burn, I couldn't resist the flames. I closed my eyes tightly, trying to snap myself back to reality. I opened my eyes, and his mouth was less than an inch away from my lips. His breath brushed against my skin, and I could've pulled away, but I found myself closing the space between our lips.

Ignacio traced the outline of my back until he hit the base of my neck, deepening the kiss. I splayed my fingers through his hair and pulled him into me. His hands glided down my sides and down to my waist. He pulled me against his hard body. His touch was heavenly, and I couldn't help but moan into his mouth.

I couldn't believe I was kissing him.

Leaving Paris

The realization that I had done something emotionally risky jolted me back to reality. I instantly placed my fingers against my lips and gasped. I'd made a big mistake by allowing myself to become vulnerable too soon. I fumbled with my keys as I tried to unlock the door.

I closed the door halfway and darted my gaze toward him. He looked confused, hurt, and desperate.

"I'm sorry, I can't do this," I whispered. "*Buonanotte.*"

I pressed my back against the door, placing my hands over my mouth in disbelief. It was amazing, and then it wasn't. It was freeing, and then it wasn't. It was hopeful, and then it wasn't.

I can't let myself kiss him again.

Chapter 18

IGNACIO

I couldn't keep Estella out of my mind. I thought of her during the day and dreamt of her at night.

Estella. Estella. Estella.

We kissed, and we were in Heaven, then we came crashing down to reality.

The way she looked at me…it killed me. After she had realized that we kissed, her eyes immediately pooled over with regret. I didn't want her to regret the kiss. I wanted her to ache for more.

I could hear Nonno talk endlessly about his plan to surprise Norah for her birthday, tomorrow. It was an important time for him, but I couldn't process any of his words. My mind was on Estella and if what we once had was really over. It was driving me crazy.

"Should we go?" Nonno asked.

"Go where?"

Nonno glared at me and slapped one of his leather notebooks against my arm. "To Salem's café. She wanted to go over my ideas; she's helping me with the surprise."

Estella.

"Of course."

Estella.

"Let's head there now. I will drive," I offered.

Estella.

On the ride there, I thought about how we would look at each other; I thought about what I would say to her; I thought about every possible minute.

I felt panic wading in and out. Estella wasn't running the front; instead, she was seated across from a male figure. I attempted to keep my composure as we walked past the pair. The thought of her being with another man bothered me.

He looked around Estella's age with scruff on his jawline and light-colored hair. I'd seen him before but couldn't put a finger on where. He spoke to Estella, she said something in return, and then he gave her a polite laugh that made her smile. It was the prettiest smile that I had seen, and I hated that he made her smile.

Nonno and I leaned against the vacant wooden counter. Nonno looked over the counter and through the window that overlooked the kitchen, in search of Salem. Minutes later, and there was still no trace of her. Nonno pressed the bell that they had on the counter to signal a new customer.

Estella turned in our direction. She acknowledged me for a microsecond and then looked at Emile. "Maria is in the bathroom; she'll be out soon."

"We're here for Salem."

"Salem should be back soon, too. Take a seat anywhere you'd like."

Emile walked over to a table in the corner of the café. We were a table away from the pair but still close enough to overhear their conversation.

"You're outstanding," he said. "You've picked up the language easily."

"It's similar to Spanish. Trust me, I'd be more of a mess if I didn't already have some base."

"Never a mess," he said, his finger grazing her hand.

She retreated her hand slightly, tugging the sleeve of her cardigan over her hand. She pushed a strand of hair over her ear and looked away in uncertainty. He softly smiled at her and collected all of his material before talking to her again.

"So, when should we practice again?" he asked.

"Saturday?"

"It's a date."

I wrinkled my nose and snapped my head in the man's direction. My reaction had gone unnoticed, which was for the best.

"See you then." They both nodded at each other before parting ways.

Estella extended her hands over the table and lowered her head, seeming to gather the courage for her next move. She perked up and turned to us with a friendly smile.

"I'll get you two a cup of coffee while you wait for Salem," she said, then lifted off the seat and dashed into the kitchen.

Estella returned with a tray carrying two cups of coffee, some creamer, and a plate of small cookies. She placed the dark green mugs in front of us. Nonno took a sip and hummed in satisfaction. I placed my lips on the rim of the mug, and a sweet, cocoa aroma hit me.

It was hot chocolate.

"On the house, of course."

"You're too good to us," Nonno said.

"Thank you," I chimed in.

Estella nodded and stepped back.

"Take a seat by us," Nonno invited.

"Oh no, it's okay. I should maintain the kitchen since Maria isn't out yet." Her eyes were glued on Nonno; she didn't dare look at me.

The bell above the door jingled, and we all turned to see who was entering. Salem walked over to us and gave Nonno a pat on the back.

"I'm sorry for being late, but there were some complications with deliveries."

"It's okay, Estella spoiled us."

Salem gave Estella an appreciative nod.

"Should we start to plan?" Nonno asked.

"Plan what?" Estella asked nervously.

"Nonna's birthday! It's tomorrow," Salem said.

Estella placed a hand over her forehead. "Ah, okay, sorry must've slipped my mind."

"We're going to close the café early, and then we are all going to take her out."

Estella tried not to react, but I noticed the panic in her

eyes when Salem asked to switch seats so she could sit directly next to Nonno and look at locations on her laptop. She nodded and awkwardly moved over to the seat next to me. She crossed her leg and shifted her body towards Salem, desperate to be a part of the conversation. I wanted to reach out, touch her, and reassure her, but she wouldn't even glance at me. I knew that I was the last person she wanted to see, but she was the only person I wanted to see.

Estella and I didn't contribute much to the conversation, despite her efforts. Salem and Nonno would ask for our opinions, and we would blatantly agree with them, then as time went on, they stopped asking us for our input.

An hour later, Nonno and Salem had devised a plan.

"We'll see you girls tomorrow," Nonno said, giving them a half-hug.

I kept my eyes locked on Estella until she looked straight at me. Her gaze flickered toward my lips, and I caught her cheeks reddening before she turned her back to me.

It looks like we've infiltrated each other's minds.

***

Leaving Paris

We toured through the countryside, absorbing the mountainous region with its ability to release all worries. Estella and I rode on our own horses while the other three took a carriage that was pulled by a pair of horses. We rode through the open fields, passing by farms and homes dated centuries ago. We waited above the vineyard where we would be met with a table filled with local products such as jams, cheeses, breads, and meats.

I glanced to the side and watched Estella stare ahead with her back straight as she galloped with her graceful horse. She looked confident yet delicate, at ease yet alert, angelic yet unfriendly. I had planned to speak to her tonight, even for a minute, but the barrier she was putting up had me question my next move.

We arrived at our destination, and Estella and I hopped off our horses' backs, handing the reins to a farmer who approached us with his hands spread out. He told us that the horses would be in the stables if we chose to ride them through the meadows after our meal. Norah, Emile, and Salem stepped out of their carriage and soaked in the beautiful view of the vineyard.

A man approached us with a cheerful smile and

motioned us toward our table. The four friends gasped at the sight of the variety of food, and Estella even smiled. I loved her smile. I wanted her to smile at me in that way.

A wine steward approached the table and gave us a detailed presentation on the top wines the vineyard was known for and gave us samples of them. Estella declined the first two cups until Salem threw a grape at her and told her to loosen up.

"It's very good, Estellita," Norah chirped, handing her the glass.

"Fine, only because it's your birthday," she said.

Her full, pink lips kissed the rim of the glass, imprinting it with a light lipstick stain. She pulled it away and thought about the wine for a moment. "It's not so bad."

"Keep it, I'll get another glass," Norah said, waving for the waiter.

"I have a feeling we are going to have to tuck Nonna in tonight," Salem joked.

"Salem," Norah scolded.

Estella hid her small smile against the glass, and of course, it made me smile. She glanced in my direction and didn't immediately give me a death stare.

So there was some hope after all.

Leaving Paris

It was a quarter to six, and everyone had indulged in the food and were admiring the violet-and-light-blue skies. They chitchatted, but I stayed back and only spoke when Nonno attempted to integrate me into the conversation.

I learned a little bit more about Estella. Nonno asked her how she knew how to ride a horse, and she told him that it was one of her favorite pastimes as a child when she went to El Salvador with her family.

"Do you guys mind if I leave the table? I want to take one trip around those meadows before we head out," Estella said.

"Of course," the couple responded.

"I can join you." The words slipped out of my mouth.

Nonno looked at me and nodded in approval. "Good idea, the sun is setting."

Estella opened her mouth slightly, ready to protest, but she closed her lips. I trailed a few feet behind her as we walked to the stables to retrieve our horses. The same man from earlier handed Estella her sandy-colored horse with a blond, bright mane and handed me my black, proud stallion. We hopped back onto our horses and whisked through the green, wispy, grassy hills.

Estella lifted her reins, motioning for the horse to trot

ahead toward the setting sun. Her silhouette against the purple and pink pastel hues of the sky was breathtaking. I whipped my reins, picking up a good amount of speed to catch up to Estella. She was making it clear that she didn't want to be around me anymore.

"Estella," I called out when I saw her galloping ahead.

I started to match her speed, and she turned her back to shoot me an annoyed scowl. "I don't want to talk, Ignacio."

I motioned the horse to go faster, and we sprinted ahead of her. She started to slow down and then stopped in front of us. Estella's face was red with anger. "What is wrong with you?" She directed her finger towards my face. "Stop following me."

"All I want to do is talk to you. I can't go on ignoring what happened."

"There's nothing for us to talk about," she said, tensing her jaw. "Nothing happened."

"Estella, you're going to tell me that we didn't kiss two nights ago?" I had my arms spread out in disbelief.

I couldn't believe that she wanted to deny that anything happened. She might have regretted it, but she couldn't forget it.

Estella crossed her arms tightly around her chest.

"Nothing happened."

Estella tried to sound genuine, but *I* knew that she didn't believe her own lie.

"If you regretted it, it's fine, but don't sit there and lie to me about a moment that I can't stop thinking about." I remembered her body, lips, smell, and voice. "At least be honest with yourself."

Estella balled her hands into a tight fists and closed her eyes. She was ready to explode, and I was ready to be cut ten layers deep with all the hate that she'd contained for years.

"You want the truth, Ignacio?" Estella demanded, getting off her horse.

"Yes," I pleaded, following her lead. "That's all I want."

"Fine! The truth is that I'm scared. I'm scared, Ignacio," she shared, her eyes glossing over. "I'm scared because I try to convince myself that I don't want to be around you, but deep down, that's all I want. I want to be touched by you. I want you to speak to me despite my stubbornness. I think about those nights in Paris. I think about the good and the bad, but it's scary. I'm scared of getting too close again only to be burned somehow. I know you told me you came back for me, but what if that was a sign? What if this isn't supposed to happen?"

Estella confessed. She confessed, and it was not what I had expected. I had my heart set on hearing her bash me and hate me for hurting her, but I received the opposite. She stood in front of me, on the brink of tears, as she let her heart become vulnerable.

"I know, I know," I told Estella, running my hands through my hair.

"No, Ignacio. You don't know. You don't know what it feels like to be wronged by so many men."

"Maybe not by so many men, but I've been wronged by my parents. I know the feeling."

Estella shook her head, regretting what she had said to me. "I'm sorry."

"You can trust me. I want this, Estella. I want you to trust me. I want to be this forever." I leaned over, reaching for her hand.

"I don't know."

"I know that your biggest problem is me, but I know that you want to solve it. You *want* to know what happens if we are together." I took a step closer to her, and she gazed at me as I continued speaking to her. "You want a love that simultaneously grounds you down to Earth yet scatters you amongst the stars." She wanted a Debussy kind of love, and

I was more than willing to give that to her.

"Stop, Ignacio," Estella whispered.

"You want to know if you can give me a second chance… You want to know if your heart will let you fall in love."

Estella slammed her lips over mine, and her hands clutched my shirt as she pulled me against her. My mouth grew impatient against hers; I wanted to absorb everything Estella before she pulled away from me. My hand traveled down to her knee, and I lifted her leg against me, gripping her tightly. Kissing her was a dream.

Except this moment was real.

And I became greedy with the reality. Our lips were dancing and our tongues tracing each other. I pulled away from the kiss and started to trail her neck with kisses, causing her to murmur out my name, which made me more possessive of her. I wanted to be the only man's name she would moan.

Estella's lips began to slow down, and she hesitantly pulled away from me, loosening her grip on my shirt.

"Estella." I sighed. "Don't run from me."

Estella bit her lips and looked over her shoulder. "It's just a little too fast."

I nodded and traced her raspberry-colored lips with my thumb. "I can do slow."

Estella hopped back onto her horse and waited for me to join her side. We rode away from the sunset in silence, but our minds buzzed with thoughts. I thought about the sweetness of her lips, and my growing need to taste them again. I would never get tired of kissing Estella.

You won't regret this, stella mia.

Chapter 19

ESTELLA

The autumn breeze whipped through my hair, greeting me and telling me it was here to stay. The winds had escalated throughout the last two weeks, but there was something different this time. It wasn't teasing; it was carried by whispers of warm fires to come. The skies were darkening, and even at six in the evening, there were red and orange hues that initiated the end of the day.

"Are you sure you're going to be okay?" Salem asked.

We usually spent our evenings together, but Salem had a date with Leonardo. He ended up staying at the café one day after our tutoring lesson, and the pair hit it off. Salem was extremely picky with men, so when she told me that she had an interest in Leonardo, I told her to go for it.

"Yes." I chuckled. "Ignacio will be here soon, anyway."

"Are you okay with that, too?"

"Yes, I'm fine." I appreciated her concern. She knew that I didn't have a good track record with men, but we had been taking it slow the past two weeks.

We didn't text constantly throughout the day; he would only meet me in public and did no house visits, and we had to keep our relationship a secret from Emile and Nonna Norah. They were the happiest they'd been in years, and we couldn't let our failures affect them.

"This would be his first time in the house," she said. "Things could get heated."

"I'm not going to sleep with him," I said. "We've hardly kissed these last two weeks." It was true—he stole a kiss one evening, but that was the extent of it. Most of the time, he would caress my hand, cheek, or arm, or kiss my forehead before saying goodbye. I meant it when I told him I wanted to go slow.

"That's the point! Suppressing desire is a recipe for disaster."

I rolled my eyes at her nonsense. We weren't suppressing desire; we were slowing it down. It was a challenge at times. I was completely and utterly enamored with his masculine beauty, his talent, his passions, his cognac-colored eyes, but I remained strong.

"We're just going to eat and watch a movie."

Salem wiggled her eyebrows as she smirked.

"Is Leonardo close?" I huffed. "You're kind of getting on my nerves."

"Okay, I'm teasing, obviously. Do you like him a lot?"

"God, Salem, I like him a little *too* much, but I'm petrified of getting burnt if things don't work out. Something goes wrong every time I fall in love with a man."

"Take your time with him."

"Of course."

"Speak of the devil."

"He's early," I murmured.

"He's eager to get down and dirty." Salem shimmied.

I nudged Salem away and walked toward the car. Ignacio opened the car door and handed me a beautiful floral bouquet, then placed a soft kiss on my cheek. "I'm early, I know."

"It's okay." I smiled, admiring the bouquet. "Thank you."

"You're very welcome," he said and circled his car to retrieve a large, brown paper bag. *"Pupusas."*

My heart skipped a beat. "What?"

"Heard it's your favorite." His eyes darted to Salem.

"Where did you get these?!"

"A woman named Rosario. She grew up in Castellara, but her parents were from El Salvador. She was more than happy to make some for you."

I couldn't believe he went out his way to find someone who knew how to make my favorite dish. That had to be the sweetest thing someone had every done for me.

Another car pulled into the sandy pathway and parked behind Ignacio's car. Leonardo exited the vehicle and opened the passenger side door for Salem.

"Be good, you two!" Salem chirped, patting my arm as she walked past me.

I opened the front door, giving him a view of the living room. It was a small, quaint cottage that had all the essentials, such as a living room, kitchen, two bedrooms, and one joint bathroom. There was no extra space for fluff, but we had the occasional plant, paintings, and small figurines.

"Wow, this is homey," he said, walking around the living room and admiring the flower-field paintings that I had hung.

Leaving Paris

I softly chuckled and crossed my arms. "I'm sure it's nothing compared to your villa."

"It was a gift from my father." He placed the bag of food on the coffee table. "Sometimes big isn't always better."

"That's true. How are you two doing? You're not working for him anymore?" Five years ago, Ignacio had been adamant about succeeding in the cooperate world. He gave up on his dream of being a film composer to work for his father. It all had to sting.

"I quit a minute before he was going to fire me."

"I'm sorry."

"Don't be; it's really for the best. I prefer it this way anyway. Wake up whenever I want, work on music again, run around the city, visiting you while you're at work."

"You're working on music?" I smiled.

"Fiddling around with some chords."

"I can't wait to hear it."

"You'll be the first to hear."

I sat on the couch, leaning slightly in toward Ignacio. He stretched his arm out across the couch and grazed his finger against my exposed shoulders. He leaned in closely, staring at my lips.

"I know you said you want to take it slow, but would I

be going too far by telling you that I missed you?"

My lips parted slightly, and I watched his light brown eyes growing warmer. My heart flickered, my cheeks blossomed like spring flowers, and the butterflies in my stomach fluttered their wings.

I missed you.

My mind repeated his words like a broken record.

Ignacio's finger trailed up the curve of my neck and up to my jaw, grazing my cheek. I was melting, withering, and burning under his intense stare.

"I'm sorry, it's too forward."

"No," I exhaled. "It's okay."

"I *really* missed you."

God, he was killing me.

I couldn't think around him; my mind was scattered. His voice became a song, and his words carried the melody. And I would lose myself in the beautiful music.

Ignacio had moved in closer, his breath teasing the middle of my neck. "I missed you, Estella," he whispered into my ear.

A shallow breath escaped my lips as a rush of heat traveled between my inner thighs. "Ignacio," I whispered.

"*Stella mia.*" My star.

I couldn't resist his accent and his endearing words. I placed my hand over his cheek and leaned in to plant a gentle kiss on the lips, but it was much more aggressive. It was desire, need, an *aching* need for his touch. My body was hungry for him.

Ignacio maneuvered himself back to a sitting position and I straddled him, cupping his neck and crashing my mouth against his lips. His fingers danced along my back and down to my lower waist. I moaned in ecstasy; his touch had a bewitching effect on me.

"First door," I said between kisses.

I knew what I was doing and, in the moment, didn't care about the consequences. I was listening to my body's desires because it craved some sort of physical culmination with Ignacio. He was the only man to have ever explored my body at all levels. I was twenty-year-old me again: naïve, curious, and full of passion.

My mattress was beneath me, and he was over me. Ignacio leaned in to kiss me, and my legs parted to allow him to kiss me in even closer proximity. Ignacio lowered his hand and placed tender kisses on my neck that made me melt into the bed. My hands reached his chest, trying to frantically unbutton his shirt.

Ignacio's hand cupped over mine, stopping me.

"Are you okay?" he asked.

His eyes meet mine, and we stared at each other for a brief moment.

"Yes," I responded with a timid smile. "Why'd you stop me?"

"This isn't slow." He sighed in frustration.

"Do you not want to sleep with me?" I whispered, feeling the insecurities coming up to the surface.

"I want you, so much. I'm using all the strength known to man to not devour you. I've waited for this moment for years, but I need to do this right. I don't want you to make a hasty decision. I don't want you regretting the decision to sleep with me again."

My heart and sweet spot achingly throbbed for this man. My heart appreciated the efforts he wanted to make to ensure a perfect night, but my sexual essence wanted to straddle him. Having my hand on his hard chest and looking into his intoxicating eyes made me want to forgo all the formalities and go for it. I didn't want to think or fight it anymore. *But he was right.*

He could see that I was agreeing with him.

Damn it.

I reluctantly nodded and released my hand from his chest. It was for the best.

"Thank you for stopping," I said, coming back to my senses.

"Of course."

Ignacio fell onto his back and placed his arms above his head, resting his head on his hands. "I have a surprise for you. Well, one of two surprises."

"Okay." I smiled. For someone who liked to know so much, I also appreciated the thought behind a good surprise.

Ignacio retrieved the item from his jeans pocket and handed it to me.

"Glow-in-the-dark stars?" I asked, pulling out one of the stars. "I love them." I had glow-in-the-dark stars painted onto the ceiling in my New York bedroom. My papa loved astronomy, and he would read to me space-related books as a child, and an interest in stars naturally grew from that. I asked for stars above me one night, and my papa made it happen.

I handed half the stars to Ignacio. "Help me?"

We spent ten minutes sticking the stars on my ceiling; we actually tried to put some effort into their placement.

Leaving Paris

"Nonno told me you're from New York—Brooklyn, right? My mother is from Manhattan."

"Really? That's pretty close."

"I received my bachelor's from the Manhattan School of Music."

"That's a tough school, but clearly you have the skills. Do you see your mother often?" I've always heard of Angelica being a mother figure, but he never mentioned his actual mother. I wondered if they were close.

"Once in a blue moon. She's busy with her career. She's an actress. Florence Amatore—or as the public knows her, Florence Lilianna."

"That's your mom?" I gasped. She was in line with Meryl Streep. She had over twenty awards and triple the nominations for all her work. Mama, Maya, and I gathered around the TV every Sunday evening and played one of her movies. We were all fans.

Ignacio hummed and then moved his attention to the stars on the ceiling. He wasn't comfortable talking about her, and I knew my star-stricken face wasn't helping.

"I'm sorry, that was just unexpected. My mom, my sister, and I love all her movies."

"It's okay. She's brilliant at her work, I won't deny her

that."

I nodded.

"You can't really see stars like this in the city," he said, changing the topic.

"No, not really."

"You must love the night sky here then."

I tilted my head and tried to think of a time when I stood in place and appreciated the night sky. I spent a lot of time looking at the sky when I was deep in thought or contemplating my next move, but never when I was at peace.

"I don't think I've ever soaked it in," I admitted. "Peacefully."

"Let's do that right now, then. Your second surprise is in the car," he said, smirking.

We walked out of the cottage and near the edge of the water, opening our field of vision to something unimaginable. We had the perfect view of the night sky; it was dark, the moon was full, and the stars twinkled. Ignacio's fingers danced down my arm until they intertwined with mine.

"How did I not do this any sooner?" I asked.

"It's hard to see what's really around us when we are

preoccupied with our own lives."

"Yeah." I sighed.

Ignacio and I admired the white-gold moon that gave the night sky a warm glow. The bright stars were scattered around the sky like flickers of paint on a black canvas. They shone through all darkness, completely invincible. Gazing at the night sky brought me hope, assuring me that everything would align the way it was intended.

"Close your eyes."

I covered them with my hands, and Ignacio guided me to his car. The trunk popped open and I heard Ignacio fumble around with something bulky.

"Open."

I opened my eyes and gasped at the sight of a brand-new keyboard set, a Yamaha one, to be exact, with the stand, headphones, and bar stool. It was all displayed on the box.

"No way, Ignacio," I said, excited and reading all the features labeled on the box.

"You have talent; I want you to practice." There was a genuine delight in his eyes. It was clearly important to him that I kept practicing. Our history made the piano an important staple of our lives—our connection.

"Thank you so much," I whispered.

Leaving Paris

"Let's eat, set it up, play a little, and go from there?"

"I would love that," I said, hugging him. Ignacio kissed the top of my head and continued to hold me. Trust and closeness slowly built over my fear of falling in love.

Chapter 20

IGNACIO

The sound of a door closing had woken me. I immediately laid eyes on a sleeping Estella with all her guards down, and she looked truly at peace.

I caressed her cheek and admired the sight of her. I vaguely remember doing the same thing before we had fallen asleep. She was telling me stories about her sister and parents, and I listened to her as I stroked her cheek.

She loved Italy but missed her family. She didn't want to talk about them at first; she thought it would upset me since I didn't talk much about my parents. I assured her that I wanted to know everything about the people who raised such an amazing woman.

I heard a loud groan come from the kitchen, and I

decided to step out of the bedroom to check on Salem.

Salem's annoyed eyes flickered toward me. "I'm guessing you're sleeping over?"

"I wasn't sure, but if you'd rather I leave, I will."

"No, it's okay," she huffed.

"Bad date?"

Salem opened the refrigerator door and scanned the inside. "It fucking sucked."

I looked at my watch and furrowed my eyebrows. "It's 1 a.m. You've been out for six hours. That's a long date, if you ask me."

"It lasted an hour because we aren't compatible. He's not into cooking, astrology, reality TV shows, Disney movies, or anything I'm interested in. Plus, he's vegan." She picked up a jar of pickles and struggled to open it. "Vegan, Ignacio! After hearing that, I headed to the nearest bar and played pool with some strangers and drank."

"That's a shame."

Salem opened the jar and stabbed a pickle with a fork.

"It was horrible. Anyway, how was your date? Did you two fuck?" She bit down on her pickle and watched me with casual eyes.

I took a deep breath and stared at her with

astonishment. She had no filter. "No, Salem. We had a great date, though. She enjoyed her surprises. Thank you for all the help." I wanted to give Estella a memorable date, and I had to ask the only person who knew her the best. Salem was happy to help with the food and gift ideas.

Salem soaked in the compliment and smiled with pride. "Anything for my best friend. She deserves the world, especially after her last relationship," she mumbled. "Dickhead," she sang.

I neared the small island and leaned against it, wondering if Salem would give me more insight into Estella's past. I knew I wasn't the only guy who had broken her trust, and I hated that she'd gone through that again. "What happened?"

She pointed her half-eaten pickle in my direction and gave me a crooked smile. She was *very* drunk. "I know what you're doing. I'm not going to tell you her story because it's hers to tell, and if she isn't ready, then you're out of luck."

I couldn't hide the disappointment in my face, and Salem noted it. "I just don't want to hurt her, Salem. She has her reservations about me, and the last thing I need is to remind her of her ex."

"You're doing good," she said simply and walked away.

"Trust yourself more. Night!" she called out, and then her bedroom door closed.

Trust myself more.

I breathed in her hopeful words and nodded in confirmation.

I trusted in myself and Estella.

We would have our second chance at love.

Chapter 21

ESTELLA

Waking up to my bedroom being lit by the fall sun was visually breathtaking. I stripped the duvet away from myself and noticed that I was wearing the same outfit from last night. My gaze traced the outline of the digital piano that pressed against one side of my bedroom wall.

"Ignacio," I whispered.

I wasn't sure how I had fallen asleep—talking a lot usually did it—but I had woken up to no Ignacio. This wasn't my first time, and panic rose in me.

At least, you didn't sleep with him this time.

I rushed out of my bed and into the main area, stopping in my tracks. Ignacio was sleeping deeply on the couch. He had a navy-blue blanket tossed over him and a pillow covering half of his face. I guessed Salem found him asleep and tossed those on him.

It was 10 a.m., and everyone in the house was fast asleep except for me. As a child, my favorite memories were the ones when I would wake up to the smell of deliciousness: plantains, refried beans, bacon, eggs, and a good day.

I worked quietly for the majority of the prepping, but once I started cooking, I captured Ignacio and Salem's attention. Ignacio had been awake and staring at me for God knows long, and Salem shortly entered with her hand over her head.

"Drank a little too much?" I asked, stirring the beans.

"Yeah, it was a rough night."

"Bad date, huh?"

"So bad."

It was the same conversation with Salem, ever since college. She had the exact same routine after having a bad date. She would never come home after a failed date because she didn't want to be embarrassed, and then she would go to a bar—legal or not—and drink a little more than average to forget about the date and also hype herself up.

"Do you want coffee?" Salem groaned to Ignacio.

Ignacio had his arms folded over the edge of the couch, and he peeked his head in my direction, his gaze glued to me. "No, thank you," he answered.

Salem placed her freshly brewed cup of coffee to her lips, and she glanced in Ignacio's direction and rolled her eyes.

I glanced over, and he still hadn't taken his eyes off me. His stare felt even more intimate, considering he didn't have his glasses on. It was the eyes. They were as beautiful as fire.

Our rustic, oval kitchen table had been set with three full plates of breakfast food, and I motioned for everyone to take their seats.

Ignacio leaned over and placed a gentle kiss on my cheek. "Thank you."

Salem doused her plantains in sour cream and stuffed a bite into her mouth. "Mmm, thanks." She reached over to the fruit bowl and popped a grape into her mouth. "Oh, guess who is in town?" Salem asked. I could tell she was trying to sound upbeat but was too hung over for it.

I shrugged my shoulders, not able to name one person that we were friends with. Ever since middle school, it had always been me and Salem. People came and went, but none of them came to mind.

"Bianca."

"Oh yes." Bianca was Camilla's younger sister—by a year—and she'd occasionally hung out with me and Salem in school. Both Camilla and Bianca were popular in high school, but Camilla was the mean one who dated the quarterback whereas Bianca floated through groups, befriending everyone she could. "She's cool." I nodded.

"She wants to come over tonight. Girls' night."

"That sounds fun." I smiled.

"Do you think I can steal you away for a couple hours today?" Ignacio asked me. "I'd like to take you out on a date."

"Sure." I liked that he didn't want to leave right away. It was nice to have him over for breakfast and integrate him into a different part of my life. We would usually see each other in the evenings, so having him around in the morning was a pleasant change.

"Shit," Salem muttered with her mouth full of whipped cream. "I told Nonna I'd be at the café at eleven to help her with the wedding cake. I'm running late."

Salem left the table without saying another word, and Ignacio leaned over, his sweet lips tangling with mine. He ran his fingers up to the back of my neck and entwined them within my messy hair.

"Is this okay?" he asked, softly.

"Mhm," I hummed and closed the small gap between our lips. He molded his hands to my head and brought me in for a deeper kiss.

I had to protect myself, at least until I knew it was okay to fall.

***

Ignacio took me on a private tour to see a medieval castle situated on a high cliff that used to serve as protection from outsiders. It was beautifully impressive on the outside, and the inside displayed even more of it, retaining most of its original appearance. It had been neglected, but most of the rooms and halls were well-perseverved with an outstanding view of the lake.

I inhaled deeply, taking in the history and romance of it all. Our tour guide, Alonso, directed us into the breathtaking ballroom and spoke about all the grand weddings that were held in it.

"It's the perfect place for a beautiful couple," he said,

nodding at us.

Ignacio and I looked at each other; clearly it was too early to think about marriage. I was still learning to navigate my feelings and fears, but I appreciated Alonso's notion. Maybe he was able to see something that I couldn't see just yet.

"We've only been dating for a few weeks," Ignacio informed.

"*Oh, scusa!*" Alonso's face turned red like a tomato, and he excused himself out of the ballroom.

"Poor guy." I chuckled, staring at the ceiling. It resembled the sky with the light blue color and groups of clouds. I wanted to lay a blanket down here on a rainy day and still look up to see a perfectly clear sky.

Ignacio grabbed my hand and twirled me in a full circle, then began to sway us from side to side. "I'm not much of a dancer, but being in a ballroom with a beautiful woman makes me want to give it a try."

"You need to stop doing that." I giggled against his chest.

"Doing what? Complimenting you?" He began to hum *Fly Me to the Moon* and twirled me once more. "Why would you like me to stop?"

Ignacio pulled me into his chest and I placed my hand over it, looking up at him. He looked down at me with awe. I had never had a man look at me the way he looked at me. In all honesty, I'd never had a man treat me as well as Ignacio had these past few weeks, and I had never felt strongly for a man until I had met Ignacio, but the fear still lingered.

"I think you're the first and only guy who has given me words of affirmation," I admitted. "It's new, and I'm not used to it."

"Ah, well, sounds like I need to do it more instead." He chuckled. "But, if you'd really like me to, I will stop." His smile flittered away for a second, until I shook my head no.

Ignacio kissed the top of my forehead, and that was the end of the conversation. We danced around the ballroom, taking large steps, fumbling over each other, and laughing at our horrible dance skills until Alonso appeared with a smile on his face.

"Should I escort you two to the lover's trail?"

"Lover's trail?"

"Yes, it is where all the misters and misses would walk to signify their courtship," Alonso informed.

"Are you asking me to officially be your girlfriend, Mr.

Amatore?" I asked with a playful smile.

Ignacio smirked and nodded.

Alonso gave us a pleasing smile and marched across the ballroom to open the grand white doors. We followed Alonso's lead, walking around the corner to be greeted by a garden tunnel resplendent with pink flowers.

"Enjoy," Alonso said, bowing down and disappearing again.

Ignacio held out his hand, but I wrapped myself around his arm instead. We slowly walked down the trail, admiring the various blooms. The sweet aroma of the flowers surrounded us and tickled my nose. There was a flower in perfect condition lying on the cobblestone path and Ignacio picked it up then placed it behind my ear. His fingers lingered, stroking the same piece of hair back as his eyes danced around my face.

"Thank you for going on this date with me."

"No, thank you for bringing me here. It was magical."

"Like frolicking through the meadows?" There it was, a mischievous know-it-all smirk that I had seen once before, five years ago. Of course, he was teasing me about Debussy.

"I believe so," I said, running my fingertips over the last blossoms of the tunnel as we walked out of it. In front of me was laid a blanket with and a picnic basket sitting perfectly on it near the edge of the cliff that overlooked the glistening, blue lake.

Ignacio wrapped an arm around my waist and guided me to our lunch spot with a triumphant look on his face. "Lunch with a view?"

"Yes, please," I sang, sitting down on the blanket and inhaling the fall breeze.

I looked over at the breath-taking view of the majority of the town, of the townspeople enjoying their day, and noticed all the different-sized boats that sailed across on the lake. I had grown up in the city, but I belonged in the country. The quietness of the town, the tight-knit community, the endless acres of land, and the fresh breeze running through my hair.

"I could live anywhere in the world and I'll always come back to Castellara."

I looked over to Ignacio who had been watching me attentively and understood that I was appreciating the town. Sometimes I wondered how he was able to read me so well.

"I don't blame you; it's breath-taking. It reminds me of my parent's home town."

Ignacio's lips slipped into a brief smile. "I like that you're very close to your family, almost a little envious actually."

"Yeah, they're the best. They, along with Salem, encouraged me to come here."

"I'll have to thank them when I meet them." He smirked.

"Oh, when you meet them, hm?"

Ignacio and I had been sitting a couple of inches away from each other, but his hand traveled across the blanket and on top of mine. "I'd like to, really. I'd like to be more to you, Estella. Is the idea of being exclusive at this point entirely out?"

"No," I responded, softly. "So, you really were asking me to be your girlfriend?"

Ignacio gave me a firm nod.

I pulled away from his gaze and stared off at the lake. The thought of being an official couple brought a swarm of emotions, mostly positive, but I couldn't ignore the hesitation. We'd been dating for a couple of weeks, with the intention of becoming more, but now, with the opportunity arising, it wasn't as easy to say yes. Being a couple meant fulfilling certain obligations. Sex. I wasn't ready for that.

Ignacio closed the gap between us, facing me to caress my cheek. He stared deep into my eyes, his brows furrowed. He could pick up the hesitation that I was feeling.

"We will still go at your pace. We can be a couple and still take it slow."

I reached over for him, playing with the collar of his shirt. "What about your pace? I just don't want you to run out of patience." It was clear that my hesitation was rooted in from my past troubles with Cesar. Cesar was worlds different from Ignacio, but I still worried that underneath his kind demeanor, he would want what most men wanted: sex, and now. That was a big step for me. I was not prepared to become intimate with a man this soon—not like before.

"It's only ever been you, Estella. You're the only person I've wanted and my pace is your pace. I'm ready when you are."

Looking into his mesmerizing cognac-colored eyes and his words echoing through my mind, I developed a primal desire to get lost in him. Ignacio ignited a passion in me that I never knew was possible, and with one swift movement, I placed my hand on his neck and pulled his lips into mine, allowing myself to feel the sweetness of his words.

"Stella mia," he groaned, gripping my waist. "I won't disappoint you."

***

Bianca splayed her long legs out on the L-shaped couch and popped a cheese bite into her mouth. "Honestly, I still can't believe she's getting married. I'm going to meet the poor man tomorrow. Have either of you met him?"

"Yeah, he's a hot Michelin-star chef," Salem said. "I'm actually making their wedding cake."

"Why?" Bianca shrieked.

"He came to me and I couldn't say no to 3K."

"I can't believe you've met him before me."

"Are your parents coming to the rehearsal dinner at least?" Salem asked.

"No, but they'll be there for the wedding, obviously. Nico will be at the dinner though." She reached over to grab a cracker from the charcuterie board.

Salem glanced in my direction, and I pulled my legs up to my chest. Niccolo, or Nico for short, was Camilla and Bianca's older half-brother. They shared the same father, and Nico would stay with them only in the summers.

Nico was the beginning of my issues with men.

I hadn't seen Nico since I was fourteen, but I could never forget him. He was my first kiss and first-ever real crush. He was three years older than me, and as children, we would play together in the summer, but once I turned fourteen, things between us changed. He would find opportunities to whisk me away from the crowd, and one day, he pinned me against the wall, looked at me with his beautiful hazel eyes, and stole a kiss.

That was our thing for the summer. I would sneak away from the girls, and he would meet me in the kitchen or in the basement to kiss me for however long he could. Nothing more happened, but it meant a lot to me as a fourteen-year-old. I thought I was special for capturing the attention of a seventeen-year-old gorgeous boy.

I was far from special to him. That was the last summer I saw him. He was supposed to visit us the following summer, but at that point, he was eighteen and interested in traveling. No one really heard from him after that.

Salem was the only one who knew about my summer with Nico. She pretty much had to force it out of me because she found me balling my eyes out after Nico left.

There was a knock on the door that sliced through the silence in the room. I stood on my feet and opened the front door, greeted by a young man who held a white paper bag.

"Estella?" he asked, unsure.

"Yes?"

The young man sighed in relief. "*Da parte del signor Amatore.*"

"*Grazie!*"

I closed the door and placed the gift on the table.

"Who is Mr. Amatore?" Bianca asked, intrigued.

"Technically, my boyfriend." I opened the bag and pulled out a bottle of wine, box of chocolates, and an assortment of baked desserts.

"Jesus!" Bianca yelped. She picked up the bottle and analyzed it. "This bottle is $500. Where are you guys finding these rich guys?"

"Have it," I said.

"Oh my God, will I be meeting him tomorrow?" Bianca asked, hovering over me. "He's certainly in love with you."

"It's a little early for that," I mumbled.

"Well, he's either in love with you or you're really giving him the best sex of his life." She gave me an expectant stare. I wasn't going to tell Bianca the truth; she wasn't that close a friend for me to tell her about the complications of the relationship.

"We aren't sleeping together."

"Hmm, well he must be in love then," she said, giving me a knowing smile. "But, seriously, get on it or you'll have trouble in paradise."

"What do you mean?" I asked, crossing my arms and giving her a bothered look.

She shrugged. "Guys don't want to wait around," she shared, casually. "They get bored and will find it somewhere else. It's sad, but all my guy friends tell me the same things."

"Seems like you need new guy friends," Salem advised, playfully throwing Bianca a grape.

"Maybe." She chuckled.

Bianca's words caused an internal frenzy. Ignacio couldn't be that kind of man; he wouldn't leave me for not loving him or sleeping with him right away. He reassured me. We agreed on taking it at my pace.

As Salem and Bianca drank through all the expensive wine and chattered, I found myself deep in my thoughts. There were feelings that I couldn't ignore resurfacing again.

Insecurity. Anxiety.

Leaving Paris

Everything Bianca had said had shifted me off track, and I was stumbling across the tightrope that I was walking on.

And I was terrified of my next step.

Chapter 22

IGNACIO

I stood out on my balcony, looking over the lake and to the little cottage that housed Estella. This dinner was our first public appearance to those close to us, and the knots in my stomach kept pulling tighter. I tried to ease my racing mind by admiring the pastel colors of the sky. Below me, caterers, party planners, and the soon-to-be bridezilla zoomed across the lawn to make sure everything was in order.

I winced at the sound of Camilla's shrieking voice. "Are you all trying to sabotage me? These flowers look dead!"

An exhausted groan came from behind me. It was Marcelo. There was no doubt in my mind that he wanted some space from Camilla, but her voice was audible from every corner of the villa.

"Tell me again why you're marrying her?" I asked Marcelo.

"Money, business, legacy."

"She's not worth it."

"Well, we can't all find a woman that we are head over heels for," Marcelo said, nudging me with his arm. "I'm excited to meet her. I don't think you've ever spoken about a woman."

"I've been waiting for her." I had never loved a woman before her. The connection, chemistry, and compatibility that I had with Estella were unreal. There had to have been some cosmic force that pulled me and Estella to the same country, same city, across from one another.

"How long have you been seeing her?"

"Dating for a couple of weeks, but I asked her to be my girlfriend today."

Marcelo chuckled. "Well, have you slept with her?"

"No, we are taking it slow." I hated lying to him; he was my best friend, and I had to lie about sleeping with Estella. I'd never told him about those nights in Paris.

"I respect that." Marcelo nodded in approval.

Marcelo placed his hands on the railing and stood up straight. "Thank you for letting us use the villa. I don't know what we would've done if you didn't offer it. Their original dinner location had been vandalized a couple of days ago. I offered my villa to Marcelo whose mind had been driven stir-crazy by Camilla. I didn't understand her appeal, but I had to support him regardless.

I patted his shoulder. "It's no problem. Go help your soon-to-be wife before this place becomes a crime scene." I shuddered at Camilla's yelling. She had no respect for anyone. Marcelo rolled his eyes and left without saying another word.

Poor man.

***

My gaze traced the outline of Estella's goddesslike body; the way she carried herself made me want to lose myself in her. The light blue, silk dress accentuated her every curve, highlighting her natural hourglass figure. I stood beside her, wrapping my arm around her waist, pulling her closer to me. All I wanted to do was touch her.

We entered through the gates and into the backyard filled with strangers and acquaintances. There were a few people that recognized me and gave me a simple smile, and others looked at me without any care in the world. I entertained many friendly strangers with a nod and made my way through the crowd and to the firepit in the back corner of the yard.

"Wow, this view of my house is incredible. It's almost picturesque."

I stood behind Estella, her body slightly leaning against mine. "I wake up every morning and look out here, then I smile, knowing that you live right across from me."

Estella raised her head and watched me through her long lashes. She had a contemplative look on her face, almost as if she was trying to read me. She lowered her head and then composed herself before breaking the distance between us. It didn't feel good to be away from Estella, and it was even more painful when she was near and I *couldn't* touch her.

"Would you like to dance?" I asked.

She crossed her arms over her chest and peeked at the not-too-occupied dance floor.

"One dance?" I asked, reaching my hand out to her.

"Okay." She nodded.

Estella placed her delicate hands over mine, and I led her to the wooden dance floor. I pulled her close to my chest, my eyes never leaving hers. She looked up at me again, and once again, I caught her staring at me, deep in thought. I wrapped one arm around her middle and with my free hand, stroked her cheek with my thumb.

"Are you okay?" I asked, softly.

Estella pressed her cheek against my chest and didn't answer my question. We continued to sway to the music in silence, but my mind buzzed with questions. I wanted to look at her and see what she was feeling because I was certain that something was wrong.

I pulled away from her slightly and stepped back, then brought her back into my arms with a spin. She landed with her hands on my chest and looked up at me with lost eyes.

"What's wrong?" I whispered.

Estella's lips opened, and before she could respond to my question, a young man approached us. His hazel eyes met mine, but then he glanced over at Estella. Estella's breath hitched, and she looked more alert.

"Do you mind if I cut in?" he asked.

I'd never seen this man before, but it was clear that Estella knew him. I wanted to tell him that he couldn't dance with *my* Estella, but instead, I released Estella and allowed her to decide. Estella looked at me with worried eyes and without receiving any confirmation, the man held her hand and pulled her into a dance. She grimaced but didn't protest.

I tensed my jaw and walked back, staring at his hand on her waist. I wanted to burn a hole through his hand; I hated that he was touching her. Estella kept her distance and her head low, not wanting to face him directly.

Was he the reason that she seemed unlike herself?

The man spoke to her, murmuring occasionally, and even chuckled once.

Estella didn't look the least bit entertained by him. I cupped my hands together, rubbing them, because I needed to do something with them other than wishing I could push him away from her. There was a gentle squeeze on my shoulder, and I turned to see Salem standing next to me.

"I can feel the scorpion coming out." She smirked.

"Who is he?" I asked, gritting my teeth.

"You look good in your navy-blue suit." She tried to change the subject.

"Salem," I warned.

"He's my cousin, Nico. They had a thing about ten years ago. They were kids, doing kid things." She was trying to lessen the severity of the situation by telling me they were young, but I was young once. Five years ago, I became completely transfixed by the idea of Estella, and here I was five years later, pursuing her.

Time and age had nothing and everything to do with it.

Salem placed her hands on my arms and led us to the dance floor. She kept her arms there while I hovered my hands a centimeter away from her waist. She definitely knew how to take the lead and eventually managed to maneuver us closer to Estella.

"I've been trying to look for you all over social media," Nico said. "I even managed to get your number, but that didn't work either."

"I deleted all my personal social media and changed my number shortly before moving to Italy."

"I've been trying to contact you for almost two months. I was in Brooklyn for a bit and wanted to take you out to eat, then I heard you were in Italy. I figured I'd see you at Camilla's wedding. You look great, by the way."

"Are you hearing this?" I whispered to Salem.

"I'm literally right here," she hissed.

"Yeah, I can't do this," Estella scoffed. I released Salem when I saw Estella walking away from the dance floor and toward the villa. I speed-walked toward Estella, managing to meet her at the door in time.

"Do you want to go elsewhere? Maybe the piano room?" I suggested.

Estella looked unwell. The color from her face had been drained, she looked weak, and she placed a hand over her forehead. "Yeah, sure." She sighed.

We didn't speak on our way to the piano room, but I walked closely beside her.

We entered the light blue room, and Estella walked toward the familiar piano, grazing her fingers over it. The way she touched the piano displayed how much it meant to her. If only she knew how much it meant to me. She danced her fingers up toward the fox-and-piano figurine, giving it a faint smile.

I situated myself on the bench and started bouncing my hands around to find the right notes, tempo, and rhythm for a song that I'd never actually played before. There were no piano sheets or any physical copies of this song. I had mentally composed it over those five years; it was all about Estella—light, wistful, romantic.

"What is this called?" she asked, placing her hand on the piano and watching me play as she stood next to me.

"Lost Star," I said, facing her.

Estella didn't say anything else. She simply stood there, watching my fingers dance up and down the piano keys.

We found ourselves in the same situation as five years ago: enjoying a night of music, returning to a small space, and playing the piano to wind down. The last move would be to undress and ravage each other like desperate lovers. My heart pounded against my chest, and for a brief second, I believed that it was louder than the piano. The need for her grew stronger with every high note that I pressed.

My fingers gracefully slid away from the piano and onto her hand. I faced her, scanning every one of her delicate features, and then her innocent brown eyes met mine. I reached for her waist, pulling her onto my lap. Her legs straddled me tightly, and my hands ran up her arched back as I watched her in fascination.

I claimed her lips, grabbing the nape of her neck, intensifying the kiss. Her lips, her touch, her lustrous perfume, her soft moans made me ache for her. I pulled away to bury my face into her neck, pressing hot kisses all over. Estella's nails dug into my shoulders, and I continued to plant kisses and worked downward to her collarbone, lining it with kisses.

"*Oh, God.*"

I hooked my finger along the strap of her dress and lowered it down her shoulder to get more access to her beautiful body. I loved her. I craved her. I loved that I craved her so much that it hurt. Five years. I needed her.

Estella held onto my shoulders and then extended herself upward as she lowered my head to her breast. My lips moved down, and I took a nipple in my mouth, sucking it gently. Estella immediately moaned and clutched my head against her body.

She loved it.

My mouth moved from one nipple to another, teasing it with a light bite. Her hips began to circle in need, and I groaned in anticipation.

"Are you sure?" I whispered, my mouth traveling back up her neck. "Tell me you want this, Estella," I begged.

"I-I…"

I pulled away, searching her eyes for an answer. She placed her hand on her chest and exhaled deeply as if she had been holding her breath. I pushed away a piece of hair that fell in front of her face and tried to cup her cheek to read her, but she pushed my hand away.

"I need to go," she mumbled, pulling her legs away

from me.

"I'm sorry," I said, reaching out to her, but she was already out the door. I followed behind her because I needed her to know that I was sorry for asking too much from her. "Estella."

"Just, give me some space, Ignacio," she responded, taking long strides toward the end of the hallway.

It wasn't possible for me to give her space when I felt that she was permanently removing herself from my life. There was something off about her ever since she'd arrived, and I had to make sure she wasn't having doubts about us. All I wanted was us.

"Estella, please, don't run away from me."

She made a swift turn to the left and opened the door to the bathroom. Estella immediately yelped and stepped back with her hands shielding her eyes. "Jesus!"

I jogged to her side and looked into the bathroom to see what had made her react. Camilla fumbled to put her dress back on, and a man I had never seen before squeezed by her to exit the bathroom. There was murder in my eyes, and he knew because once he brushed past me, he ran down the hallway.

"Get out of the bathroom, Camilla," I ordered.

Camilla usually had a confident, better-than-you attitude, but not at that moment. She was terrified and had every reason to be scared.

I gripped my neck in irritation and walked around in a circle, trying to decipher my feelings. I wanted to sort out the issue I was having with Estella, and instead had to deal with finding out my best friend's fiancée was having an affair days before the wedding. My heart slammed against my chest, aggravated by the whole situation, but I had to remain calm.

"We need to find Marcelo, and you will tell him what happened here. It may be the only redeeming thing you've done in your life."

Camilla nodded and then followed closely behind me as I led her back to the party. Estella could've left, but she lingered behind Camilla. Perhaps she didn't have too much confidence in Camilla either because I certainly didn't.

Camilla deserved to be humiliated in front of her friends and family, but I wasn't going to do that. I called for Marcelo from the sunroom and watched him quirk his head to the side.

"What's going on?" he asked, and then he looked over my shoulder. "Who is that with Camilla?"

"Estella." I sighed.

Marcelo brushed past me and offered his hand out to Estella. "It's nice to finally meet you. I'm glad you could make it to the party."

Estella simply shook his hand and then looked at me. My eyes darted to Camilla and then to Marcelo. Marcelo dragged his hands across his face and exhaled.

"What's going on now?"

"I'm sorry," Camilla cried, exaggerated. It was clear that she was apologizing for getting caught. "I didn't mean to…"

"Spit it out," Marcelo said, gritting his teeth together.

Camilla schooled her face to appear devasted, but it was too contrived. She wasn't going to tell him unless he pulled it out of her. I didn't have the patience to deal with Camilla, and I shouldn't have expected her to own up to her mistakes. It might've been a selfish move, but I had my own relationship to worry about.

"Estella and I found her having sex with another man in the bathroom."

"I didn't mean to," Camilla repeated.

Estella rolled her eyes and turned her back to us and headed toward the door. I couldn't let her leave without talking to me. I glanced at Marcelo, and he could tell that I had a lot more to deal with than Camilla. He gave me a firm nod to reassure me that I wasn't needed, and I quickly followed behind Estella.

"Estella, wait," I called.

She walked past the grand front doors and searched the lot. I wasn't sure who or what she was looking for, but I knew she was desperate for a way out. When she realized that she had no other way to leave other than to walk on foot, she headed toward the entrance gates. I didn't want her to leave, but more than anything, I just wanted her to be safe.

"Estella, let me take you home." I hoped that maybe she'd open up in a more private setting.

"Ignacio," she cried. "I want to be alone."

"Talk to me, *please*."

Estella balled her hands into a fists and waved them in front of her in frustration. "I *can't*!" She covered her face and exhaled deeply. "I can't do this, Ignacio. I can't give you what you want."

She had given me everything that I had wanted. All I wanted was a second chance, nothing more. Estella was enough for me. I didn't need the title, the sex, or even her love—not yet anyway.

"Is it about yesterday? I'm sorry if you felt pressured to be exclusive. We can take a step back. Or is it what just happened in the piano room? I'm sorry for that, too; I won't test those waters until you're ready." My mind was buzzing with all the things that I could've done wrong.

"No, it's not that," she groaned, continuing to pace.

"Then what is it?" I reached over to her, sliding my hand around her waist and bringing her into me.

"I just…I don't…I can't." She continued to stumble over her words as she looked down at the ground.

"Estella, I wanted a second chance; you gave it to me. I haven't asked for anything more. What you're giving me now is enough for me."

Estella released an exaggerated and exhausted laugh. "If I don't either give you sex or love, you'll leave." The way she said it sounded forced as if she didn't believe it entirely herself. "I'm not capable of giving you either right now, and I don't want to disappoint you. I don't want you to resent me for wasting your time, money, or energy."

I stared blankly at her and then shook my head in confusion. She couldn't possibly believe that I was looking for something in return other than her company and trust.

Could she?

"I would never resent you; if anything, I'm grateful for you. I don't need sex; I don't need to hear that you love me tomorrow or even the next month. I simply desire *you*. We can talk, laugh, play the piano, swim with our clothes on, anything and everything. All I want is to have you here with me, and staying."

This wasn't how I planned on professing my love to her, but it had to be said. I had to make her realize that she meant so much more to me.

I was able to close the space between us, sliding my hands up her arms and bringing her into my chest. Estella remained motionless in my hold. We stood in this position for a minute, and right when I thought she would finally understand what she meant to me…she pulled away.

"I'm sorry, Ignacio."

A yellow taxi pulled in front of the gates, and a man exited the vehicle, extending his hand out to his cheerful date. The man attempted to close the door, but Estella reached her hand out, grabbing hold of the handle.

"Estella," I whispered. "Don't go."

She stared at me with heavy eyes one last time and then proceeded to get into the taxi. I watched the tires of the taxi roll through the pebbles and onto the road, taking Estella away from me.

My heart wasn't beating against my chest anymore. It wasn't booming with the love that I had for Estella. It was bleeding. It was as if a shard of glass had been jabbed into the center of my heart, obstructing the flow of blood, air, life. The peace in me had been replaced by emptiness and echoes of love.

I'd lost her again.

Chapter 23

ESTELLA

Ignacio's pleading face came to mind.

I hated that I did that to him, to us, but there was no other way. How would I have told him that I spent hours the night before thinking about him the last couple of weeks, feeling guilty that I hadn't nor couldn't reciprocate the love that he had given me? How would I have explained to him that the wall I had built around my heart was too stubborn, too guarded for his love? Ignacio would only try to break those walls down by doing everything he humanly could, and if all of his attempts failed, I would never forgive myself for giving him false hope.

I came to Castellara to grow, to have my own space because that was what I needed in order to sort through my feelings.

The front door started to jiggle, and I flung myself out of bed to meet Salem. She didn't come home last night, and all I wanted was my best friend. I wanted to have ice cream, watch a movie, and cry out all the guilt and pain that filled my heart.

"Oh, Salem," I exhaled, knowing that she'd just had a one-night stand.

Salem lifted a tired finger. "Don't judge me."

"I'm not—just judging how awful you look."

"As if you look any better," she said, flinging her black heels to the corner of the room. "Are you okay?"

I shook my head no. The tears were at bay, but the floodgates wanted to spring open.

"Estella," she whispered as she approached me, bringing me into her arms.

I gripped her tightly, as if she was the only person that could keep me grounded. "I had a fight with Ignacio, and I broke up with him. I'm just so scared of taking it to the next step and getting hurt."

To open up. To trust. To be vulnerable. It was all so painfully hard for me.

"I knew Bianca would plant some doubt into you," she

mumbled. "Estella, you two have a lot of history, but you're never going to know how it ends if you leave him. The relationship is fresh; you're so hard on yourself."

"I can't go through another heartbreak. I mourned for him once, I don't want to do it again."

"I don't think you'll have to." Salem wiped away the tears from my cheek with her finger. "I know there's a lot going on in that mind, and take the time you need to sort it out, but you two will be okay at the end of it."

Salem extended her arms out and watched me take a deep breath.

"Maybe…"

She gave me a tired smile and shook her head.

"So, who were you with last night?" I asked, wanting to move onto a different subject. I wouldn't mind talking about Salem's scandalous night. She always had the best stories, and that was what I needed to take my mind off Ignacio.

Salem widened her eyes and then sheepishly walked past me. "It doesn't really matter."

"Salem," I groaned. "I really need the distraction."

"It's just some guy."

"Some guy?" I asked, crossing my arms.

Salem never withheld information when it came to a one-night stand. She would always start the conversation with a rundown of the man with storytelling descriptions.

"Do you regret it?" I asked.

"No way," she said, walking to the fridge and taking out the leftover food from the night before.

"Italian, I'm guessing?"

"Mmm, yeah." She stuffed a piece of food into her mouth.

"What's his best physical quality?"

Salem blushed. "Too many to count."

"Salem!" I whined. "What's his name?" I needed to know about the man who made my best friend turn into a schoolgirl. Men usually didn't affect Salem like this, and now I was beyond curious.

"Promise me you won't get mad?"

"I promise," I exhaled, walking over to the little island and leaning against it.

Salem was skeptical at first, but she took the chance. She knew that if I were to ever be mad, it wouldn't be forever.

"It's Marcelo," she squeaked and lowered her head to shield herself from my reaction.

Not exactly what I wanted to hear.

Leaving Paris

The thought of Salem having sleep with a man who'd ended his engagement that same night, *and* that man being Ignacio's best friend, didn't sit well with me. There was a swell of emotions in me, and all I could do was stare at her intently.

She looked happy.

I had to be happy for her despite my reservations.

Salem straightened herself when she realized that I wasn't going to react at all. "Are you okay?"

"I'm as fine as I'm going to be," I said. "As long as you had fun."

Salem placed a cracker over her red-stained lips. "It was probably the best I've ever had."

Images of Ignacio's lips running up and down my lips, neck, and breasts came to mind. All the fine hairs on my arm and back rose at the thought of his touch and urgency. Only Ignacio had that effect on me, but it terrified me.

My feelings for Ignacio were real and strong. Refraining myself from sex was more a self-preservation tactic because the moment we slept together, I'd be in love with him. Ignacio would become my source of life, and if it were ever cut off, I wouldn't be able to recover.

Salem tapped my back. "Let's get you in bed; you don't

look the best."

"I don't feel it."

***

It had been ten days since I had last seen or spoken with Ignacio. Every aspect of my life had gone well, except for the part where I ached for Ignacio. I tried not to dwell on Ignacio or love, but it was difficult because Marcelo would appear at the end of the working days to visit Salem. Seeing Marcelo reminded me of Ignacio and how he used to visit me after work.

I helped Salem in the morning, and in the evenings, she would receive help from Maria. My pottery business was picking up—and with my need to avoid Marcelo—Maria would substitute for me more often, so I could stay in the studio until late at night.

I removed my dirty apron and balled it up, throwing it onto the table in frustration. Someone had placed an order requesting one of every item that I'd featured on my business website. It was a small business owner's dream come true and I was excited about it at first, but now I felt like a fraud. Making art wasn't the same anymore. I enjoyed the routine of it, but my heart wasn't fully in it. I wasn't putting my soul into it, and I felt like I was stealing the customer's money by giving items that weren't wholeheartedly made.

"I'm going to Milan for the opening of one of my new restaurants. I won't be back until the weekend," I heard Marcelo tell Salem.

That was their first official break. They had seen each other every day since the party which meant the relationship was serious, at least for Salem anyway.

"Try calling me every night, okay?"

"I'll try, but with the opening and keeping an eye on Ignacio, it might be difficult."

"Oh yeah," she said. "How's he doing?" She tried to keep her voice lower as she asked him. Most of the time I would wear my earbuds to listen to music as I created, but even music didn't sound right. It just sounded like chaos and noise, not art.

"Not great," Marcelo exhaled.

"She's not doing too good either," she said. "Drowning herself in work—her usual."

"I'm sure they will figure it out," Marcelo said before leaving the restaurant.

Leaving Paris

I waited a good two minutes until I turned off the studio's light and walked through the black curtains to head into the kitchen. Salem did her usual late-night inspection and then gave me the nod of approval to leave.

"Ready to go?" she asked, locking her arm with mine.

"Yup!" I said, trying to sound enthusiastic.

I was so far from it because going home meant having to sleep, and the second my head hit the pillow, Ignacio took over my dreams.

***

It was a Friday night, and I spent it at a beautiful seaside restaurant in Lilla for Emile's birthday—one day early. There was an uneasy lingering feeling—maybe hope—that Ignacio would stumble across the restaurant and we could lock eyes, and I'd know that Ignacio and I could have the relationship we deserved.

"Thank you for this wonderful dinner." Emile gave a big smile.

"You're welcome," Salem and I said in unison.

I shouldn't have taken credit for the birthday; Salem did most of the planning. She looked for the restaurant, made the reservations, and made sure we had the perfect seat. All I did was pay for half of the bill.

"Where will Ignacio take you tomorrow?" Nonna Norah asked, placing a delicate hand on Emile's arm. Emile placed his hand over hers, giving her a different smile. A smile that was very much in love. It tugged at my heart.

"We will be having a picnic."

"A picnic?" Salem asked, confused.

Emile offered her an understanding smile. "He loves picnics. It's something we used to do with Angelica. My birthday is on the thirty-first, and Ignacio's is the first of November, so his nonna would take us on a picnic to celebrate. He always found comfort in them; I suppose he's feeling nostalgic."

My mind wandered to the day that we had a picnic by the old castle, and I remembered how at peace he looked throughout it.

Nonna Norah gave Emile a wistful smile as she comforted him by rubbing his arm. Emile looked at her with glossed-over eyes and then managed to still lift the corner of his lips. They genuinely loved each other and had gone through the same misfortunes of love. I wondered how they both managed to move past the hurdle of giving love a second chance.

"Did you still want to walk around the area?" Salem asked the lovebirds.

"Yes, but I need to use the restroom," Emile said, lifting himself up slowly.

"On second thought, so do I," Salem said, wrapping her arm around Emile's shoulder, and the pair walked toward the restrooms.

"We should wait for them outside," Nonna Norah suggested.

I gave her a nod and linked my arm around hers, guiding us out of the restaurant. The sun was starting to set, and there was a beautiful contrast between the colors of the sky—blue and orange. Admiring sunsets was one of my favorite pastimes, and it was the only good feeling I'd had in the past two weeks.

"What's going on, my Estellita?"

"I'm just admiring the sky."

"You are, but you're also thinking, my dear."

"Yeah." I sighed. I wasn't going to lie to Nonna; she was a grandmother and always knew what was wrong with her loved ones.

"Is it Ignacio?" she asked, bluntly.

I whipped my head in her direction, shocked that she guessed correctly. She wasn't supposed to know about us, nor even suspect it.

"I wasn't born yesterday." She chuckled. "I know you two are interested in each other."

"How?" I asked.

"Why don't you tell me what's going on in the beautiful head, and then I'll tell you how I found out?" Nonna Norah was giving me a deal that wouldn't be fun on my part, but she knew that my curiosity would get the best of me.

"Did Salem tell you?" I questioned.

"No, she didn't."

I pulled my cardigan closer to me and reluctantly agreed to the deal. I didn't tell her the extent of our history, but I did tell her that Ignacio and I'd had a connection ever since we met. She loved the idea of me and Ignacio together; she'd secretly thought we would be a good couple. I admitted that we tried to date, but my past relationships had prevented me from moving forward. I was scared of lowering my walls, in addition to not wanting to feel the guilt of disappointing him if I couldn't give him what he wanted. It was a mix of emotions and worries that convinced me that love wasn't something I could do.

Leaving Paris

"I mean, you and Emile, you both have lost your significant others and still managed to give love another try. How did you put your heart out there again, knowing that there could be heart and so much to lose?"

Nonna Norah gave me a sympathetic look. "Estella, if you think of love as a game, then you've already lost. That's what's wrong with you young people." I was taken aback. "Love is a gift, not a game. Love is something you give, and it might not go into the right hands at times, but at least it was given. You never lose by giving love. I had the gift to love Fernando for nearly fifty-five years, and that is something I'll carry in my heart. He passed away, but I never lost him because his love is a memory I'll carry with me forever, and with Emile, I know the same will happen whether I have three days or fifteen years left with him. I will always give love another chance because real love makes you stronger. The stronger you are, the braver you are from that love, the freer you'll feel."

I tried to process her words.

"Can you laugh with him?"

"Yes."

"Cry with him?"

"Yes."

"Does he make you happy?"

"Yes."

"Do you feel like the other half of you is missing?"

I closed my eyes and nodded slowly. "Yes."

"Don't let him go."

I heard Salem chitchatting with Emile behind me. I didn't want to talk about Ignacio with Emile around, and I guessed that by my expression, Nonna Norah knew that.

She cupped my cheeks with her silk hands. "I know you have the courage to love one more time. I believe in you; now you need to believe in yourself. Plus, Emile raised a good man."

I nodded, thanking her for her faith in me because that only made one of us who had faith in me. "Wait, you didn't tell me how you knew?" I whispered quickly.

"It's the way you two look at each other when you're together. It's a look of longing."

The longing overwhelmed me—it was suffocating—and now I knew why. We were longing for someone that we believed we couldn't have fully, but that was all wrong. I allowed that idea to drown me because I've always been scared to love again. Truth was that I longed for him.

"And the guests from Camilla's party spotted you and

Ignacio together," she snickered before walking off to meet Emile. "I may have not been there, but I have eyes and ears everywhere."

Of course.

Nonna Norah was right; I had to be brave in order to be set free.

I knew what I had to do even if it meant putting my heart on the line.

Chapter 24

IGNACIO

All I felt was dread as I pulled into the driveway of my villa. From the outside, it was lit up at every angle and welcoming, but once inside it was far from a home. I always felt like an angry ghost that roamed the halls of its haunted mansion. Sometimes, being outside was more comforting than stepping foot in it.

I couldn't get Estella off my mind, and she was all that I dreamed about. I'd spent the past few days in the corner of a high-end bar in Lombardy while Marcelo focused on his restaurant's opening. I would repeatedly go over Estella's words, and that only made me think about the things that I should've said to her.

I wanted what she wanted.

I wanted to love, to lust, to trust, to need. It was as simple as that.

The large, wooden doors opened, escorting me to my dark and lonely castle. I didn't bother bringing any of my belongings inside. I didn't care. All I wanted was to go to my bedroom balcony and look out across the lake to see if Estella's light was on. It gave me a sense of comfort to know that she was across from me and just *there*.

I walked out onto the balcony of my bedroom and leaned against the ledge, looking straight ahead to the cottage that sheltered the only woman that had captured my heart. Thinking about her made me happy, then I'd feel my heart physically withering, knowing that we wouldn't be together.

My phone vibrated in my pocket, and I eagerly reached for it. I wanted it to be Estella and was disappointed when it wasn't her. It was my father. He rarely called me or kept in contact with me.

"Hello?" It was difficult to keep my voice composed.

"Ignacio, how have you been?"

"Not the best."

"Well, maybe I can help with that."

I remained silent, equally disappointed and intrigued.

Disappointed because parents normally wanted to know what made their children upset before providing a solution, but at least he wanted to help. I had to take what was given.

"I'd be lying if I said we haven't noticed a downfall in the company's performance. We've gone through two men in the past couple of weeks. They couldn't perform the way you performed, Ignacio. Maybe I didn't appreciate the work you did here."

"You didn't."

"Let's put that behind us." Apologies were too hard for him. "I need someone competent by my side. I'll be leaving for Paris tomorrow evening for a major deal and I would like you to join me."

My broken heart swelled for a moment. Was my father actually asking me to join him again? Was it possible for him to miss having me by his side? Or just miss me in general? It was overwhelming to think that he wanted me to be a part of his life again. I was used to people leaving my life—especially him—so when he wanted to return, I almost wanted to immediately open my arms.

"I need to think about it." Maybe there wasn't much too think about. I had nothing going for me in Lilla or Castellara. Estella used to consume all my time, and now that she wanted nothing to do with me, I had all the time in the world. A big part of me wanted to say yes, but another part of me held onto the hope that Estella would return.

"What is there to think about?"

"I just need to talk to someone before I make this decision."

"You are a grown man, Ignacio. You don't need Emile's approval."

I had to talk to Estella, not Nonno. I may have considered letting him back into my life again, but I wasn't going to tell him about Estella. He'd only find her to be a distraction, especially if she continued to encourage me to play the piano.

"Let me know tomorrow by noon." My birthday. I wondered if he remembered.

"I will."

The line disconnected.

I leaned against the railing, focusing on the darkening sky and the rustling winds. Every call or text that I send to Estella would go ignored. I needed to tell her in person that I might be leaving Italy.

The sound of water crashing below lulled me into a

hypnotic state, in which I closed my eyes and was met by the image of Estella. My heart went to my throat. We weren't able to say goodbye five years ago, but I was going to say goodbye this time around. That's all I wanted from her.

"Ignacio," I heard her voice call.

My eyes snapped open, scanning every inch around me. There she was sitting on the edge of my pool and looking back at me. I leaned against the ledge, in complete awe and confusion. She waved for me to come down, and in a blink of an eye, I met her in the backyard.

Estella sat on the edge of the pool, kicking her legs in the water. I kicked off my shoes, pants, and glasses, and slowly unbuttoned my dress shirt as I kept my eyes locked on her. The cold air greeted my bare skin.

My head collided with the water, and it consumed me into a warm embrace. The contrast between cold air and then immediate heat was amazing. I truly felt free, ignoring the rules of gravity by experiencing weightlessness. I spread my arms open, moving toward the deeper end of the pool where Estella sat.

I emerged from the water, the droplets trickling down my face and my breath labored. I gripped the edge of the pool and made sure I was directly in front of her bare legs. She sat there, watching me as I admired every inch of her, her face sweet and delicate, her body embraced by a silk dress, her wavy hair loose and cascading down her shoulders.

"I've missed you." I hovered my hand over her legs, tracing the silhouette that the pool lights had created. "What are you doing here?"

"I needed to see you," she exhaled, sliding her hands down her leg, and she placed her hand over mine, letting it rest on her knee. There was so much warmth in her touch, it made all my insides hum. "I'm so sorry for leaving you, Ignacio. I was so scared of everything. I had convinced myself that I wasn't capable of loving you fully, giving you what you deserved. I didn't believe in me, or us, and that was the biggest mistake I've ever made. I'm still scared, but I want to love you."

I stared at Estella in disbelief. Was she really admitting her true feelings for me? It was all before me: Estella and her confession. She trusted me enough to be vulnerable, to lower her walls down for a rare moment.

"I understand if you don't want to take me back, but just know that I do want to try again with you," she said, twiddling with her fingers. "If I haven't lost you already…" she added with sadness in her voice.

"You would never lose me, Estella," I declared, my hands running up her legs. She'd never lose me. I was certain she could never lose me. "Come in the water."

"I don't have a swimsuit."

"Neither did I. Come in with your dress."

Estella bit down on her lip and contemplated it for a second. She went from unsure to confident in a mere second. She slowly lifted herself up and stood at the ledge of the pool, sliding one arm out of her dress, followed by the other one until her dress fell down her body, pooling around her feet.

My eyes wandered up and down her beautiful body. She was almost naked, wearing white, lacy panties, and her long hair covered her breasts, but the slightest movement would have changed that.

Estella dove into the water with ease, and within five seconds, she broke through the surface. The water cascaded down her hair, and the longing look that she had on her face made my heart skip a beat or two.

We swam in circles, staring at each other with need in our eyes. Teasing each other. It almost felt like a competition to see who would give in first. I lost. There was no way I could resist the invitation of her coy smile. She had the ability to bring a man to his knees.

I rushed toward her, pulling her against my chest, feeling her breasts pressed against me. Estella wrapped her arms around my neck and enveloped my midsection with her legs. I didn't waste a second longer and pressed my lips against hers. I gripped her back, deepening the kiss with a desperation that said I was afraid of losing her again. I could feel her melt into me as she moaned against my lips, submitting to the idea of us.

My hands traveled down her back and to her thighs, gripping them with desire. I tasted the inside of her mouth, enjoying every blissful moment that she was giving me. I kept waiting for her to tell me to slow down, but she continued to kiss me. She wanted me to keep going because every time I paused to think about the moment, she would pull me closer into her. She didn't want me to think; she wanted me to explore. She was trusting me with her body again.

Her whole body.

I disconnected from her lips and trailed her graceful neck with kisses until I reached her breasts, placing a nipple in my mouth.

"Ignacio," she moaned, her nails digging into my back. I didn't know what that was, but it was incredibly sexy. It brought out a primal instinct in me and I groaned under my breath as I narrowed my eyes at hers. I needed to explore more of her, and I couldn't do that in the water.

"I need to show you how much I've missed you," I whispered in her ear.

Estella tightened her grip on me and nodded. I carried her out of the pool and into the villa to my bedroom. The mattress was beneath her, and I watched her splay over the bed, ready for me to unravel her. I didn't waste another second and hooked my fingers on the edges of the lacy fabric that clung to her skin, tossing it aside.

I took in the image of Estella's body—vulnerability and trust—and I wanted to show her that she was safe in my hands. I'd cherish her, protect her, and love her the way she deserved. I trailed kisses between her legs, savoring every moment that led to the inner part of her thighs. With every deep kiss that I placed, she tasted sweeter...absolutely divine.

Estella sucked in a deep, ragged breath as I began to indulge in her sweetness. "Ignacio."

She pounded her fists into the bed and opened her hands only to ball the sheets in her hands.

I wrapped an arm around her leg, bringing her closer to me as my other hand traveled up her body to mold my hands over her perfect breasts. Greedy, I was being so greedy, but I wanted all of Estella.

"Fuck," she gasped faintly.

I pressed my mouth deeper into her depths, sucking her sweet spot, teasing her by pushing a finger in, slowly sliding it in and out. I could feel her blossoming under my touch, and it only made me want to explore her even more.

I moved my head in a sensual way, losing myself in her taste and smell. Her legs tightened around my head, and her moans filled the room.

"Ignacio, I need to tell you something." She gasped, her fingers running through my hair.

I slowed down my pace to look up at her. "You're going to come?" I teased, lightly blowing air in between her legs, watching her circle her hips around in desperation. I lowered my head back down and returned to my original speed.

"You were my first and last," she muttered quickly and covered her face.

I stopped immediately.

My heart crashed against my chest, and my mind brought forward all the memories from that night in Paris. She'd seemed nervous, but I thought that was normal for anyone who was going to sleep with someone new—I sure was. I remembered how she pressed her lips against my neck when I entered her, connected with her and became her prisoner. I remembered how our moans filled the room when we rocked against each other.

"It was my first and last time too."

"Really?"

"Just you and only you."

Estella was everything to me. I plunged my hungry lips against hers, and she grabbed my head with both hands, kissing me until she was breathless.

The thought of delving into her beautiful depths again, to be inside her and take care of all her needs, release her from all her worries, was driving me insane. I wanted to love her with everything I had.

Estella shoved my underwear down and could see how much I wanted this. A small hiss escaped my lips when her warm hand encapsulated my cock. She rubbed her hand up and down with ease as I threw my head back, my eyes rolled all the way back. If she kept it up, I wouldn't make it a minute longer.

"Lie down, Estella."

Estella's chest rose and fell with anticipation as she looked at me with her sweet brown eyes. I hoovered over her, and nuzzled my head against her neck, inhaling her as I entered her. We both let out a small cry of ecstasy, and she clung to me as if I was the only solid thing that could keep her grounded. I pushed in and out, pressing my body against her scorching chest, and moved myself deeper into her. Her soft, tan legs hooked around my lower back in response.

"Ignacio," she moaned into my mouth.

Being inside Estella overwhelmed my senses; I couldn't imagine sex getting any better than this. Sex with Estella was ethereal, she evoked sensations that I never knew I was capable of feeling, and I just wanted more. More. More. So greedy for her.

I held onto her as I rolled onto my back, allowing her to be on top. My eyes never left hers and I watched her grind her hips against me, placing both of her hands on top of my chest, her breasts pressed together, and her light moans and whimpers being sent in my direction. My hands traveled up her waist and towards her back, feeling her soft and smooth skin radiate so much warmth. There was no place left undiscovered, so my hands roamed freely.

Estella lowered herself, and I wrapped my arms firmly around her, bringing her even closer as my lips tasted her. "You're mine, Estella. I'm going to love you like this for the rest of your life." I continued to push into her, losing myself in Estella's musical moans.

"Yes, yes, yes," she moaned. "All yours, and you are mine." Her lips crashed into mine again, owning me. If only she knew that she had owned me all this time. It would always be Estella.

We lost track of time in my bed. We went two, three, four times in different positions throughout the night. We were making up for lost time—those five years we missed out on each other.

If love were a game, then Estella had won.

She won ten times over, five years ago and forevermore.

Chapter 25

ESTELLA

It actually happened.

I slept with Ignacio.

Sun rays filled the room with light, lulling me out of my restful night. I was sprawled across Ignacio's bed with nothing on but his navy-blue sheets tangled around my legs and Ignacio's arm around my chest. I peeked over to the side and watched Ignacio still fast asleep. I lightly brushed one of his curls away from his face with my finger and admired how handsome he was.

I was sleeping next to a statue that the angels had carved out themselves, and yet, out of all the women in the world, he was in love with me. He wanted me. I was enough for him.

Ignacio's dark lashes began to flutter slowly, and then his eyes focused on my face. He smiled widely, and the butterflies in my stomach swirled around in giddiness.

"Happy Birthday," I cooed.

"Mmm, a happy birthday indeed," he replied in his deep, raspy voice that made those same butterflies flip around in a frenzy. His face came closer to mine, and his sleepy eyes closed as his lips touched mine. He slid his hand to the back of my neck, through my hair, and brought me closer to him.

I shifted toward him, and my body ached in a beautiful kind of way. "What would you like to eat?" I asked against his lips.

"You," he groaned in response. His hand was no longer in my hair but making its way down to my ass. "I want you for breakfast, lunch, and dinner."

"I think it's a little too late for breakfast." The clock on the wall read 11:25.

"Brunch then," he said, hungrily. Ignacio bit on my lip as he gripped my thigh, pulling my leg until it hooked around him.

I giggled against him, unable to contain the happiness that overwhelmed me. "Ignacio, I want to make you something to eat." The first meal of the day was a big part of birthdays in my household, and I wanted to have the same tradition with Ignacio. I wanted to make a meal that would set the mood for the day.

Ignacio placed a patient kiss on my forehead and smiled. "Okay, I'll wait for after brunch," he said with a chuckle. "Although, you would be the best meal of the day."

"I'll be your dessert," I replied and grazed his lips with mine before jumping off the bed to raid his closet for a shirt.

There was nothing much in the fridge except for eggs, tomatoes, herbs, and shredded cheese so I made omelets. Smooth jazz played in the background as I continued to scurry around the kitchen in hopes of finding something that would elevate the dish. There was a loaf of bread tucked away in one of the cabinets.

"I thought I lost these for a second." Ignacio came in from the backyard as he slipped on his glasses. "I haven't had a birthday breakfast in years." He looked at the dish and then pulled out his phone to read incoming messages.

I wondered if he'd received a text message from either of his parents. I couldn't imagine what he had gone through as a child, not having his parents there to love him.

"It's the best I could do considering what you had in your fridge," I said, handing him his plate.

"It's amazing, thank you." He leaned over the counter to place a light kiss on my lips. "I see you've found Lucia's bread," Ignacio said, taking a bite of said bread.

"Who's Lucia?"

"She's my house manager—a little, old woman who manages to make the place function perfectly without ever being seen." He took a big bite of the omelet and smiled with genuine contentment.

"Is she here now?" I whispered.

"I give everyone who works for me my birthday off, so no."

"Was she there last night?" I whispered again. I wouldn't have wanted her to witness everything that happened in last night's pool session.

"No." He chuckled. "She leaves after six and only stays overnight if I'm traveling."

"Good." I sighed.

"So, we have this big house to ourselves. What would you like to do?" He had a hopeful smile on his face; he definitely wanted to finish what he'd started earlier in the bedroom. To be honest, I wanted the same, but I also wanted to finish what we had started in the piano room the night of the engagement celebration.

"Can you play *Lost Star*? I want to hear it again," I asked, circling the island to be near him again. We had spent so much time apart that all I wanted now was to be close to him whenever possible.

Ignacio pushed his finished dish away and then turned around to place me in between his legs. He slid his hands around my waist and brought me into him, looking at me as if I was the reason for of all his happiness. "Whatever you want, *amore mio*," he whispered against my lips. His words created a beautiful warm surge through my body that embraced my soul, an embrace so tight that it felt like I was levitating.

Ignacio lifted me with ease and kissed me repeatedly until we reached the piano room.

We took our places on the bench and I scooted close to him to watch him perform his magic. He started to play the soft, sensual song. It had a French-jazz style to it, but I didn't expect anything different considering it was fitting for that night. I closed my eyes, thinking about the moment Ignacio approached me, handed me a peony and spent the rest of the night charming me with his talent.

I pressed my thighs together in an attempt to conceal my desire for Ignacio. Having a handsome, talented man play a passionate song that he composed for me was beyond attractive, it was surreal. It was my biggest dream come true.

And to think I almost gave up on us.

The song came to an unfortunate end, and I made my way to him. I straddled him, running my fingers through his disheveled hair as he gathered my hair to press kisses around my neck. The softness of his lips and his light stubble on my skin had me growing impatient, and I ached for more of him. Every bit of him felt wonderous against me.

My phone vibrated on top of the piano, and I ended the call without seeing who was on the other line. The distraction was not welcomed\ when I wanted to lose myself in Ignacio. His sing-song chuckles danced around my ears.

Ignacio's mouth trailed up my neck, and his soft lips grazed mine before crashing into them. Ignacio's strong hands molded around my back, supporting me as he kissed me harder, faster, hungrier.

Leaving Paris

My phone vibrated again, and I flicked through my screen to put my phone on silent but noticed it was Maya who had been calling me. She rarely called me.

Her text message alarmed me: **CALL ME ASAP. 911.**

I frantically tried to call her as I stumbled off of Ignacio and out of the piano room and through the grand hallways with blurred vision. I wasn't sure what happened, but any positive emotion had been eviscerated, and all I did was panic.

I crashed through the bedroom door, waiting for the line to be picked up, and Ignacio followed behind me. "Estella?" he called tenderly as he reached out for me. "What's wrong?"

"Estella," Maya's voice came through, sounding low and cautious. "It's Dad."

In a matter of seconds, I went from feeling on top of the world to plummeting down back to Earth.

Chapter 26

IGNACIO

"I have to go to New York," Estella spoke, her voice rippling with emotion. "My dad, he was robbed in his market and ended up having a heart attack. He's currently in a coma." She crashed into my chest and muffled her cries against me.

I pulled her into a tight embrace and kissed the top of her head. "I'm going with you. I'll set everything up; you go home and prepare your luggage."

"Really?" Estella asked, looking up at me with damp eyes.

"I've lost you twice; I will not lose you again." She was my angel, yet I was her guardian.

Estella cupped her gentle hand over my stubbled cheek, then leaned forward to take my lips but held me at bay with her hand. I inhaled her sweet scent of pomegranate, peonies, and vanilla. I'd never kissed a woman that awakened my body and connected with my soul with such sensuality. I didn't want there to be an end to the kiss, but Estella slowly and almost unwilling stepped back.

"I'm going to put my dress back on and head to the cottage."

"Take my car; take the time you need to make your preparations, and I'll call you with the flight information."

"Thank you," she whispered, her eyes lingering a little while longer before breaking contact and rushing out of the room.

I immediately pulled out my phone to call Pamela, my mother's manager. She knew the best airlines to call and prepared for my stay every time I decided to stay in New York.

"Ignacio, there is a flight departing from Italy to New York City at 1:15 p.m. on Black Crimson Jet. Would you be able to make that flight?" Pamela informed.

"Yes."

"While you're on the line, could I wish you a Happy Birthday? It would be a nice surprise for your mother to hear that you'll be in town for your birthday. Would you like to schedule a dinner with your mother tonight?" Pamela always found an excuse to schedule a meeting with my mother. I wasn't going to New York for pleasure; it was solely to be with Estella.

"Not tonight," I said, short with her. "Anyway, she hasn't wished me Happy Birthday yet so I'm sure she doesn't remember."

"Ignacio, it is 6:30 a.m. here. She is asleep."

I rolled my eyes at her lie. My mother had woken up at 6 a.m. every morning after she discovered yoga. The instructor held her lessons at 6:30 a.m., and my mother would never miss a class; that's how she'd operated for the past five years.

"I expect to hear back, Ignacio. Have a safe flight. Mr. Bardin will be awaiting your arrival at the airport," she said, followed by a click.

Speaking of parents, I had to inform my father about my decision. There was no way I'd leave Estella to go to Paris, not after last night and establishing that we wanted this relationship. Paris would've been an escape from my problems, and now, I had no need for it.

"Ignacio, calling with good news?" he answered.

"I'm not going to Paris with you."

"Why not?"

"I belong here."

"There isn't much Lilla or Castellara can offer you."

"It's enough for me. I'm sorry to disappoint, once again."

Father huffed. "That is what November first is all about. Disappointment."

A part of me thought I'd heard it all from my father. I was wrong. Those words stung. They left a permanent scar: a reminder that my whole existence had been a disappointment for him. There was no salvaging this relationship.

"I'm no longer your son. Goodbye, Alessio."

Happy birthday to me.

***

Our plane arrived in New York at 6 p.m., allowing us to have a good portion of the day left. Estella needed to see her father before visiting hours ended, and I wanted to spend the last few hours of my birthday with Estella.

"Brooklyn Hospital Center," I informed Bardin.

"Right away, sir," he said, turning on the BMW.

Leaving Paris

Estella's leg bounced up and down as she looked out the window. Every time we hit a red light, she would push her leg into the floor and form her hand into a tight ball. I reached over to place my hand over hers, giving it a gentle, reassuring squeeze. I had been trying to comfort her ever since we boarded our flight. She didn't eat anything on the plane, tossed and turned in her seat, and either had her leg bouncing or chewed on the side of her thumb.

Bardin had hardly come to a full stop in front of the hospital when Estella opened the car door and ran inside.

"Go get some dinner," I said quickly, tossing him a fifty-dollar bill, and I rushed out of the car to catch up with Estella.

She had finished speaking with an older woman at the information center and placed a sticker over her shirt. "He's in the ICU, Room 232," she said, handing me an extra visitor's tag.

She had no time to waste and immediately headed to the elevator. She repeatedly pressed the up-arrow in hopes that it would arrive faster, but we waited a long minute before the doors opened.

We speed-walked down the white hallways, breathing in the sterile smell, watching nurses with their noses in a clipboard or transporting monitors and saddened by mourning loved ones. Estella scanned the room numbers, seeming like she was on the brink of tears, and all I could do was watch the woman I loved look utterly and completely lost.

"Over there, Estella," I redirected, holding her hand and leading the way.

She stood in front of the wooden door, staring at it with fear and hesitation. I placed my hand on her lower back and gave her a reassuring smile. "Everything will be okay."

She took a deep breath, watched the door, and turned the handle.

Chapter 27

ESTELLA

Hospital rooms had always made me feel strange. The plain walls, the constant beeping of monitors, a television playing in the background to fill up the emptiness of the room, but we knew that nothing could mask the eeriness of it all. Except, Papa's room was different. It was the standard room, but cards lined the windowsill, a teddy bear holding a get-well-soon heart had been placed on the night table, and a rainbow, tie-dyed blanket lay at the end of his bed.

I moved a seat toward his bed and slowly sat down, bringing myself to the reality of being in a hospital with my unconscious father beside me. I'd known a day would come when I'd have to see my parents in bad shape, but I hadn't expected it so soon. He had turned fifty a couple of weeks before I left for Italy.

"Oh, Papa." I sighed, placing my hand over his still hand. "I'm here now."

I didn't sleep on the flight, and all the energy I had used to search for my papa's room had drained me beyond belief. I placed my head on his hand, wishing that he could place his hand on top of my head to comfort me. That was his thing. Whenever I needed to reconnect with him, he would place his hand over my head and bring me into his shoulder. I'd inhale his cheap cologne that he adored yet it burned my nostrils.

I inhaled deeply this time, and no cologne. There was no reciprocation on my papa's end which made my eyes swell and my throat constrict. He was lost in some sort of limbo, drifting between life and death, and although he was in front of me, it was just a shell.

"I can't lose you," I whispered.

There was a subtle knock on the door, and I turned around to find a woman dressed in scrubs smiling at me. Her brown eyes brought warmth into the cold, sterile room.

"Hi, honey," she greeted. "The eldest daughter, I

suppose?" She scooted in between me and Papa to record the readings displayed on the monitors.

"Yes," I responded. "How is he doing?"

"He's in a stable condition. I have a feeling he'll be back with us in no time."

Her words brought comfort, and I held onto them tightly because that was all the hope that I needed at the moment.

"Thank you."

"You're very welcome, sweetheart."

The nurse left, and I spent half an hour in the hospital room, resting my head on his hand and hoping that what the nurse had told me was the truth. I wanted to be with him longer, but visitation closed at eight, and I was sure that my sister would want to say goodbye to him. She wouldn't be able to see him too often throughout the week considering she had school and extracurricular activities. Our papa might be in the hospital, but Mama wouldn't want her to miss school. She'd want to keep the routine going, and I had to support her; it was the only control she had for the time being.

With every step I took to the waiting lounge, my head fogged up more. I desperately wanted to go home, but even that wouldn't fill the emptiness that had consumed me the past hour. Drawing near to my loved ones, my eyes connected with Ignacio who smiled at me, and the hollow cavity in me filled up for a second. A good second.

"*Amor,*" Mama called, standing up to wrap her arms around me. She was usually one to look years younger, but it seemed as though the past twenty-four hours had aged her significantly. I pulled her in tightly and took a deep breath to let her know that we had each other.

"You will be staying at the house, right?" she asked in the form of a command rather than a question.

"Yes."

"Good, Maya will need good rest before going to school. She said she didn't sleep well at Martha's and Wilson's last night."

"They made me sleep on the old couch. I could hear my bed crying for me on the other side of the wall," Maya said dramatically.

"Don't worry, I'll be staying there my whole visit."

"Very good." My mom nodded.

"I could've slept over at Alana's, but mom said no," Maya mumbled, upset. Alana was Maya's girlfriend of three months. Mama had nothing against their relationship; she was just someone who was old-school and preferred premarital couples to sleep in different houses.

Mama tossed Maya a dirty look and then flashed me a smile. "*El es guapo y educado,*" she said in a hushed tone into my ear.

I rolled my eyes and was unable to hold back a smirk. Mama thought Ignacio was handsome and well-mannered. Well, I had to agree with her on that. She'd go crazy if she knew that he came from wealth. Every Hispanic mother secretly wanted their daughter to marry a rich man.

"*Hablaremos más tarde,*" I whispered back. I wasn't interested in talking about my relationship.

Mama narrowed her eyes and clicked her tongue. She clearly wanted to know more right then and there. "Let me know when you'll stop by tomorrow; I may need you to bring me some of my belongings and then we can talk too."

"I will."

"And Maya," my mom said, pulling Maya's hoodie back and unplugging her earphones. "Please, keep on top of your work. I know it's hectic, but we need to stay strong."

"Yes, yes." Maya shrugged.

"It was very nice to meet you, Ignacio," my mama said, holding her hand out.

Ignacio gripped it gently and nodded. "Pleasure was mine, Ms Salvador."

Mama placed a kiss on my shoulder, since that was the only spot she could reach without going on the tips of her toes, and then forced a kiss against Maya's hoodie. They were more or less the same height as each other. My papa and I were the ones who had more length to us.

"Please, my loves, stay safe," she said before walking back to Papa's room.

"I'm hungry. Do you mind if we stop to get some food? I'm thinking burritos," Maya asked casually.

I looked up at Ignacio. "What would you like to eat? It's your birthday after all. It's the least I can do considering the hectic day we've had."

"I think burritos sound good," Ignacio agreed, peering over to Maya who had the happiest expression on her face.

"Sounds good," I said.

"And chips with guacamole?" Maya asked, flashing me an appeased smile.

"You're pushing it."

"My dad is in the hospital; come on, spoil me a little."

I nudged her to the wall in annoyance and she smirked. We'd missed each other; we didn't have to say it, but it was a fact.

***

"Thank you for the food, Ignacio," Maya sang as she leaned her head back to devour her last bite of burrito. "So good." I insisted on paying, but Ignacio had paid for the order before I could take my wallet out.

Maya collected all of the trash and walked into the kitchen to place it in the bin. I could hear her open the fridge door and scour for more food. "Estella, did you happen to bring some snacks from Italy?" she called out.

"Maybe."

"Sweet," she hollered in a singsong voice.

"I said maybe."

"Maybe means yes—just a tip, Ignacio," Maya said.

"Noted," he responded, winking at me.

"I'm going to shower. Do you mind placing the snack on Mom and Dad's bed while I'm in there?" Maya asked, walking into the living room with a diet coke in her hand. "Preferably something salty."

"You're sleeping in Mama and Papa's room?"

"Yeah, about that," she said, crooking her neck to the

side, signaling me to follow her. We walked into the kitchen, and she bounced her knee as she debated whether to tell me what she'd called me in for.

"Yes?"

"Well, as much as I want to be home, I'm terrified of staying here, and I'd feel safer in their bed. What if, *they* want to break into our house?" Maya looked genuinely nervous, and that wasn't usual for her. "Do you think your boyfriend would want to stay the night? It could be nice to have that male spot fulfilled, at least for tonight. You can even sleep in the same bed; I won't tell."

"I can ask him," I said, nodding understandably.

"Okay, thanks, and don't forget the chips," she said, heading upstairs.

Ignacio swiped through his phone, looking bored at what was on the screen. He noticed that I had walked into the living room again and slid his phone into his pocket.

"Everything okay?" he asked.

I pulled my sweater close to myself. "Well, we are a little nervous about staying the night here. Maya has brought it to my attention that the group of boys who broke into the market could break into the house, as well, if it's a personal vendetta they have against my father," I said, pinching the bridge of my nose.

I heard Ignacio stand up, and then his strong arms encircled me. "If that is your way of asking me to stay the night, then I will. I'll have Bardin leave my suitcase here instead of in Manhattan."

"Okay, and I can show you to my room in the meantime," I said, leading him up the stairs. I had been gone for two months, and everything felt foreign already. I ran my hands up the wooden railing, something I'd touched since I was a toddler, yet it felt like I touched it for the first time.

There was a stronger-than-usual smell of lavender and jasmine upstairs; it was Mama's signature plug-in scent. Or was it that I had been gone and had forgotten about the pungent smell? The sense of unfamiliarity heightened when I took the first step into my bedroom.

I turned on the bedroom light and looked around the bland room. There was a bed with a light blue comforter, a white dresser with random items that I never used on it, and above it, a shelf of my ceramic projects from all through high school. On my desk, there were old textbooks of the history of piano, classical music, and guidebooks on Italy, headphones, a sketchbook with my future ceramic project ideas, and a vintage polaroid camera.

"It's a little…underwhelming." I sighed, doing a double take and making sure I didn't have anything embarrassing lying about.

"There's nothing underwhelming about seeing the room that your girlfriend grew up in," he replied, placing my suitcase by the entrance and walking toward the dresser to examine the shelf above it.

With a closer inspection, I groaned and covered my cheeks. "Don't look at those." My older work wasn't my best, but the fact that I had created five ceramic pieces of the Disney princesses made me shudder. Not so much when I was eighteen—I loved the idea of finding your prince charming in a blink of an eye. Now, as a twenty-five-year-old, it felt out of place.

"It was for a senior project," I said.

"They're amazing," Ignacio said which took me by surprise. I expected him to think I was childish for doing anything related to princesses. "You're incredibly talented."

"I wouldn't necessarily say that…" I trailed off and timidly walked beside him. He was being too nice because my ceramic figurines were short, bulbous, and didn't have too much detail, but maybe I was being too hard on my eighteen-year-old self.

"You are, Estella. I'll always be your number-one supporter."

I looked up at him and watched his eyes ping from each figurine to the next with amazement. That thought made my heart flutter. I never had anyone admire my art the way he did.

"Were you the one who placed that massive online order?" I asked, running my hand down his arm.

"Yes." Ignacio intertwined his fingers with mine and pulled my hand to his lips.

"Why?"

"I was convinced that you didn't want anything to do with me at the time, and if it were true, I wanted to do one last thing for you."

"I don't deserve you."

"You deserve the world, *stella mia*."

Chapter 28

IGNACIO

Estella walked out of the bedroom in an oversized red T-shirt, and I nearly pounced off the bed. She seemed startled to find me on the bed as she dried her hair with a white shirt. I had been sitting on the edge of her bed, shirtless and with black briefs on.

I gave Estella another once-over and had to compose myself. I'd seen Estella in many outfits but seeing her in an oversized shirt with her legs on display had to be the sexiest thing I had seen on her. Nothing could beat effortless beauty.

"You look beautiful," I said as she approached the bed.

"Thank you." She sighed, plopping onto her bed and grabbing a pillow to stuff her face in it.

"What's wrong?" I lay on my side, propping my head up with my hand. With my free hand, I ran my finger down her soft skin.

Estella lowered her pillow. "I feel bad. You spent your birthday on a long airplane ride, the hospital, and out of the comfort of your home."

I pulled the pillow away from her to take in the beautiful sight of Estella. She was all I ever wanted for my birthday. "A day ago, I thought you'd never want to see me again. All I wanted was a greeting from you for my birthday, and today, well, I spent every hour of the day with you. I received more than I asked for. You are the best gift, *stella mia*."

I expected my words to bring Estella some comfort, but she seemed bothered. She placed her hands over her face and groaned lightly. "I still feel bad."

"Don't."

I plopped onto my back, and I extended my arm out, inviting Estella into my chest. She rested her head on my shoulder and placed her hand over my chest. "This is all I wanted."

Estella sighed deeply. "I forgot to ask you, how are you doing with all of this? I'm sorry if any of this is reminding you of that night in Paris." I had not once thought about that incident. In between recalling my father's words and worrying about Estella, I couldn't think about anything else.

"Honestly, it hasn't affected me. My mind has been preoccupied with other things."

"Me?" She deflated.

"Yes, and that's okay. You're important to me, Estella."

"Anything else?"

"My father called last night before I saw you at the pool. He wanted me to go back and work for him, but I'd be stationed in Paris."

"What did you say to him?"

"I didn't give him an answer until this morning. I told him no because I didn't want to be away from you. He was not happy with my decision and called my entire existence a disappointment. I'm cutting him out of my life." I'd never be the son he wished for, and he'd always resent me for that.

Estella turned to me, gazing at me with her soft eyes. "Ignacio, your father will never be half the man you are.

I took in her words and smiled lightly. Estella could see something in me that I couldn't even see in myself.

Estella softly chuckled and grazed my hand with her

fingertips.

"What's on your mind?" I asked.

"I'm remembering the night we met."

"Oh," I drawled out. "What part exactly?"

"Not a part, just the feelings. So many butterflies. You were just different from the other guys I've interacted with in the past. You weren't looking at me like I was someone to conquer; you looked at me like you just wanted to genuinely connect with me. And we did. Once I touched your hand, everything felt balanced. It still feels like that when I'm with you."

I couldn't have said it better myself. When we were together, even in the beginning when things were tense, my world started to shift for the better. We were two magnets, and when we got together, there was no easy way to separate us. I never wanted to separate myself from Estella; she had fascinated me from the beginning and was the woman that I wanted. I knew without a doubt.

"*Amore mio*," I said, breathing her in.

Estella squeezed me slightly, and then over time, her composure relaxed. Within minutes, she had fallen into a deep slumber. I continued to stroke her hair with my free arm, enjoying the weight of her love, even in her sleep.

Leaving Paris

***

Estella's angelic and slumbering face had created a frenzy in my stomach. She slept with her mouth slightly agape, breathing deeply, and her hair perfectly framed her delicate cheeks. I pushed a wavy strand behind her ear and danced my fingers down to her neck.

"*Stella mia*," I softly called.

She hummed and nuzzled her face deeper into the comforter.

I pulled her hand to my lips and placed a tender kiss on top. "Friday, 6 p.m."

"What about it?"

"Go on a date with me."

"I'd love that."

Estella's smile disappeared as quickly as it came, and she looked at her bed, then the walls and took in the whole room. Reality was setting in, and there was no stopping it.

"I have a lot to do today," she said, shuffling the sheets away.

I reached for her hand and held it tightly. "I'll help you. We will take pictures, take note of the missing inventory at the shop, clean up, and make phone calls. All of it."

"Thank you."

Walking in the city for even a block made me miss the countryside. Both sides of the street in the city reflected the other—just red-bricked townhouses, small trees planted every fifteen feet, and one trash can that overflowed with junk.

I looked beside me and was reminded of why I was here: Estella. Then things didn't look so bad. The trees were a paint palette of earthy tones, the birds were chirping, and the sun shone brightly on us. This was all I needed.

The Latin market was on the corner of the street, and Estella stood in front of it for a brief second. Her shoulders rose with uncertainty, and then they sank back down. She pulled the keys out of her purse and unlocked the main door.

The good news was that there was no exterior damage to the store, but I couldn't say the same for the interior. It seemed like the intruders used a bat or something similar to destroy their inventory. The metal chip racks were bent out of shape; cans and bags of food were busted open; colored drinks were spilled on the floors, creating tar-like puddles in some areas; the cash register had been broken into, and coins were scattered across the checkout section.

Estella placed her hand over her mouth, and her eyes grew fiercely upset. Her head snapped to the front corner of the market.

Estella noticed that the intruders had smashed their security camera. She pulled out her phone from her back pocket and started scrolling quickly. She played the recording, and over my shoulder, I could see a video of three men wearing ski masks. Two of the men were approaching Estella's father while the other one headed straight to the camera, smashing it, and the video ended.

Estella clenched her eyes tightly and took a deep breath. She circled back to the front of the Latin market and walked behind the checkout counter. There was hesitancy in her walk. Estella leaned down and picked up a picture frame. She stared at the photo for a moment before her hand quivered.

It was a picture of her family, sitting on a picnic blanket under a cherry-blossom tree. The frame had been broken, and she gently tucked it underneath the counter and turned her back to me as she raised her hand toward her face. I wasn't sure if she was wiping away her tears or in a deep state of thought.

"If I find out who did this, I'm going to sucker-punch

them straight in the face," she said, turning back around without showing any signs of crying. She was too livid to cry; she wanted to get some sort of revenge.

"The police will find out who did this."

"I hope I find them before the police."

I walked over to her, and she extended her arms out, wrapping them around my waist as she placed her head on my chest. She inhaled, then her breath trembled as she exhaled. All I could do was help her in the moment, but I also wanted to find the men who did this to Estella's family. She didn't deserve this pain.

Estella and I divided the rest of the tasks evenly to lessen the amount of time spent at the Latin market. The destruction of her family's business and her father's health was a running thought, and it was apparent from the grim frown on her face that she couldn't stay all day here.

We worked fast, efficiently, and in silence. Estella stood in front of the market, her hands on her hips, but the more she scanned the room, the lower her arms fell. I waited for her frown to perk up, even for a second. Nothing. The market was back to its original state, but the damage had been done already.

The dainty bell above the door jingled, and Estella

swiftly turned, her face contorted into confusion.

The young man at the door looked around Estella's age with unruly dark brown hair, and he wore a black, flannel jacket with black, slim jeans. Estella didn't look angry at him which made me believe it wasn't her ex, but she certainly looked disappointed.

Estella grabbed one of the two clipboards from the counter and handed it to me. "Do you think you can double-check the inventory for the cold drinks?"

"Sure," I said, staring at her a little too long, in hopes she'd let me know she was okay. Estella gave the boy a cautious look, and he slowly walked toward the counter, his eyes meeting mine. Estella looked over her shoulder and nodded in assurance that I could go.

She believed by sending me to the other end of the store that I wouldn't be able to hear her conversation with the young man. My auditory system had been trained far more frequently than the average person. Not much could get past me. I understood that she needed privacy, and I wasn't proud of myself for eavesdropping, but I had to make sure she was okay.

"Sebastian," she greeted, cautiously.

"He already knows you're in Brooklyn."

"Goddammit."

Estella gave him a pleading look, one that came too easily for her. The young man lowered his head and shrugged. "I'll do my best to have him leave you alone, but he has a mind of his own."

Estella nodded, appreciatively, and her demeanor shifted slightly. "So, um, how's your mom doing?" She folded her cardigan over herself tightly.

"She passed away two weeks ago. It's been hard for us, especially Cesar. He's been drinking too much."

Estella visibly shuddered at his words and then shook her head. "I'm sorry to hear that, Seb."

"Thank you," he said, fiddling around with the chipped corner of the counter.

"It was nice seeing you, but I think it's best you keep your distance for now. I don't want your brother to get the wrong idea. He's the last person I need to deal with right now."

"He hasn't taken your absence very lightly; he might try to reach out, but I'll try to stop him."

"Please."

As Sebastian scanned the Latin market, he saw that I was watching them. I wasn't going to divert my eyes or look guilty for being caught because I had nothing to hide. Estella was my top priority, and if someone was going to complicate her life, I wanted to be fully aware.

"Who's the *gringo*?"

"My boyfriend."

Sebastian's eyes widened for a second and then he just shook his head like having me around was a bad idea. Based on their conversation, Cesar was a relentless man. Clearly, he knew who he'd lost, but I'd be damned if he even tried to come close to Estella. I wouldn't allow it, and now I knew that, I had to up the security. I wasn't going to take this matter lightly.

"Be careful, both of you."

Estella rolled her eyes and shook her head. "I won't hesitate to call the police if I see him around—let him know that. I don't want him around me or my family."

She was no longer facing him and looked down at her clipboard, running her pencil down the whole sheet to appear busy. The young man seemed to have finally accepted her words and swiftly turned around and walked out of the market.

Estella peeked over the clipboard and gazed at the door with a thousand-yard stare.

Chapter 29

ESTELLA

I knew that I had to confront Cesar at some point, but I didn't like the idea of seeing him anytime soon. I didn't come back to complicate my life; I came for my family, for my father who was in a coma.

Cesar had to wait, and better yet, not come around me at all. Cesar felt like a lifetime ago ever since I had left for Italy. I couldn't succumb to him and his disastrous ways after coming so far.

Ignacio knew that there was tension between Seb and me—the way he looked at me expectantly. There was so much I wanted to tell him about my past and about Cesar, but I didn't have the energy to do it right now. We had been in the honeymoon phase for only a night before I received news about my papa; I didn't want another major issue in the mix. The less he knew, the less he had to worry about. I had it under control.

Ignacio's car stopped in front of the hospital, and we both stepped out of the car to have a little more privacy.

"What time should Adler and I come for you?" Ignacio asked.

Adler was his new driver, a man who looked and acted far different from Bardin. Adler sat up tall, made eye contact with us but never spoke unless prompted, nothing like the friendly Bardin.

"In three hours."

"Okay."

"Can you stay the night with me again?"

Ignacio's face softened. "I'll stay every night if you'd like."

"I would love that."

Ignacio cupped my chin and gazed into my eyes. "I'm here for you, however you need. I hope you know you can talk to me."

I nodded, reminding myself that I was with one of the most understanding men in the world. I patted his chest and looked up at his cognac-colored eyes that swirled with concern.

"I would like to explain what happened at the market, but later in the evening," I said.

"I'll be all ears," he said, his lips pressing against my forehead.

Pulling away from him made me feel like a fish out of water. My chest tightened up, and my head started to fog up. The thought of Cesar running around Brooklyn with his eyes on us was unsettling and maybe even dangerous.

I turned on my heels and hoped to meet Ignacio's warm eyes, and I did. Ignacio watched me enter through the hospital doors and gave me a slight nod. I made my way to Papa's room with a little more assurance. I wanted Ignacio with me at all times—I felt safer—with him, but I couldn't ask him to follow me around like a puppy when I knew he had other people in New York.

"Hey," I replied, entering the hospital room.

Mama placed her finger over her lip and then tilted her head toward Papa. "He's sleeping."

Maya warned me that there were moments when Mama would believe that Papa was just sleeping. We all knew that he wasn't *just* sleeping, but no one would say otherwise. If that was her only method of being able to process everything, then so be it. Who was I to take that away from her?

"I'm sorry," I whispered and pulled a seat next to her. "Have you eaten?"

"A salad from the cafeteria. Did you bring my things?"

"Yes." I reached for her floral travel bag from my backpack. "Will you be staying at the hospital tonight?"

"Yes, your father never liked sleeping alone."

I nodded.

"Will Ignacio be staying over for the night again?" she asked casually.

I made my best attempt at a poker face, but I could feel the blood washing over me. "What?"

"Martha saw him go in at night, and then saw you two walking out in the morning." It took a lot for me to not roll my eyes.

Martha was the self-appointed watchdog of the block. She would sit by the bay window, knitting through all hours of the day until it hit dinner, which she had on the table near the window, and then she'd turn the lights off by 9 p.m. Growing up, I hated knowing that I was being watched every time I stepped out of my house, but then I learned she did it because she hoped to see her husband as he patrolled around the area. Even after retirement, it seemed that she refused to do anything else.

"What was the sleeping arrangement?"

She already knew the truth, but she didn't need to know the whole truth. After all, she was still an overprotective mom, even if I was twenty-five years old.

"Ignacio stayed in my room. I stayed in Maya's room because she didn't want a man in her room, and she slept in your room," I answered.

"Sounds about right." She nodded. "Well, I'm glad he stayed with you two. I was worried about my girls the whole night." That was not what I expected. She must have trusted Ignacio because she wouldn't even let Cesar go upstairs when we were dating.

I leaned my head against her shoulder. "We're fine; you just worry about Papa. I'll look after the house and Maya."

Mama rubbed my head and sighed. "Thank you, and tell Ignacio I said thank you, as well."

"I will."

"He seems like a good man, better than that Cesar," she said his name with disgust.

"I know you never liked him. Honestly, I don't even think I liked him."

Looking back at it, I wondered why I lasted as long as I did with him. He was the biggest mistake of my life. He never brought anything good into the relationship. Everything had to be about him, and no one could be happy if Cesar wasn't happy.

Everything was easy with Ignacio; even breathing was easier around him. He was a reserved man, a man who didn't show much emotion at first glance, but that reserve melted away within seconds. Ignacio had mastered keeping his emotions at bay with strangers, but in reality, he wore his heart on his sleeve, and I loved that about him.

"I love him. Ignacio." The words danced out of my mouth. It was the first time that I'd admitted it to myself. I had spent so much time suppressing my feelings for him ever since we'd met, but now, it was just a fresh breath of air.

Mama grabbed my arm, her brown eyes drilling into mine. "Did you say you love him?"

"Yes," I answered, a little more cautiously.

"Ah, our daughter is in love," she cheered, nudging Papa's leg.

The relationships I'd had before couldn't even compare to what I had with Ignacio. If I was experiencing love now, then I never knew what love was before.

"And he's rich," she whispered to Papa.

"Mama!" I scolded.

"*Que!*"

"It's not always about money."

"Money helps, *hija*."

"Wait until you find out that he's Florence Lilianna's son."

I stared at her, expecting a priceless reaction. She nodded, my words not fully processed yet.

Then it hit her.

"*QUE!*" She placed her hand over her heart and plopped her head onto my shoulder.

"Oh, you will get that big, sparkly engagement ring," she said, fanning her hand out.

I lowered my head back on her shoulder and started to giggle as I imagined a ring. It wasn't quite the conversation I was expecting to have with my mama today, but I was glad we had it. It lightened the mood. We both needed that laugh. Things didn't feel as complicated anymore.

***

"Goodnight, Nacho!" Maya hollered before I closed the bedroom door.

"Nacho?" I asked.

"Her nickname for me," Ignacio huffed.

"Maybe I should call you—"

"No," he said and proceeded to place a kiss on my lips. "How are your parents doing?" He held me in his arms.

I simply stared at him, in awe of his question. Cesar had never asked me how my parents were doing; he didn't care for them. He would fight with them about my curfew or about when I could see him next. Everything was an argument waiting to happen with him, and when my parents did attempt to stop me from seeing him, I would fight back, but only because I felt like I had to, not because I wanted to. It was hard to love him.

Ugh! I hated comparing them; it wasn't fair to Ignacio.

"You seem a little preoccupied."

"Yes, sorry," I said. "Mama is doing okay, and Papa is as stable as he can get. Sorry, just have a lot on my mind still."

"I can tell." He tenderly grazed my cheek with his thumb. "Do you want to talk?"

My mind and heart were racing at a million miles an hour, and I couldn't process anything. My hand flew up to my forehead, and I pressed on it, sighing when there was a brief moment of relief. It felt like there was a tight band around my head.

"Sit," Ignacio said, easing me down onto the bed.

I pulled my knees into my face when a sudden onset of chills ran across my body. Ignacio placed my Brooklyn College fleece blanket over me and ran his finger over the bulldog patch on it.

"My mascot was a polar bear," he shared.

"Did you enjoy college?" I asked.

Ignacio laughed dryly and shook his head. "You don't enjoy college when you're in a music school. All we do is breathe, eat, and live music. Alongside classes, we also had to devote hours to the art."

"No parties, no girls, no nightlife?"

"I recall going to two nightclubs, and I did date a girl or two. They were time-consuming, and when I had a bit of time for myself, I realized it wasn't worth it." It brought a smile to my face that he'd decided to make time for me. Heck, he'd traveled across the ocean to be with me.

"How about you? Is that where you met Cesar?"

I glared at him, and he raised his eyebrow. It was clear we were going to have this conversation, and I pulled the blanket tighter against myself, feeling the cold surrounding me again.

There was no point in avoiding this much-needed conversation, I conceded.

"That's where I met his brother, Sebastian. We were good friends, but after college, we didn't speak much. On New Year's, I was waitressing at the Russo's restaurant, and Sebastian, Cesar, and a couple of his friends dined in. It was a busy night, but we managed to catch up, and Cesar started to show some interest in me. After that night, Cesar would come around Papa's market on the days that I worked and would chat with me. He asked me out on a date, and eventually, we made it official on Valentine's Day."

Ignacio looked at me with guilt in his eyes. "I listened in on your conversation with Sebastian earlier today. It's an automatic thing, really."

"Oh great, bionic ears."

"Something like that." He sighed. "I'm sorry."

"It's okay," I assured him.

"Estella, did he hurt you?"

My teeth started to clatter, and I leaned into Ignacio, wanting him to envelope me in his warmth. Ignacio lifted up the comforter and slid underneath it, lying down on his back and extending an arm out to invite me into his arms. I shuffled into his embrace and placed my head on his chest while the rest of my body pressed against him.

"You're safe with me," Ignacio whispered.

"I know," I breathed.

No words were exchanged for sixty seconds. It was a long, contemplative minute. There was an internal battle between wanting to share my past and feeling like it was a burden to the relationship. I always thought leaving the bad in the past was the best option, but now with the bad creeping into my present, I wasn't too sure.

"Yes," I answered, finally.

Ignacio's arm tightened around me, but he didn't say anything. He didn't have to say anything to show that he had been fueled with anger. I could hear his heart racing.

"How did he hurt you?" His voice was almost a whisper.

A wave of nausea came over me, and I gripped onto Ignacio's shirt, recalling the moments that created deep lashes over my heart. "It started with teasing, then he controlled what I wore or did, mocked me about my weight, and blamed me for every bad thing that had happened to him. He constantly wanted to be around me, but not in a romantic way—almost possessive." I paused, not wanting to expose the true lengths he'd gone to in our relationship.

Looking back at it, I was ashamed for staying in a relationship that only took from me. Every moment I had been with Cesar, I would forget to breathe because being with him felt like I had a weight locked around my ankle and I was thrown overboard into the dark depths of the ocean.

"Did he physically hurt you, Estella?" Ignacio asked, forcing the words out of his mouth.

"I'm so stupid," I cried, burying my face into Ignacio's side.

"God, no," he assured, squeezing me even tighter.

"But I am because he mistreated me, and I stayed."

"It's so much more complicated than that. Love is blind."

Ignacio's words were supposed to bring solace, but they didn't. I wasn't sure what they made me feel. I still felt like a fool for enduring the unnecessary.

"Cesar took me out to a beautiful restaurant in Manhattan. I wore a dress that upset him, and he started commenting on my body, and I told him that he had to work on his manners. He dragged me out of the restaurant and was rough, but I manage to run away." I inhaled deeply, finding it hard to catch my breath. It seemed like I had performed a five-minute-long speech despite it only being a couple of sentences.

"Do your parents know?"

"Oh, God no. Papa would kill him."

"I would help him."

"I hate him, but I'd never wish death upon him or anyone."

"Have you gone to the police?"

"No."

"Are you afraid of him?"

"I try to tell myself that I don't have to be afraid of him, but really, I'm so terrified." I was on the verge of crying.

"He will never hurt you again," he whispered, running his long fingers through my hair.

I wanted to believe him. Demons lurked around the corners but lying in Ignacio's arm and enveloped by his warmth, nothing frightened me at that moment. That was all the peace I needed for the day.

Chapter 30

IGNACIO

On the ride back to Manhattan, my knee wouldn't stop bouncing, and my hands automatically balled into tight fists. Never in my life had I wanted to hurt someone as much as I wanted to hurt Cesar Ramos.

I didn't feel great about prying into Estella's life, but I needed to know who the threat was in her life. All I needed was a name, and Maya gave it to me during our early morning sittings. Estella wasn't an early riser, which was to my advantage. I gathered as much information on her ex-boyfriend as I could, and Maya didn't hold back. She had told me that if he suddenly disappeared off the face of the planet, she wouldn't think twice, and then winked in my direction.

Leaving Paris

Murder sounded enticing, but not something I wanted to actually accomplish. The reality of the situation was that I couldn't touch him without being provoked. There wasn't much I could do aside from being vigilant. I hoped that was enough until we boarded on Sunday, and until then, I had to ease her stay in New York.

"How long has it been since you've seen your mother now? Five years?" Adler asked.

"I don't know," I responded.

I knew exactly when I'd last seen my mother. Nonna died in the summer, and I visited my mother shortly after in hopes that she would be able to fill the maternal hole that I desperately needed. Nonna was more than a grandmother to me; she raised me when my biological parents decided that their needs were more important than mine. I thought that my mother would understand my need for a connection with her after losing Nonna, and she did for a day and then told me that she was too busy to tend to her 'emotionally exhausting' son.

My father called me a couple days later and offered me a job at his company. I told her that I was leaving to be with my father, and she didn't bat any eye. She wanted me out of her way. There was no way for me, her son, to be a part of her life.

Now a part of me, or more so seventy percent of me, didn't want to have lunch with my mother. I didn't see the point in sitting down and going over the last five years when she could've just been a mother during that time and contacted me to show that she cared. I texted her on holidays, her birthday, and all that was reciprocated was a 'Thank you, my sweet boy' response.

I had my reservations about my mother, but if I'd learned anything from the past week, it was that no one was guaranteed another day. Estella would've never imagined that her father would fall into a coma from a heart attack at just fifty. If anything were to happen to my mother, I'd at least want to say that I'd tried to reach out before her demise.

The restaurant that my mother selected didn't surprise me. It was on the eighteenth floor, a penthouse lounge that had everything glittery and gold—two of her favorite things. The restaurant was known for serving high-ranking celebrities such as my mother. I'd only wished she didn't feel the need to abandon me to become successful.

Florence Amatore. I noticed her sitting in a private booth in the corner of the lounge. There was never a time when she was undone. She was a woman of class, pose, and femininity. Her honey-brown hair gently grazed her straight shoulders, her hands were perfectly manicured, and she wore a classic cream ensemble, giving her an angelic look. She certainly knew how to deceive her audience.

"Hello." I leaned over to kiss her cheek and was instantly greeted by her signature lilac perfume. It had been her scent ever since I was a little boy, and oddly enough, brought a little sense of comfort.

"Oh, my sweet boy," she said, placing a tender kiss on my cheek in return.

I took my place in front of her and crossed my arms over my chest. "How have you been?"

"I'm usually very busy. I finished a movie yesterday, and I will be starting a new project in a week. Busy, busy, busy." She flailed her hands.

I nodded and stared at her while she fiddled with the stem of her wineglass. I waited for her to reciprocate the question, but I didn't hold my breath. She wasn't good with personal conversation. My mother could talk anyone's ear off on a superficial level, but conversations about emotion were nonexistent. It made her uncomfortable.

"Where will you be flying for your movie?" I asked, not interested, but it was better than sitting in deafening silence.

"Vancouver, Canada."

"I've never been to Canada."

"Oh, it's so beautiful. Beautiful."

God, someone put us out of our misery.

The waiter appeared to take our drink orders, and I was fine with water, but my mother had ordered her favorite red wine. The waiter disappeared and reappeared within seconds and poured her wineglass halfway, but she motioned to him to keep pouring until it barely hit the rim. He proceeded to hand us our menu and left us to suffer in discomfort.

"I see that you still love your wine," I commented.

"Very much—it's my coffee." She laughed dryly.

I looked down at the menu, and my mind couldn't process any of the food descriptions. I couldn't think about food when I was sitting across from a woman who didn't know how to be around her own child.

"I'm buying; you pick out whatever you'd like to eat," she said, slipping on her glasses and looking over the menu.

"I'm not too hungry."

"Neither am I, but I need to include fiber into my diet, so I will have a salad."

I nodded and leaned against the lounge chair, closing my eyes and taking in the jazz music that played. It wasn't what I studied, but I loved everything about the genre. The complexity of the chords, the syncopations, and the improvisation. It reminded me of freedom, and Estella.

"Do you still play the piano?" my mother asked.

"I started playing recently again."

"Oh, that's so wonderful." She leaned over and reached over for my hand, squeezing it. "Do you remember when you used to play for me as a little boy?"

She brought up the memory with fondness in her voice, but it was far from a fond memory for me. The nights following after my father had spoken to my mother about separating, she hadn't been well. She appeared in my bedroom one night, with a glass of wine in her hand but several already in her system, and tenderly brushed her fingers through my hair to wake me. She pleaded with me to play one song for her to help her go to sleep, and I did.

Little did I know that she would wake me every night at midnight for a month, so I could play with her. It was a lot for a nine-year-old boy to have to be responsible for his mother's emotional well-being. Every night, the songs became slower, sadder, and soul-churning. She would have me play for hours on end until she allowed herself a 'good' cry. At times, she would vocalize what she wrote in her diary. Too many times, I heard her say she regretted the path she created for herself, that she wanted to end her life, and that every day was too much of a pain to bear. And I couldn't do or say anything. I had to endure her suffering.

"How could I forget?" I answered, watching her take a sip of her wine. Her dependency on alcohol was one of the main reasons I didn't drink often. It left more than a physical bitter taste on my tongue.

My pocket rang, snapping me out of my memories.

Estella: Papa is awake!

A large smile broke across my face reading her message.

Me: That's amazing news! When will he be home?

Estella: Doctors are running tests on him. Maybe Friday night, or Saturday morning.

We would have to move our date to another day. I didn't expect nor want her to miss her father's homecoming, but Estella was a step ahead of me.

Estella: Can we do the date night tomorrow? I hope it's not too much of a hassle to do so. I can help as much

as I can; I'll still act surprised!

Me: There is one thing: Do you think Maya could stay over at a friend's (or girlfriend's) house? I'd like to stay out the whole night with you.

Estella: I don't think she'll mind at all, lol. Our little secret though, okay? Both Mama and Papa would kill us all.

Me: All your secrets are safe with me.

My mother cleared her throat, and I looked up at her, noticing her I'm-ready-to-know-more smirk. "May I ask who is putting a big smile on my handsome son's face?"

I didn't want to tell her about Estella, only because she would never be around to meet her. Correction, she would want to meet her once just to get it out of the way and never ask for Estella again. I knew my mother and her intentions with people, yet I couldn't stop myself from sharing about the girl who had contributed to some of the best days I'd had.

"Her name is Estella."

"Estella Salvador," she said, matter-of-factly.

"You ask me with such innocence that it makes me think you know nothing."

"This is why I have numerous Best Actress awards," she

shared, doing her triumph shimmy. "Pamela told me a little about your plus one. Now tell me *more* about her. What are her aspirations, goals, desires?" She narrowed her eyes, trying to see into me, but there was nothing for her to read.

"She's an artist. She wants to create sculptures, figurines, and whatever else her heart desires."

"Does she own an art studio?"

"She shares a space with her friend back in Castellara."

"Ah, is that where you met? Is she Italian?"

"It's a long story, but no, she's not Italian."

I rolled my eyes before she could go on a tangent about not having an Italian daughter-in-law. Mom wasn't fully Italian herself, but she just wanted a reason to complain about someone she knew absolutely nothing about, and I wasn't going to allow it.

"You two will never meet, so don't get too upset."

She gasped. "Why would you say that?" She had her manicured hands over her chest.

I furrowed my eyebrows and looked at her oddly. "I'm sorry to have offended you. It's just, you're hardly around for me; I don't expect you to be around for my girlfriend."

There was something in her eyes that I'd never really seen in her before until now—guilt. A part of me believed that my mother purposely decided to abandon me with my grandparents and that she didn't care about me, but maybe I was wrong. Maybe, she had been haunted by all her actions after all these years.

Her eyes grew heavy with sorrow, and she reached into her purse for a tissue. There were no tears, but she pressed the edge of the tissue to her eyes. "I know I haven't been the best mother, and knowing what I know now, if I could go back in time to spend time with you, I would. I regret that you spent most of your childhood with your grandparents. I'd like to make it up to you now; let me be here for you now. Let me be your mother," she whispered, cradling my hand.

I studied her face, trying to see if she would break character at any second, but she didn't. She was a fluid woman, a woman with many sides, and I wasn't sure who I was talking to at that moment. Regardless, I decided that there was no harm in taking a chance with her. If she failed, I knew that she was a liar, and I wouldn't allow her to make a fool out of me again. And if she succeeded, then it would've been the best move on my part.

"I was planning on giving Estella a date night that she would never forget. I had mostly everything in line, but now the date is a day earlier, and I still have a lot of the little details to figure out. I could really use your help," I offered. "It isn't something that is specifically to do with me, but it's still personal."

"I would love to help you. She's very lucky to have a man like you in her life." My mother sighed, giving me a look that only a mother could give to her child.

"I suppose we should eat something heavier than salad with a busy day ahead of us?" she said, reaching over for the menu again and calling over the waiter to let him know that we would be staying for longer.

"I'll get the steak and vegetables."

My mother gave me a large smile, and for once, I really hoped that she would keep her promise of being more active in my life.

Chapter 31

ESTELLA

There was so much to do in so little time. My date with Ignacio would be in the evening, and I still had to pick an outfit along with fix my hair and face. I also wanted to plan a surprise welcome brunch for Papa who would be back home Saturday around noon. I wouldn't have much time with him, considering my flight would leave Sunday in the afternoon, so I had to make sure I had plenty to do with him on Saturday but also not exhaust him.

There was a knock on the door, and I had Mama on the phone. I wanted her advice on what to make and to do on Saturday, but she was more concerned about my date night.

"Estella, I know you are an adult, but please, do not get pregnant tonight."

"Oh God," I groaned.

"Also, please, make sure your sister doesn't sleep over at her girlfriend's house. She's too young for sleepovers with her girlfriend."

"At least she wouldn't get pregnant," I joked.

"Estella Noelle! I'm very serious."

There was another knock on the door.

"Yes, Mama, I know. I like teasing you, that's all."

I walked toward the door and looked through the peephole before opening the door. I used to open the door without looking, but with Cesar knowing my whereabouts, it was better to take precautions. It was Adler, lost in a tower of boxes.

"Give me a minute," I whispered to my mom and placed my phone on the end table by the door.

"Adler," I greeted, with a timid smile. "What is all this?"

He carried three white boxes with pink bows on them. Seeing a strong, serious man like Adler lost in a sea of boxes kind of made him look more approachable. "To Miss Salvador, from Mr. Amatore."

"You're not serious?" I asked, nervously.

I was shocked by all the gifts, but it wasn't the first time that I had been surprised by them.

"Oh, one more thing," Adler said, and walked back to the car to retrieve a large bouquet of pink peonies with an envelope. He handed them over to me with great care and offered me his best smile. He wasn't one to show much expression, but this whole situation revealed that he was a softie.

"Could you please give me a little insight on tonight?" I asked in a hushed tone.

"You know I can't do that."

"Just give me a street. I know you've been driving him everywhere."

Adler pretended to zip his lips and walked back to the car. I stood in place, waiting for him to drive away.

"I need to make sure that you're inside," he called.

"I am," I said, my hand on the door.

Adler gestured for me to go back into the house and I complied, closing the door behind me and moments later, appearing by the window.

My phone vibrated in my hand, reminding me that I was on the phone with my mom, but also that I'd received a text message from Adler. I had his number in case of emergency.

Adler: Music. A lot of music.

I smiled from ear to ear and waved at him as he drove away.

"I'm sorry, but Ignacio just had boxes of gifts delivered to me."

"Video-chat me—I want to see what he got you," she urged and ended the call.

I gathered all the items into the living room and propped my phone against the couch to allow Mama a good view of my gifts.

I video-called Mama, and she told me to open the gifts from smallest to largest. She was excited for me, and I loved that I was able to share this experience with her.

I opened the smallest one and revealed diamond drop earrings. "Oh my God," I whispered as I gave Mama a closer look. They were white-gold and diamond-wire bezel-drop earrings. They were simple, minimal, but definitely luxury.

"That's our mortgage for the month easily." She gasped.

"This is too much."

"You deserve this. You deserve the whole world, *hija*."

I grabbed the medium-sized box and immediately gasped at the sight of nude pointed heels. "Oh, wow."

"Very beautiful."

"I really can't believe he's doing this." My cheeks were

burning hot. I'd never been gifted items from a man, let alone items that could pay my parents' monthly mortgage. "I still think this is too much."

"*Ay!*" Mom scolded. "Open the last one."

It was a beautiful, jaw-dropping dress.

I lifted it from the ruffled box and admired the underwire dress that had a slight flare at the hem. It had diamante trim outlining the neckline, bust, and straps. My hand touched the glittered mesh fabric, and it glistened under the sun's rays that penetrated through the window.

"You're going to look gorgeous. I want a picture of you two, okay?" She rustled around with the phone. "I'm going to wake your father up, so he can eat and take his medication. Be safe, and I'll talk to you later."

She ended the call, and I bit down on my finger as I gazed at all my gifts. Overwhelmed was an understatement. I didn't know what to think. There was some anxiety in the mix, only because I'd never been spoiled to this extent. It almost felt wrong, but maybe because I was just so used to Cesar's treatment. All he did was take, and now, I found someone who only wanted to give.

I took a deep breath and lifted up the bouquet of peonies that were wrapped in light pink tissues. I loved my gifts, but the peonies were my favorite because they reminded me of that night in Paris. Ignacio approached me, handing me a peony like it was second nature. He had a reserved confidence to him, which only made me more attracted to him.

I swayed on my way to the kitchen, humming a tone that popped to mind, and prepared my arrangement in a magenta vase. I leaned over the counter, admiring the beautiful bouquet and reminding myself how lucky I was to have Ignacio in my life. The sun shone brighter than normal, the birds sounded chirper, and I was certainly floating on cloud nine.

***

I texted Adler, telling him that I would be done with my hair appointment in five minutes. He didn't go too far. Ignacio had told him to stay around the area until it was time for the date. He didn't like juggling Adler between Manhattan and Brooklyn.

The autumn air tousled my shiny, wavy hair, and I didn't mind. It gave it a second-day look, which all girls knew looked better than on the first day, oddly enough. I pushed the strands away from my face and jumped at the sight of the man walking toward me. Romeo.

Romeo was Cesar's best friend and right-hand man. I used to call him a yes-man because he would agree with Cesar without any hesitation. There could be no logic in Cesar's decisions, yet Romeo would be the first one to give them a seal of approval.

"Wow," he called. "Don't you look so done up and pretty?"

I eyed him and crossed my arms, facing the street again.

"I gave you a compliment; you should say thank you."

"No, thanks," I responded.

Romeo huffed and walked in front of me to be in my line of vision. His soulless, beady, black eyes penetrated through me. "You came back from Italy being bitchier than usual."

"Go away," I said, walking away from him.

"But I've missed you, Twinkle Twinkle."

I hated that stupid nickname that he and Cesar made for me. They were drunk out of their minds and created parodies out of children's lullabies. Cesar started to sing "Twinkle ,Twinkle Little Star" and then pointed at me. "Twinkle Twinkle never wants the winkle winkle," he sang, causing his idiot friends to laugh until they couldn't breathe.

"I can't say the same." I hated that I responded to him; it only kept him entertained. He loved getting under my skin because he knew that Cesar would never say a word to him.

"Ouch, Cesar wouldn't be happy to hear that."

"Fuck Cesar and everyone he knows," I responded, harshly.

"Damn," Romeo said, snapping his head back. "There's a little bit of bite in that bitch, huh?"

I continued to walk down the street, my arms across my chest and my gaze down on the sidewalk. I could feel him following closely behind me. I turned on my heels and looked him dead in the eyes.

"Please, leave me alone."

Romeo grabbed the sleeve of my sweater and pulled my arm against him. "But we miss having fun with you."

I looked at my arm as if it was on fire. Before I could snatch it away, tires screeched against the road, and the BMW skirted in place beside us. The sudden drift caused Romeo to release my arm and look behind him, only to be approached by an upset Adler.

Leaving Paris

"Do not touch her again, understand?" Adler warned, his jaw tensed. Adler didn't look a day over forty, but his short hair, bearded face, and muscular build made him look more intimidating than needed. He had endured more than the average person, being ex-military, and it was clear through his constant stoic expression.

Romeo gave me a sideways glance, puzzled by the sudden bodyguard, and then jogged away without saying another word to either of us.

I could see why Florence Amatore hired Adler to be one of her personal bodyguards and driver. No one would ever dare question him or even bat an eye at him, for that matter. I wondered why he wasn't with Florence instead, considering she was an A-list actress with paparazzi at every corner. What was he doing giving me gifts and picking me up from the salon?

We entered the vehicle, and Adler drove to the townhouse so I could adorn myself with all of Ignacio's gifts. It was a ten-minute drive, but the silence made it feel like an hour. Adler parked in front of the house, but he didn't step out of the car as usual. I could open my own door—I would rather do it on my own anyway—but I knew that he wanted me to speak first.

"You're going to tell him, right?" I asked, softly.

"I have to, Estella. He told me about your situation, and I told him I'd handle it." It hit me then that Adler had been assigned to protect me.

"They're just a bunch of idiots. I'm sure you've spooked them."

"That's the point."

"Let me tell him, okay? He's put a lot of effort in tonight, and I don't want the mood to turn sour with this news. Cesar has ruined all the good in my life for the past year; I don't want him to ruin this night."

Adler was mulling it over. He was a serious man but not evil. "Very well."

"Thank you." I sighed.

I opened the door before Adler could open his, which made him huff in frustration. "You need to stop doing my job." He wanted to sound stern, but it didn't faze me.

"Easy money." I shrugged.

I headed toward the bricked stairs and turned around, seeing Adler watching me. "Who's watching Ms. Amatore?"

"Another bodyguard—she has us on rotation." I wasn't going to hold it over him for lying. He was only doing what Ignacio ordered him to do.

"I bet you're nicer than him."

"Not necessarily true."

"I believe otherwise."

Adler tried to fight off his smirk, but I saw the corner of his lips turn slightly upward. "Have a good evening, Miss Salvador."

"I certainly plan on it."

No one would get in the way of my night with Ignacio.

Chapter 32

ESTELLA

I couldn't figure out what to do with my hands. I placed them on my lap, clasped them together, held onto the headrest of the passenger door, and also gripped onto the leather seat. I was beyond nervous. I had to remind myself to breathe.

Adler seemed entertained and attempted to relieve my anxiety, but it didn't help. His efforts to find the perfect radio station failed miserably because I told him to turn it off. I had no knowledge of the Manhattan area, but I noticed an increase in college students in red apparel, some even carrying instrument cases.

We were at the Manhattan School of Music.

"That's why you said a lot of music," I chirped, my

nervous feelings subsiding momentarily. "We're going to see a performance?"

"Yes."

"Awesome," I whispered, lowering the window and leaning against the edge. I never understood everyone's fascination with New York, despite being born here. I viewed it as a dirty, smelly city with obnoxious people, blaring horns, and busy roads. It was always chaotic, but today, it felt different.

Under the pastel sunset colors, seeing young adults laughing amongst friends, and with the man that I loved just a short distance away, everything seemed to be realigning.

We went down Claremont Avenue, and the BMW made a gentle stop in front of the Performance Center entrance. I undid my seatbelt and flashed a smile at Ignacio through the window. We had only been apart for a few hours, but it had felt much longer than that.

Ignacio wore a beautifully tailored, navy-blue suit that went so well against his tan skin. He stopped Adler from opening the door and reached for the handle to open it himself. Our eyes met, and everything went in slow motion. His touch radiated warmth, and he eased me out of the vehicle, and once I stepped out, we didn't utter a sound. We took in the sight of one another, and at some point, time froze.

"Wow," he exhaled. "You look heavenly."

All the blood rushed from my heart and to my cheeks. "Thank you," I whispered.

Ignacio offered his arm, and I delicately placed my hand on him. "And you look great, too," I added. "As if you walked out of a magazine." We walked into the spacious center, and I allowed Ignacio to guide me through the unfamiliar yet inviting area.

We stopped in front of the Alan M. and Joan Taub Ades space. The melodies of the cello and violin wafted outside of the performance space. I held tighter onto Ignacio's arm in anticipation, practically on my toes in excitement. The only live performances I had experienced were the jazz groups in Paris, five years ago.

Ignacio motioned for me to close my eyes, and I did. I heard him open the doors and felt him gently guide me into the space. The music was more audible, a rendition of a popular pop song that I couldn't place a finger on. Either way, it was better than the original.

"Open," he whispered in my ear.

Leaving Paris

The venue had been bathed in candle lights, giving the room a warm and intimate ambience. There was no other light source. The talented musicians were completely surrounded by flickering candlelight, and there was a black grand piano next to them with a vacant bench. Outside the ring of candles, there were two white chairs with gold trimming.

"A private performance?" I whispered to him in awe.

"Exactly," he said, holding my hand and moving it upward to swirl me into his arms.

"Aren't you romantic?"

"For you, yes. Should we sit?"

"Yes!"

It was a surreal experience, hearing the musicians play their renditions of pop music and working their way down the timeline until they began playing classical music. The sweet vibrations traveled through the floor and walls and onto my skin. I rested my head on Ignacio's shoulder, letting all the music unfold and absorbing it with pleasure. Our love for instrumental music had been the seed that fueled our relationship from the beginning.

I looked down at Ignacio's watch to check the time. I had been so immersed in the music that I couldn't believe we had been watching the performance for almost an hour. The piano still hadn't been occupied, and I wondered when the piano player would make an entrance.

I watched Ignacio ease himself away from me, and fixing his suit, he flashed a mischievous smile, then I connected the dots when he strode toward the piano.

He's going to play for me.

At the age of thirteen, I begged Mama and Papa to tell me how they met and how they fell in love. We were sitting at a restaurant, and the question had come to mind. The manner in which they spoke about their first encounter and their growing love was so effortless. They bounced back and forth in their story, everything perfectly aligned and told like a true romance. I had propped my head on my hands and admired their love for each other. Mama told me that when you know, you know. *It'll hit you like the strongest force on Earth,* she said, which sounded scary. *But it isn't really,* she assured me.

The sensation of the wall built around my heart tumbling apart, each heavy brick being broken down into nothingness and exposing my vulnerable heart—that was when my heart let me fall in love with him. It would be an indelible moment etched in time, the time in which love conquered all for me.

I didn't expect it to happen, nor did I believe it really would after everything I had endured in the past year. Love with Cesar was hard, brutal, suffocating, but with Ignacio, it was second nature. This love didn't hurt; this loved healed.

Ignacio and the musicians played one song together: *Clair De Lune by* Debussy. It was my favorite classical song, and hearing it being played by Ignacio only made my heart tighten. The combination of the strings and the piano felt similar to being in a romance movie. Everything seemed so perfect.

The musicians bowed after completing the piece, and Ignacio stood up to give them a handshake of gratitude. I followed his lead and vocalized my appreciation for their masterful work. The violinist and cellist informed me that they were students at the school, recently graduated, and were touched to have been a part of the arrangement.

They left, and Ignacio led me to the piano, and we sat on the bench, admiring the grandness of the instrument. My fingers danced on familiar keys, playing a simple melody that took months to create, and Ignacio built onto it without another thought.

"I'm so jealous of your ability to play," I said.

"You'll learn in no time. You just have to work with me." He smiled.

"We'll get back on it when we return to Italy."

"Back at Emile's house or do you feel comfortable enough to go in my piano room?" he teased.

I lightly nudged him. "I've seen your piano room—it's okay. Emile's piano room has more character."

He wanted to be offended but couldn't. "I can't deny that." He chuckled.

"There's a difference between having a piano in a cottage and a piano in a mansion. The piano in a cottage is more inviting than a piano in a mansion."

"I understand completely; it's about the intimacy. Pianos communicate with you in a wordless language, and the closer the piano is to you in a small room, the more intimate the conversation sounds. That's why I enjoy playing with you in general, being able to communicate with you in a more intimate setting."

"You have no idea how much I enjoy playing with you, Mr. Amatore."

"How much?" he asked, leaning in slowly as his fingers ascended to the right of the piano, creating a chirpy cascade of notes.

We had kissed plenty of times before, but sitting in front of him, with his lips inches away from me, made my stomach turn into knots. I felt younger, like a teenager in love. Inexperienced, jittery, skittish. God, he turned me into a nervous schoolgirl. I knew he'd have this effect on me for years to come even when I wasn't as young and beautiful.

I brushed my lips against his, a surrendering sigh escaping them, and Ignacio pulled me in hard to melt his lips against mine. My fingers laced onto the back of his head, craving his sensational touch.

"I'm deeply in love with you," he whispered against my lips.

The pressure in my heart had exploded, and I realized a frenzy of butterflies escaped. "I love you too, Ignacio." It was my first time saying it to him. Ignacio pressed his forehead against mine and then leaned in slowly to kiss me.

"Say it again," he whispered.

"I love you, Ignacio."

"Again."

"I love you," I breathed out, watching him absorb my words.

"I'll never get enough of those words."

Ignacio faced the piano again, and his fingers played a dreamy interlude.

"I love seeing you process," he shared, looking at me as his fingers performed magic. "What do you think about it?"

I chimed in, my right hand playing familiar notes. "My melody," I whispered in awe.

Ignacio had transformed my melody into a sonata. It started with an ethereal feel to it as if one was lost in another reality, floating in a dream, but then when it was least expected, it spiraled into a melancholic serenade. The dream had now turned into a lonely limbo; it was a piece that was written from a dark place.

Ignacio's composure and face had changed as he began to play it, he put in all of his emotions into the piece. His eyebrows furrowed deeply as he slowed his playing, reliving a moment in his life. All I wanted to do was soothe the pain out of his face, to touch him tenderly, but it was clear he *had* to express himself. This was a part of the sonata, his part of his story.

The pace started to step up, the tempo became livelier and his expressions became lighter as his fingers danced around the keys, circling back to a tone full of yearning.

Ignacio's body moved with the careful rhythm of the sonata, the notes filling me with the desire to clasp my heart tightly. It wasn't sad, but there was an anticipation, I felt it with all my being. It was that feeling of hope, that things could either go as planned or not. The need to know was suffocating, but the right outcome would make it so worth it.

Then it was all worth it because love prevailed. The sonata cascaded into a beautifully breathtaking harmony that locked in all your emotions. That feeling of waking up to birds singing, the sun beaming on your face, with the love of your life next to you. That was all we wanted to live for. We wanted to live to love.

"What are you calling it?" I asked, with my head on his shoulder and my eyes closed.

"Leaving Paris. It's about the last five years without you, and then finding you again."

"I love it." I shook my head in disbelief. "The fact that you pulled all of this off so suddenly amazes me. You've done so much for me today."

"You deserve so much more than this." He sighed. "I want to give you the world."

I placed a soft kiss on his cheek. "You are my world,

Ignacio Amatore."

Ignacio gave a cheerful, sweet smile, and it was all the love I would need from him. It extended from his eyes and into my soul. There was nothing else I wanted more than him and his pure smile.

"My mom helped me with a lot of this."

"Your mom? I thought you two weren't on speaking terms."

"We don't really talk, but she asked me to meet her for lunch yesterday. It was uncomfortable in the beginning, but you came up in the conversation, and everything went smoother. She helped me with most of the date, really. We were together for hours, collaborating, talking, laughing; it was great. It was all I ever wanted from her."

"I'm so happy for you. I'm so glad that you gave her that chance."

"I'm happy, as well. She wants to meet you," he said. "She wanted to meet tomorrow for dinner, but I know you'll be busy preparing for your papa's arrival. I told her that we'd be back in December, if you like. Christmas in New York is phenomenal; Castellara could never beat it."

The happiness inside of me grew strong and fierce. I squeezed Ignacio's arm and nodded excitedly. "I would love that—maybe a joint Christmas function? Oh my God, we would all be in the same room as your mom. That's insane. We could have a potluck."

Ignacio looked at me again with a loving smile and partook in my fantasy. "Our food blanketing a long buffet table, beautiful winter decor lining the penthouse's floor-to-ceiling windows, Frank Sinatra playing in the background, and I'll wistfully pull you into me, and we'll dance in the living room."

So, this is love.

And to end all the fascination and awe, leaving me in pure disbelief about the connection that we genuinely shared, Ignacio began to play *So This Is Love*, another Cinderella love song. I wasn't sure what universal strings were being pulled for us, but I didn't question it. This was most certainly love.

***

Ignacio had reservations for a rooftop restaurant, but I had asked if I could surprise him instead. He was taken aback and amused. He let me take the reins, and I knew exactly where to go for our outing. Or a rough idea.

Salem's father had a close friend named Julio, who owned a Mexican restaurant in Manhattan called La Cantina. I had been there once with Salem, as a senior in high school, and the food was beyond magical.

Ignacio asked me to order for him, to add to the surprise. I went with a taco box; it had everything that you needed.

"I think I have the perfect place for this," he said.

We hailed a cab and headed toward his penthouse–a gift from Lilianna, but Ignacio rented it out most of the time. The vibrant turquoise building was modern and like nothing I had ever seen in New York and located in NoHo.

"We are going to the rooftop," he said, holding the door open.

The rooftop was maintained, but you could tell that no one went up there. The outdoor furniture seemed to have never been touched by another person. It all looked new, despite the building being around for years.

We edged closer to the black railing, taking in the view of all the historic buildings, bright lights, and night sky. It felt like I had been taken out of my reality and plopped into a movie scene.

"This isn't real," I whispered.

"Very real," Ignacio whispered in my ear, circling his arms around me as he hugged me from behind. "It's even better when you have someone to share it with."

And that's exactly what we did. We sat on a bench that overlooked the city and chit-chatted about our favorite memories as children whilst munching on our delicious tacos.

Ignacio opened his blazer jacket and reached in, pulling out what looked to be a napkin. He handed me the folded material and looked at me expectantly. I hovered the napkin over my lip, but he flinched and pulled my hand down. "No, no. Open it."

"Open it?"

He nodded.

I opened the folded-over piece of napkin, and my eyes lingered over the drawing of a woman surrounded by musical instruments. It wasn't any drawing; it was my drawing from five years ago. It was the doodle I had drawn as I sat alone in the booth, listening to the jazz group slowly finish their gig for the night.

"But, how?" I gasped. "You've kept it all this time?"

"I snuck it into my pocket when I was on the phone that night we met and you were upstairs playing on the Fazioli.

I thought it was pretty neat and always kept it in my desk drawer. I would look at it on certain nights that I thought about you." His hand rose up to my cheek, and he touched me as if I could vanish from him.

"I suppose I really left an impression on you."

"You have no idea."

A surge of emotions tugged at my throat. The way he looked at me, the way he touched me, it was the way I'd always wanted to be loved. He slowly leaned over, his eyes watching my lips attentively, and then he branded me. We'd kissed many times before this, but this seemed to solidify the moment. It said, "Here we are, Universe, back together again for good."

***

There were no words to describe his penthouse. We walked through the grand entry that opened up to an entertainment space, and the living and dining rooms were adjacent with an abundance of art on the walls. The main attraction of the contemporary living room was the brown piano that glistened next to the lit fireplace.

I opened the door to his bedroom, and there was

another fireplace that instantly invited me to the room with its roaring fire and the black-gray marbling that created a nice contrast. The room was Scandinavian minimalism—what I had expected from Ignacio.

My feet were planted by the side of the bed, my hand grazed over the pressed, white sheets, and then it started to sink in that I had to tell him about my interaction with Romeo before anything else happened. It was either I do it tonight, or Adler would tell him in the morning.

"Estella, we don't have to have sex. I know you've gone through a lot. I wanted to give you what you deserve. Don't ever feel obligated to give me anything in return." He pulled me into his chest, his arm circling my waist.

I laid my hands flat on his chest and looked at him. "I need to tell you something."

There was worry and confusion in his eyes. "Is everything okay? Was it all too much? Too little?"

I felt his heart pounding against his chest. "It was all perfect."

Relief washed over him temporarily, but the longer I went without talking, the more he was ruminating on what I wanted to share.

"This is horrible timing, but I need to tell you. I had an

interaction with Cesar's best friend, Romeo."

He tilted his head. "What kind of interaction?"

"He was harassing me. I tried to walk away from him, but he grabbed me." Ignacio's chest rose, and I patted him gently. "It's okay. Adler came on time and scared him off."

"Adler witnessed it and didn't tell me?" Ignacio wasn't taking it well.

"*I* told him I'd tell you, okay? Don't be mad at him. He gave me until tonight."

Ignacio's eyes wandered around my face as if he were searching for something. His lips were pulled in tight like he wanted to talk to me but didn't.

I breathed deeply as my hands slid to the nook of his neck, and I gripped onto it as I lifted myself up to place a tender kiss on his lips. Ignacio's hands found their way around my waist, and he held me tightly.

"Talk to me," I whispered. "I'm sorry for ruining the night."

"I can't lose you, Estella," he whispered back, fear lingering in his voice. "You're the only person I've ever wanted in my life. You make everything so right. I've lost people, and it fucking hurts. I need you, and if something were to happen to you…" He closed his eyes tightly, and the tears that trickled down were enough to let me know what he wanted to say.

"Ignacio," I cooed softly, wiping away his tear. "I love you. Nothing will happen to me."

"Estella, you need to report them. Men like that will not hesitate to do more harm to you. I can only do so much on my end."

I wanted to protest, to tell him that they were ego-inflamed idiots and that they would let it go. I didn't want to relive everything that had happened to complete strangers, but I had to let go of that fear. I had to look out for my future—our future.

"I know. I know that's why you assigned Adler to us."

Ignacio closed his eyes and gave me a firm nod.

"I'll go tomorrow," I promised. "Will you go with me?"

"Of course. We are in this together, *stella mia*."

Our bodies were so close, our lips two inches away from each other, our eyes locked, and our attention only on each other. This was intimacy.

"Have you ever gone out in nature on a dark, cold night after a bad day and looked up at the sky, noticed a bright star, and gazed at it with sheer amazement?" I nodded in response to his question. "Then doesn't that star give you comfort, some joy for life, some spiritual alignment?" I nodded again, keeping the tears at bay. "Well, you're that star for me."

God, my heart could explode into a million pieces.

I wanted him. I wanted this. I wanted it all. The good, the bad, the ugly, the second chance of love.

"Thank you for not giving up on us," I said as I took his mouth hungrily like a starved woman. Ignacio cupped my face, kissing me back as if I would evaporate into thin air at any second. Our tongues intertwined, lips intermingling, and our bodies wanted to be joined together, too. Ignacio's mouth left my lips and trailed down my neck, kissing feverishly down until he reached my shoulders.

Ignacio spun me, slowly unzipped my dress, and I let it fall, exposing all my bare skin except the thin, black fabric that covered the area between my legs. He cupped my breasts as he soaked in my euphoric expression. I moaned at his burning touch and closed my eyes. We had longed and craved for this moment again, and the journey here had felt like an eternity, but I was glad we had made it.

"I don't want to go another day without you," he said, his voice low and full of love. He shifted forward and sucked my erect nipple as his hands danced up my back. I gripped the back of his neck as his mouth explored my breasts. He made me come alive in more than one way. I caught a faint whiff of cologne that evoked all the early memories of our relationship. That night in Paris. Music. Intimacy. Sex.

I started to undress him, and he hastily finished the job. We moved onto his bed without hesitation, and I held his sculpted muscles in my hands, feeling his rock-hard erection underneath me, his hands exploring my body as if it was our first time again—it was all too intoxicating. I was on sensory overload; everything felt surreal.

"I need you," I begged against his lips.

He gripped me as he positioned us near the edge of the bed and lifted me up to slip his cock under me. The lacy fabric had posed a nuisance to his manhood, but that didn't stop him from getting what he wanted. Ignacio slipped the thin, silky fabric off, and I climbed back on his lap, sinking down onto him. *Holy shit.*

I was a quivering mess, simultaneously wrapping my legs around his waist and gripping his neck tightly. With the fire casting a glow behind me, I was able to stare into his inviting eyes, losing myself in them. Ignacio traced the outline of my body and stopped at my thighs to grip on them. His fingers dug into my skin, imprinting himself onto me.

There wasn't much hard thrusting; it was just the rocking of our hips, our bodies aligning with each other after so much turbulence. We kissed each other's lips, chin, and neck as our hands explored each other. We were plunged into each other like a stellar collision—becoming one newer, brighter star.

Chapter 33

IGNACIO

Everything about Estella was addictive. Her voice, her personality, her body...*Jesus*. Last night might've been my third time having sex, but she showed me how sex was supposed to feel. She scorched herself into my veins, consuming every fiber of my being and marking me for life. I knew that my life began when I met Estella, and it had to end with her.

The sunrise acted as a curtain, a beautiful display of the sun blooming over the horizon. I looked over to the other side of the bed and watched Estella still lost in a deep slumber, her bare back exposed. I ran my fingers through her tousled waves and inhaled deeply.

This was all I wanted. I waited years for this moment

again, and nothing was going to get in the way of it. I would make sure of it.

"I won't allow anyone to ever come between us again," I whispered to Estella.

***

As it came closer to noon, I noticed Estella growing paler. We were going to the police station to put in a formal request for an order of protection. There was no doubt that she would receive one because of the harm he'd caused her months ago. Apparently, she'd had to shut down all her social media at some point because he would have harassed her—easy win, but it hadn't been that easy for Estella.

"I can't shake the feeling of being the bad guy for asking you to do this," I admitted, leaning toward her.

"I should've done this before I went to Italy," she said quietly. "I figured that I didn't need to do all of this because I'd be gone for a year, and a lot can change in a year. I just didn't want to relive everything…it hurts." She folded her arms across her chest and pressed herself against me. I understood her completely.

I wrapped an arm around her, holding her tightly. "I'll

protect you; I hope you know that."

"I know," she whispered.

The process wasn't complicated, but it was daunting. Estella reached over for my hand on occasion, needing extra reassurance while discussing details about her relationship with Cesar. It was in our best interests for Cesar and I to steer clear of each other because if I faced him, I would make him regret ever treating Estella less well she deserved.

"Thank you for coming with me," Estella said as we walked out of the station. "I actually feel a little better." She scanned her surroundings and drew in a deep breath.

I placed a gentle hand on her lower back. "Good."

"You're staying over tonight, right?"

"Of course."

"Good. I still need you at night." She adjusted her shoulders to match her confidence—not completely there but more than before.

"I'll spend every night with you, if you let me."

"Last night was unbelievable," she said, reminiscing.

"It really was." I looked down at her and caught her beautiful smile. I kissed her lips hard and pulled her into a tight embrace.

"I'm not sure how you'll top our future dates."

"Oh, I have so much more up my sleeve." I might've exaggerated, but I did have at least two more date ideas that I wanted to execute in the near future.

I watched Adler drive closer toward us, and once he parked in front of us, I opened the door for her. She shimmied down, and I entered after her. Adler immediately locked the doors and proceeded to drive toward Estella's townhouse.

Estella exited the vehicle before Adler could open his door, and she pointed a firm finger at him, gesturing him to remain seated. She enjoyed being quicker than him, and I could tell that he found her entertaining. Estella walked over, and I lowered the window to kiss her goodbye.

"Enjoy your time with your mom."

"Are you sure you can't come?" I asked.

"I want to clean the house, set up the decorations, and marinate the chicken for tomorrow. Chicken and waffles will be on the menu." Her smile was even more beautiful when she was giddy with excitement. She was so loved, and that was the best thing a person could have in life.

I extended my hand out of the window and placed it on her soft cheek. Feeling her was one of my favorite pastimes. "Okay, I'll try to be back in a few hours." I couldn't shake off the feeling that it was too soon to leave Estella.

"Take your time, really," Estella insisted.

"Call me or text me if you need me."

"I will. How about I text you every hour?" Her fingers danced up my hand and to my watch.

"Thank you. I can have Adler return if that makes you feel safe."

"I'm not going to have him drive there and back. Give him a break."

I watched a flicker of a smile appear on Adler's face from the rearview mirror.

"Very well."

"Have a little trust in me."

"It's not you that I don't trust. It's them."

"I'll be okay. I'll lock all the doors."

"Please."

"I will see you later, Mr. Amatore." God, the way her lips looked when she called me that. I couldn't wait for the day when I could give her the same name. Ms. Estella Amatore had an amazing ring to it.

Forty minutes later, and I arrived at my mother's opulent penthouse. I forgot how everything in the penthouse was either gold, marbled, or cream-colored. She

Leaving Paris

prided herself in being a maximalist.

One of her house managers escorted me into the tea room, my mother's favorite room and mine, as well. The walls were painted white with gold accents throughout and on the ceiling, there was a grand chandelier that hung over the table arrangements, and a Samick ivory-and-gold piano in the corner of the room. I appreciated it when a piano was the statement piece of the room, and although the piano was gorgeous, it was outshone by everything else around it.

Mom entered the room, and three men dressed in white chef's uniforms followed behind her with a selection of scones, sandwiches, cake, and teas. She had enough to serve up to twenty people, but that was my mother. Go big or go home.

"*Figlio mio.*" She smiled as she approached me, cupping my face and kissing each cheek. "Tell me everything that happened last night. How did she enjoy the clothes, music, and Garden Rooftop Restaurant?"

"We didn't go to the restaurant," I said. "We opted for fast-food and eating on the rooftop of my building."

"It is quite lovely up there," she said, stroking my cheek. Her hands were cold and shaky. My mother might've been an actress with a deceiving smile, but I knew when she wasn't feeling well. Today was one of those days, and I wondered if she'd try to conceal it from me, or if I'd have to pry it out of her.

"We had the Samick tuned earlier this morning. Do you mind playing for me before we eat?"

"Anything you'd like," I said. "I owe it to you after last night."

"You don't owe me anything," she said, tapping my cheek before walking ahead.

Mother gazed through the window in deep thought as I played. The world knew her as a chameleon, but I wondered if she was ever understood by anyone. I was her son and knew a little more than the average person, and I wished we hadn't missed out on so many years.

We both watched the blue skies fade into a dark gray color, clouds rolling in, and raindrops streaking the great windows. The pitter-patter of the rain and the keys of the piano mingled together, and the melancholy melody ignited *something* in me.

Almost an hour in, I realized that I'd never attempted to teach my mother how to play. She was the one who funded most of my studies; she had always supported my musical career, yet I had never seen her even touch a key.

"Mamma, would you like to learn how to play?"

She moved her attention back to me with shock in her eyes. "You haven't called me Mamma since you were thirteen."

I didn't notice that until she pointed it out. "You're right."

"I'll leave the music to you, though, thank you." She went back to look out the window.

"Should we eat soon?" I asked, watching her house manager check on the food and then on us.

"Another five minutes."

Five minutes passed, and she kept her word. We sat across from each other and although we were inches away from each other, the grandness and emptiness of the room made the ambience feel haunting almost.

Mother helped herself to a sandwich and a tea cake. "So, you won't be back until Christmas time?" she asked.

"Around that time."

"Thanksgiving is in a few weeks. Why not stay until then?"

"We are both eager to go back to Italy. She has orders to fill, and I'm in search of a new place." That was a last-minute decision; I hadn't even shared the news with Estella.

I wanted a smaller place in Castellara to be closer to Estella and Nonno. The country suited me more than the modern town of Lilla.

"You don't like the villa your father gave you?"

"I'm looking to downsize. I don't need a million rooms, two different living rooms, a wine cellar, a saloon, and whatever else."

"Keep me updated. I don't want you finding something old and unsuitable."

"I'll most likely buy a decent-sized cottage and renovate it. It'll be a great home to raise children." The possibility didn't seem too far away.

"Children," she whispered. "I could have grandchildren," she whispered in amazement.

"Yes." I laughed. "When we are ready."

"So," she said, placing a napkin over her mouth to hide her giddiness. "Estella may be the one then?"

"I know she is," I declared.

"You don't understand how happy I am to hear that you found a woman to love and care for you the way you deserve." Tears started to cascade down her cheek, and she was quick to blot them away with her napkin. She wasn't one to cry in front of others, but I saw it, and it was touching to know that she genuinely felt happy for me. I may have only reconnected with Estella less than two months ago, but I knew she was the one for me five years ago.

"I wanted to talk to you about something," she said hesitantly. "Two things actually."

I'd expected this conversation. She had been off for the whole visit, but I couldn't decipher what she would want to talk about.

"You've grown up to be an amazing man, and it saddens me to not have been there for you more. I wish things could be different, especially now that we are getting closer, but I have to tell you that I might not have much time left with you." She placed her delicate, cold hands over mine and squeezed them tightly. "I wasn't meant to be your mother for long."

Her words were so vague yet so powerful. I didn't understand what she was telling me. Was she leaving me by choice or not? With our history, I assumed the worst and wanted to explode on her for playing pretend with me, but I allowed myself to remain calm and collected until she proved otherwise.

"I'm not understanding you."

"I have stage-four skin cancer, melanoma."

The words sucker-punched me in the chest. *Cancer?*

"You're being treated, correct?"

"The survival rate is low, *figlio.* I can be treated, but I won't win in the end."

I pulled my hand away and covered my forehead, processing her last sentence. The severity and darkness of her words wrapped me like a cocoon. "Fuck!" I yelled, slamming my fists onto the table, the set of cups and plates shifting. Mother didn't move a muscle.

I grabbed onto her hands and pulled them into me. "You reentered my life, Mamma. You weren't supposed to leave me again. I lost Nonna, and now you?"

She didn't utter a sound. What could she say to console her angry, betrayed son?

"How long have you known?" I asked.

"I learned that it wasn't looking in my favor early September."

"And you're now telling me? Almost two months later?" I tried to not sound upset or mad with her because I wasn't. My anger wasn't directed at her; it was directed at the situation. A part of me wished she hadn't told me, but another part would've been devastated to learn about my mother's passing even if we weren't on talking terms. She was my mother after all; I could be troubled by her unloving acts, but I still loved her.

"How long do you have left?" My heart carried the weight of a million bricks, and it still pounded against my chest.

"With the chemotherapy, radiation therapy, and other therapies, a little less than three years since it's so late. Without it all, maybe less than a year."

"What do you mean *without it*? You need to live."

Mother held my hands with all her effort and kissed them. "I do, but not if it means I lose myself. I don't want to live three more years if it means being skin and bones."

As much as I didn't want to understand that, I completely did and hated myself for it. I wanted to tell her to keep fighting for however long she could, that we'd now found each other and should try our best to keep each other in our lives, that in three years she could see me getting married, having a child, but I couldn't. It would be completely and utterly selfish.

I leaned into my mother, holding her tightly, and allowed myself to mourn for our past, present, and future. It was the first time in nearly twenty years that I had cried in my mother's arms—the tears that pleaded for help, pleaded for this moment to be miraculously salvaged.

"With every blessing, there is a curse," Mom whispered into my ears.

The words sounded familiar, but I was too emotionally heavy to recall the origin of the saying.

"Your nonna used to say that."

She was right. I would hear her say it whenever my mom and dad had scored a new job opportunity, which meant being tossed to my grandparents. I never understood it until now. They would prosper in wealth and status—the blessing—but ruined their relationship with me—the curse—but that wasn't something they would know until years passed. And now, my mother had the blessing of having me in her life, but the curse of having to leave so soon. Blessing and curses had to be received in full measure. There was no picking and choosing but solely accepting what is and will be.

"She was a wild, crazy woman, but I loved her as if she was my own mother. I always thanked her for raising you. I can't take credit for the man you are now, as much as I would love to." She chuckled, softly.

"Maybe we'll stay another week."

Leaving Paris

"I would love that, but I need to tell you the other thing before you decide to keep me around in your life."

I raised my eyebrows. There were many reasons that I shouldn't have brought my mother back into my life, but I moved past it all. With guilt and disgust taking over her face, I started to become unsure of my decision.

"It's about you and Estella. Five years ago."

My world halted, and I narrowed my eyes at my mother. There was no way she knew anything about mine and Estella's past. The only other person who knew about our history was Salem, and she wouldn't tell a soul.

"What?" I asked, my voice low and short. The longer my mother maintained eye contact with me throughout the silence, the more impatient I grew with her. "Speak."

"Do you remember how you stayed with me a couple of days after your nonna passed and then you left?"

"You kicked me out."

Mother closed her eyes and nodded. "Yes, I told you to go, and shortly after, your father swooped in and took you to Paris?"

I nodded.

"Once you were situated, he called me and told me that you were doing pretty well over there with him. I thought,

'Maybe he was a better parent than me', and I accepted that I failed as a mother, but I was wrong about both of those things." She sighed deeply.

"You need to tell me what's going on, now."

"I heard that you and your father were attacked at night, and I contemplated on whether or not to reach out. After all, your father made it clear that I wasn't a suitable mother, but I called. Your father answered, told me that you two were in a cottage, but there was no need to worry because nothing happened, and he had everything under control."

"How did you speak to him? We weren't allowed phones." She was lying.

My mother looked at me and simply shook her head. "Really, do you believe your father would go without his phone?"

I believed that, for once, he was putting us first. Our safety was more important than his business calls, but from the telling of her story, I was wrong.

"Your father had revealed to me that he'd had someone follow you throughout Paris. He found out that you were the co-owner of a jazz club, that you weren't staying at the luxury apartment he bought for you, that you had the Fazioli flown in, and that you were seeing a girl."

Estella.

"He had someone attack you, and the same person threw a couple of punches to your father. He did enough to worry you and have you drop everything that was a threat to him. Except, he complained that you were longing to go back to Paris, and he realized that your love for Estella was the biggest threat."

It all started to make sense; everything was connecting like pieces of a puzzle. "Did he have her scholarship revoked?"

"He paid the university fifty thousand for them to reject her and send her home before you went back to Paris."

I pushed myself out of the seat and kicked it away, making my mother flinch. Anger and betrayal overcame me. I placed my hand over my forehead in an attempt to fight off the major headache that was coming on. It was all boiling over, and I didn't know how to handle it all.

"Why?" I yelled. I knew why; it was all a game to my father. Every obstacle was a challenge to overcome, even if it meant ruining the lives of others.

"Your father wanted to prove to me that he could keep you around longer than I could."

I towered over my mother and shook my head. "Why

didn't you say something back then? I lost five years with Estella!"

"You weren't talking to me, and I had disappointed you enough."

"It would've been the perfect opportunity to redeem yourself," I seethed. "But you didn't."

In a matter of minutes, I went from knowing that I was going to lose my mother and wanting to keep her around, to wanting to walk away from her and never see her again. My father played with my life as if I was just origami, and my mother did nothing to stop it.

"I'm very sorry, Ignacio."

I snapped my head away from her and paced back and forth. "So, all this time, you've known about Estella. You helped me plan her date, you asked me questions about her, and you involved yourself in my life as if you cared."

"I do care, Ignacio."

I rolled my eyes.

"And I only knew what your father told me about her, which wasn't much."

It dawned on me that this might not have been the end of father's games. He'd attempted to pull me back into his company when Estella had broken things off with me, but it had failed. Could it be possible that he would try to hurt us again?

I pulled out my phone and noticed that not only was my phone on silent, but I hadn't received any messages from Estella. I immediately dialed her number, and it went straight to voicemail.

Estella may have fallen victim to my own enemies, and I was a bridge away from her.

Chapter 34

ESTELLA

I would be with my family again soon and wanted to make sure that everything went according to plan. The house had been cleaned from the top floor to the basement—I had tackled stacking all our old boxes to one side of the basement like Papa had wanted to do before I left for Italy. The basement was a small under-renovated area that stored items we hadn't touched in years, and Papa wanted to slowly convert it into his own space. If we were staying another week, I would've persuaded Ignacio to help me transform the area.

I tossed boneless, skinless chicken thighs around in the bowl with milk brine. I had texted Salem for advice on how to make the perfect fried chicken, and she'd suggested marinating the chicken in a milk brine overnight. I covered the bowl and placed it in the fridge.

I leaned against the counter, swiping the imaginary bead of sweat that was on my forehead. I wasn't sweating, but I had been active the whole day. I tapped my pencil against my lip, looking over the list of things I had to do before tomorrow morning.

The final item on the list: hang the welcome-home banner. The best spot to hang it had to be over the window that provided our dining table with light. I placed a wooden chair on one side and stood on my tiptoes to thumb-tack the banner onto the wall.

It took three attempts to get the perfect alignment, and when I deemed it good enough, I decided to go upstairs to retrieve my phone to assure Ignacio I was alright. It had been almost two hours, and I hoped that I hadn't caused a panic. The last thing I wanted was to interrupt his time with his mother. He never spoke much about her, but now they were repairing their relationship. I wanted it to stay that way because he needed her.

Midway upstairs, I heard a jostling noise coming from the back end of the house. I didn't make a sudden move and tried to listen for the noise again, confirming whether it was real or my mind playing tricks on me.

There was another thump coming from what I determined to be the laundry room, and I tiptoed the rest of the way up the stairs. The back door of the laundry room started to rattle even more audibly, the knob being fiddled with. Then, a loud crashing noise caused me to gasp out loud, notifying the intruder that I was aware of them.

"Estella," I heard a menacing, male voice call for me from downstairs.

I could recognize that voice from a mile away; it was Cesar. The room started to spin at the thought of seeing him again. I stumbled, my back landing against my closed door, and I watched him move his way upstairs. Mentally, I was in fight mode, every part of me ready to put up a fight, but physically, my body couldn't move until the final second.

I opened my bedroom door, locking it immediately, and ran to retrieve my wooden chair to place it under the knob. I had an advantage in the situation; I had another way to exit the room, and Cesar wasn't aware of it. I snatched my charging cell phone, and my fingers stumbled over each other in an attempt to contact the police. There was a strong crash against the bedroom door, I jumped in reaction, and dropped my phone as it connected to 911.

"Did you think you'd be able to come to Brooklyn and not say hello to me?" Cesar screamed, his voice penetrating through the walls. "Did you think you could come here with your arm wrapped around another man, you little whore?" He lunged against the door.

I scrambled onto the floor to grab my phone and ran into the bathroom, making sure to lock it. I whispered to the dispatcher my location and the situation, and mid-conversation, I heard my old chair snap and Cesar attempting to open the bathroom door. I went into Maya's room through the second bathroom door and reached for her desk chair to stick under the doorknob. That should've distracted him enough to buy me time in escaping back downstairs and for the police department to arrive.

"I see how he dresses, what he drives, and what he does for you. He may spoil you, but you're nothing more than trash. Do you hear me?" I knew that his words were spoken from anger, but they still cut ten layers deep into me. I wiped the hot tears away from my face and opened Maya's bedroom door.

I pressed my body against the wall, steadily walking against it to get closer to the stairs without being seen or heard. Through the walls, I could feel the vibrations of Cesar's weight crashing against the doors.

"I know you hear me, Twinkle. He will discard you, but not me. Look at how I'm fighting for you." His voice became softer, almost an attempt to sound tender, but then his voice rose with fury. "Do you fucking hear me?"

My heart felt like it was in my throat from hearing his voice, and I bolted down the stairs. Every fiber in my body was running at a hundred miles an hour, and as I turned the sharp corner to run down the two steps that led to the front door, I fell straight onto my face. My head lifted slightly, and I watched blood pour out of me, but I managed to reach for the front doorknob. And right when I thought I would escape without being ever touched by Cesar again, my head flung back with great force.

The sudden motion felt like a cracking whip. There was a hot, prickling sensation surging through my neck, and dizziness immediately followed. I wasn't just seeing one Cesar, I was seeing many.

He flung me against the floor, my body crashing against the hardwood, nearly knocking the wind out of me. Cesar stepped one foot on each side of my body and leaned down, pinning my wrists to the ground as he pressed his pelvis down on me.

"You let him fuck you, didn't you?"

I ignored his question and continued to squirm under his weight.

"Dirty, dirty, whore. You've only known him for what, two months? But you had me waiting. ME."

There was a loud crack, and I yelped in pain from his hand smacking me on the cheek. He peeled his hand off, leaving a burning sensation behind.

"I'm going to show you what you missed out, right here…right now. And after I'm done using your worthless body, I'm going to drag you out of here by the hair and take you somewhere far away. We'll see if your boyfriend will pay good money for you, but little does he know he'll be paying for broken goods." Cesar moved his face down, a millimeter away, shifting his weight onto my chest and squeezing my face with his free hand. "I'm going to break you, Estella," he seethed.

If his plan for me wasn't to kill me, I would've begged for death myself. Being in a relationship with Cesar was a nightmare, but the thought of being his captive until I was found would be a living hell.

Ignacio, I need you.

Then I heard my phone vibrating against the hardwood. It had to be him; he had to know that there was something wrong.

"Go fuck yourself," I screamed at the top of my lungs.

There wasn't much fight left in me, but with my heart pounding against my chest, every thump loud, furious, and seeking vengeance, I did what I could only think of doing. With all my might, I jerked my head up to slam it against his head, causing us both to wail in pain. Cesar hesitated for a split second, and that was enough for me to push him off of me and escape.

I wasn't sure if it was me growing unconscious or hearing things, but a siren wailed in the distance. The possibility of making it out alive was enough for me to run for the front door again, and I opened it to find cop cars surrounding the area, officers out of the vehicle with their guns in the air.

Mid-breath, my eyes locked with Ignacio who ran past the officers to catch me as I collapsed down the stairs. My body drifted off, in and out of consciousness, in the comfort of his arms.

Leaving Paris

"Estella, my star, you're okay, you're okay. I'm so sorry for leaving you. I'll make all this go away. Stay with me, *stella mia*." I heard Ignacio sob before I closed my eyes.

Chapter 35

ESTELLA

I gasped, shuddering as I gained consciousness. Bright white lights penetrated my eyes, not helping my blurred vision. As my eyes refocused, I could hear the sound of machines beeping, pumping, and voices coming from the hallway. I looked down at my wrist which had a strip of tape that held an IV in place.

I leaned my head back against the bed because the little movement I had done pained me beyond belief, and in addition, my head throbbed. I needed some relief. Actual medication. My hand aimlessly patted around the rough-textured quilt, and before I could press the call button, someone entered the room.

Ignacio.

"Estella," he gasped, jumping to my side. "God, I'm so glad you're okay." The agony behind his voice devastated me. He closed his eyes firmly, and he opened them when I reached for him.

"You came for me."

"Of course. I just knew that you needed me."

"I know," I said, a faint smile escaping my tired lips.

"I'm so sorry for leaving you alone."

"Don't blame yourself, okay?" There was guilt in his eyes. He would never forgive himself for this despite it being no one's fault except Cesar's. "I'm okay. You're okay. We made it."

He nodded.

"Where are Mama and Papa?" I asked, more alert. "Papa can't know; his heart is too weak."

"Mama and Maya know, not Papa. Not yet anyway."

I placed my hand over my chest in relief. "Okay, good. How long have I been here?" I asked, my voice dry.

"About a day." His face was pained.

"I've been unconscious for almost a day?"

Ignacio nodded slowly. "You sustained a lot of head wounds, Estella."

Hearing him mention head wounds made my head

throb in pain. I had never felt this much pain in my life. "I need medicine."

"I'll get someone to help."

Ignacio opened the door and leaned half of his body out, calling for the nurses. A nurse walked in to check my vitals. She asked me general questions and then shortly after, handed me two pills.

"The doctor will be in shortly."

"Thank you," I whispered.

Ignacio reached for my hand and held it firmly against his lips. "I could've lost you."

"But you didn't, and now, he's gone."

Ignacio sighed and placed a delicate kiss on my hand. "Yes, he's in custody with multiple charges: first-degree burglary, stalking, assault, and other charges which have had him committed to prison for years."

"Burglary?" I croaked.

Ignacio nodded. "Sebastian came forward a couple of hours ago and brought proof that Cesar had orchestrated the robbery and attack. He knew it'd lure you back to Brooklyn."

I knew that Cesar was scum, but I never expected them to stoop that low and attack Papa for revenge. My stomach twisted in disgust that I had brought such a vile person into my house and family. I wanted him to rot in prison for however long.

"I also extended your flight," Ignacio said.

I nodded, but then replayed his words again. "Do you mean *our* flight?"

Ignacio shook his head no.

I glared at him. "What are you not telling me?" Ignacio wouldn't leave me behind if it weren't for a good reason.

Ignacio reached over to stroke my forehead, but I gently pushed it away. "Estella, I need to go to Italy for some unfinished business." There was a glint of something in his eyes and I couldn't pinpoint it. We were treading on unfamiliar territory.

"Did something happen over there?" I readjusted myself upright. Every bit of my body hurt, but if I had to make a flight with Ignacio, I would go.

"I don't want to stress you."

"By not telling me, it is stressing me."

He nodded, his face was pained.

"Talk to me." I danced my fingers to his hands.

Ignacio sucked in a deep breath and cupped my hand. "I want to go to Italy to settle some unresolved issues with my father."

"Your father? Why? I thought you were going to leave him behind."

"I am, but I can't after learning what he did."

I couldn't imagine what had happened between the time of my attack and now that prompted Ignacio to want to leave. "What did he do?"

"He knew about you, five years ago. He had someone follow me for some time and realized that I had this entirely different life outside of what I was presenting. He knew about the jazz club, the studio above with the Fazioli, and you."

"No," was all I could muster to say. My mind started jumping to conclusion, and I groaned from the physical pain. My heart pounded against my chest, and I couldn't take a proper breath. Behind me, I could hear the escalating beeps of the heart-rate monitor.

"My father planned that attack, the month-long incognito, your scholarship being revoked. He did it all to keep me under his thumb because my life is a game to him. I need to go over there and—"

"And what?" I asked, restless. "If you go back to Italy to confront your father right now, you're only going to let him know that you're prepared to keep playing this game for the rest of your life. It needs to end."

"Estella, I almost lost you twice. I'm not prepared to lose you again."

"And you're not." I gave his hand a tight squeeze.

"I've learned that my father is ruthless and will not stop until he gets what he wants. If he hurts you, I will never forgive myself."

"I'm going to be okay."

"That's what you said before Cesar attacked you."

"And I'm here to tell the story, aren't I?" The corner of my lips raised up in an attempt to diffuse the tension in the air. Ignacio and I were usually on the same page, but he had been filled with a need to seek revenge and take control. This is what his father had wanted all along.

"You need to let go, Ignacio. For me, please."

Ignacio closed his eyes and shook his head. It was a battle against his heart and mind. "I don't want him to hurt you."

"You'll hurt me more if you leave me."

Ignacio's eyelids fluttered open, and he stared deeply at me with his fiery eyes. Those words clicked in place for him. He had been convinced that he needed to face off with his father in order to prevent further harm, but he'd be hurting me the most if he left. There was nothing more that I needed than his love and presence, right now.

"God, I'm so sorry, Estella." Ignacio wiped his eyes and pressed his lips against my hand. "I'm not going anywhere."

"Promise?"

"Yes, *stella mia*."

I sighed deeply, allowing my body to melt into the pillows and mattress beneath me. It wasn't that comfortable but reveling in Ignacio's promise made all the difference.

***

IGNACIO

"Ignacio, could you open this for me?" Alma handed me a glass jar.

She had been zooming in and out of the kitchen, making the final touches for our Thanksgiving dinner. There were times that she needed no one's help, and then times she wanted someone around to help. Her back-and-forth reminded me a lot of Estella, but good thing I was able to keep up.

"Ignacio, could you take the turkey out of the oven and place it here." She pointed to a vacant spot in the middle of the table.

"That's my job!" Fernando huffed, fumbling over the cloth napkins that Alma had him origami.

"Please, *amor*, you're still in recovery."

"Oh, but you had no problem having me carry four stacks of soda cans out of the delivery truck yesterday," he muttered low enough only for me, Maya, and Estella to hear.

Estella smirked at me. "He's so jealous," she mouthed.

"Ignacio!" Alma hollered again.

I jogged into the kitchen and went straight toward the oven. Alma nervously eyed me as I carried the turkey over onto the table. It was the last piece of the puzzle. I'd been full of butterflies about the day because it had been twenty years since I'd last had a Thanksgiving dinner. Celebrating the holiday with Estella was all I could ask for, and I enjoyed being with her family.

The wooden table had been blanketed with a tan tablecloth, adorned with maple-leaf garlands, little pumpkins, a bouquet of red peonies, and all the homecooked food.

"When will your mother be here?" Alma asked.

"She should be here shortly."

Estella walked over, slipping an arm around my waist and looking up at me. "It's going to be okay."

When Estella returned home from the hospital, I told her about my mother's cancer diagnosis and that she had known what my father had done to us. Estella told me to give my mother another chance, that she may genuinely be feeling guilty for being neglectful. I had dinner with her a little less than two weeks ago to discuss everything while I was more level-headed.

Through her words, her movements, her tears, I could tell Mom wasn't acting. She had even told my father that if he ever threatens or harms me and Estella, she would release incriminating documents that could ruin his whole career. She was confident that he wouldn't do anything with such a life-altering threat hanging over his shoulders.

In her own chaotic way, my mom had set my life back on course. Estella and I were having a great time together in New York. It was a whole different routine, but it was fun. There were many jazz clubs nearby that we explored at night, and we'd help around with the Latin market, go to her old ceramic studio to practice throwing on the wheel,

Leaving Paris

or go to a rehearsal studio to work on the piano. We were growing with each other.

The doorbell rang, and Alma rushed to answer. Estella's family had met my mom for dinner a week ago. It went on for about an hour, and everyone was able to get acquainted. Alma and Maya were stunned to have met her but quickly grew comfortable talking to her. My mom and Alma have been working on a friendship, and Estella thought it was adorable.

Mom walked in, and Adler follow behind and set down a crate of wine and a pink bakery box. Estella gave him a hug and then saw him off as he left. She had invited him for the dinner, but apparently, he had a date with a woman that worked at Estella's old ceramic studio. Estella loved knowing that Adler was on his own romantic journey.

Everyone gathered around the table, and Alma opened up the dinner with a quick, thankful prayer. We dove into the meals, and our conversations picked up. The table was not only filled with delicious food but laughs, stories, and closeness. It was my second, and favorite Thanksgiving dinner.

Everyone called it a night around 8 p.m. Estella and I walked my mom out and then planned on going to my penthouse. Our steps were a bit lumbering from having such a full stomachs, but we couldn't have asked for a better night.

Adler arrived promptly, opening the door for my mom, allowing her to slip in.

"How'd the date go?" Estella asked, cheerfully.

"It went very well," Adler responded. "She's pretty great."

"I'm so happy for you two." Estella clapped her hands lightly.

Adler gave us an appreciative smile and disappeared around the car and drove off. Estella and I stood on the sidewalk, quiet and absorbing the dark tranquility of the night sky. My fingers danced around the space between us and I reached over to grab Estella's soft hand.

"I definitely miss the night skies in Castellara."

"I miss them, too, and I can't wait to go back with you, *stella mia*."

I twirled her around and brought her into my chest, swaying with the only woman I'd ever loved under this cold, fall night. There may not have been any bright stars above us, but it didn't matter because she was the only star in my night sky.

Epilogue

ESTELLA

THREE YEARS LATER

The sun was sending us farewells with a pastel display of colors, a slight breeze whisked through the trees, and the clattering of plates and laughter echoed from outside. It was a beautiful sight to see my entire family gathered out in the backyard, enjoying the last few days of summer. Ignacio's film score played in the background, filling the country air with perfection.

I recalled the moment when Ignacio decided to start writing music again.

He was desperate to create a piece for our unborn child; he wanted it to be the first instrumental piece our baby heard when it entered the world. He wrote for weeks and weeks until he declared it perfect. It was the night that marked the twentieth week of my pregnancy. I sat on the bench with him as he played it on the piano, and that's when it happened.

It was a subtle kick that caught me off guard, but I gasped, and Ignacio cupped my stomach. Our baby kicked again, and I teased that the baby wanted to hear the rest of the music. Ignacio continued to play the piece, and there was another kick. We looked at each other and nearly teared up that our baby seemed to have a strong connection to music, and not just any music, but his dad's music. Ignacio continued creating masterpieces, and Emile sent them out to his connections, and shortly after that, Ignacio had a contract with a film production to write the music for an upcoming romance movie.

The bundle of joy in my arms placed his tired head on my shoulders, signaling that he was tired but resisting. He'd had a busy day filled with so much attention, presents, and a little bit of cake to celebrate his birthday. Our baby boy, Lucio, was officially one year old.

I reached over for the silver rattle that lay in a bed of blue tissue paper and handed it to Lucio. Florence had personalized it with his name and three musical notes. Lucio gently banged it against my chest, and I feigned pain which made him laugh.

"Silly boy, you should try to sleep," I whispered to him.

He slapped his little round hand against my chest. That was his way of objecting.

"I guess it's Daddy's turn to try to put you to sleep, hmm?"

He perked his head up with a wide smile, showing me his four little teeth. He was certainly a daddy's boy, and it made me a little jealous, but not too much because Ignacio was an outstanding father. He was kind, patient, and attentive. He constantly placed us first because our happiness was his happiness.

We went back downstairs, and through the back door, everyone cheered again at the sight of a very lively Lucio.

"He's ready for round two of partying," Maya joked. She, along with the rest of my family, had been visiting us in Italy for two weeks. It was Maya's and her girlfriend's last hoorah before they started college at NYU, and my parents wanted to come down since they hadn't seen us in months. I missed them, but I loved my life in Italy.

We owned a renovated cottage made out of light-colored stones, vines coming down the edges of the house, four bedrooms with bathrooms, a perfect-sized pool, an art studio with all-natural lighting, and acres of green. Ignacio had bought the old cottage and with a lot of interior design research, we built our perfect home a couple of months shy of Lucio's arrival.

"More like round two of attempting to put him down to sleep," I mumbled, handing him over to Ignacio.

"No, gimme the little gnocchi!" Maya yelped with pleading hands.

Ignacio gave Lucio a kiss on his chubby cheeks and handed him over to Maya. Maya wrapped him in her arms, and Alana leaned over, cooing over him as she played with his fingers. They were going strong for three years, and I had no doubt that after college, they would be their own happy little family.

Maya and Alana walked back inside with Lucio. I knew exactly what they were going to do. They were all going to lie down in their bed together, close all the blinds, put on their starry-night projector, and listen to their chill music. For the past two nights, I would tiptoe into their room and fetch a sleeping Lucio. It took a lot of patience and silence to not wake him as I lifted him off their bed and walked

Leaving Paris

down the hall to place him in his crib. He was going to miss them when they left.

"Well, thank you so much for that delicious meal, Ignacio. I didn't know you could cook, too," Mama swooned. She never held back on the compliments and eye fluttering; it was cute. I liked that she adored him as much as I did. Even Papa would throw in his own flattery along the way. Sometimes, I was convinced they liked him more than they liked me, but I didn't blame them. I'd found myself a keeper.

Mama and Papa cleared up the plates and glasses even though we'd told them several times throughout their visit that they didn't have to lift a finger, but they always insisted. They were always finding ways to feel needed.

The cool breeze tousled with my hair, and I lifted my head up, feeling the wind caress my skin and welcoming autumn. The month of September would always hold a special place in my heart, especially in Italy. It was the month of my son's birthday, the month that I met my amazing husband, and the month that my life changed for good.

"Have I told you how beautiful you look today?" Ignacio said, leaning over his seat and pulling me into his lap with one solid tug. I circled my arms around his neck and gazed at his fiery, brown eyes.

"Only three times," I teased.

"God, you're so beautiful, so beautiful," he repeated in his sultry voice until I laughed and begged him to stop. "Marry me, Estella."

I lifted my hand, showcasing the beautiful engagement and wedding ring that enveloped my finger. "I did."

"Marry me again."

"Ignacio," I whispered with a blush. "I think all of Marcelo and Salem's wedding planning is getting to your head." They were going to be married in five days, and of course, it made us feel extra-romantic, extra-tender, and extra-sentimental.

"You're right, and it's made me think. Do you wish we had a large wedding? Traveling around Europe to find the perfect dress, location, bakery, flowers, and more?" His eyes filled with guilt. "I know we did it all suddenly, but we are happy, right? You're happy?"

"I'm transcendentally happy. This is my Heaven."

Ignacio laced his fingers in my hair, gingerly pulling me forward, and kissed me long and slow. His tongue intertwined with mine, and I moaned against him;

everything about him felt amazing. I melted into him, and he held me with a love so divine.

Years ago, I was scared to fall in love, but I did. I fell and fell harder than I could've ever imagined. I let myself fall, and like a beautiful composition, it was slow, fast, chaotic, harmonic, and most of all, it was heavenly.

The End

Made in the USA
Middletown, DE
19 November 2022